RAMPAGE OF THE DESERT WOLF

Look for these exciting Western series from bestselling authors William W. Johnstone and J.A. Johnstone

The Mountain Man
Luke Jensen: Bounty Hunter
Brannigan's Land
The Jensen Brand
Smoke Jensen: The Early Years
Preacher and MacCallister
Fort Misery
The Fighting O'Neils
Perley Gates
MacCoole and Boone
Guns of the Vigilantes
Shotgun Johnny
The Chuckwagon Trail
The Jackals
The Slash and Pecos Westerns
The Texas Moonshiners
Stoneface Finnegan Westerns
Ben Savage: Saloon Ranger
The Buck Trammel Westerns
The Death and Texas Westerns
The Hunter Buchanon Westerns
Will Tanner: U.S. Deputy Marshal
Old Cowboys Never Die
Go West, Young Man

RAMPAGE OF THE DESERT WOLF

WILLIAM W. JOHNSTONE
AND J. A. JOHNSTONE

PINNACLE BOOKS
KENSINGTON PUBLISHING CORP.
kensingtonbooks.com

PINNACLE BOOKS are published by

Kensington Publishing Corp.
900 Third Avenue
New York, NY 10022

PUBLISHER'S NOTE: Following the death of William W. Johnstone, the Johnstone family is working with a carefully selected writer to organize and complete Mr. Johnstone's outlines and many unfinished manuscripts to create additional novels in all of his series, like The Last Gunfighter, Mountain Man, and Eagles, among others. This novel was inspired by Mr. Johnstone's superb storytelling.

All Kensington titles, imprints, and distributed lines are available at special quantity discounts for bulk purchases for sales promotion, premiums, fundraising, and educational or institutional use.

Special book excerpts or customized printings can also be created to fit specific needs. For details, write or phone the office of the Kensington Sales Manager: Kensington Publishing Corp., 900 Third Avenue, New York, NY 10022. Attn. Sales Department. Phone: 1-800-221-2647.

Kensington Books Hardcover Edition: June 2026
Pinnacle Books Trade Paperback Edition: September 2026

ISBN: 978-0-7860-5214-1
iSBN: 978-1-4967-5734-0 (ebook)

10 9 8 7 6 5 4 3 2 1

Printed in the United States of America

The authorized representative in the EU for product safety and compliance
is eucomply OU, Parnu mnt 139b-14, Apt 123
Tallinn, Berlin 11317, hello@eucompliancepartner.com.

Rampage of the Desert Wolf

Chapter 1

As the sound of gunfire erupted, shattering the warm, peaceful morning, Smoke Jensen wheeled around and gazed up the main street of Big Rock, Colorado. His hands flew to the Colts holstered on his hips, and his strong, supple fingers closed around the guns' walnut grips.

Several men charged out the front door of the train station at the end of the street, a couple of blocks from where Smoke stood on the boardwalk in front of Louis Longmont's restaurant and saloon.

On the far side of the large, redbrick depot building, a train was stopped next to the platform, steam still belching from the diamond-shaped stack of the big Baldwin locomotive.

The men who had just hurriedly exited the station wore long dusters and bandanna masks over the bottom halves of their faces. Their hats were pulled low to further obscure their features. The guns in their hands spouted fire and lead as they sprayed bullets around the street to discourage any interference with their getaway.

Smoke didn't have any idea what those owlhoots had stolen, but he didn't intend to let them get away. Their indiscriminate gunfire was threatening innocent bystanders, and Smoke needed to put a stop to it.

He pulled both irons, stepped into the street, and walked toward the outlaws, alternating shots left and right.

The five men might not have noticed Smoke at first, but they became aware of the threat the hard way as one of them went down hard, drilled through the body. The man next to him yelled a warning to his companions. All four of them threw a storm of lead toward Smoke.

Angling across the street, Smoke left his feet in a dive as slugs tore through the air around him. Dust puffed up as he hit the ground on his left shoulder and rolled.

That roll carried him behind one end of a watering trough. Outlaw bullets thudded into it but couldn't penetrate.

Smoke came up on one knee, leveled the Colts over the water trough, and returned the fire. Another outlaw jerked halfway around as a bullet caught him in the upper left arm, but he managed to stay on his feet.

The masked men had been trying to reach their horses, which were tied to a hitchrack in front of the depot, when they burst out of the building. Smoke's deadly accurate fire had drawn a curtain between them and that goal. The four men still on their feet retreated behind a parked wagon, the closest thing that offered them any cover from Smoke's bullets.

The people who had been in harm's way when the shooting started had scattered. Smoke risked a look for anyone cut down by the flying lead and was glad to see that none of the townspeople were lying in the street.

After crawling around behind the water trough to put himself in a better position relative to the outlaws, he began thumbing fresh cartridges into the Colts' cylinders.

While he was doing that, a gun blasted unexpectedly to his right. A bullet plowed into the dirt only a couple of feet from him. He jerked his head up and saw that the man he'd shot in the chest wasn't dead after all. Mortally wounded, more than likely, but he had pulled himself up onto his feet and now staggered along in front of the boardwalk, thrusting a revolver toward Smoke.

Muzzle flame spewed from the gun again, but Smoke was already rolling toward the boardwalk. The bullet ripped a gouge on the trough's side where Smoke had been stretched out a heartbeat earlier.

Before Smoke could lift one of his Colts and return the fire, a man stepped out from the recessed alcove of a building not far from him. This man had his gun out and he crouched slightly as he loosed a shot at the wounded outlaw. The bullet punched a second hole in the man's chest, spun him around, and dropped him limply on his face.

Smoke looked at the man who had gunned down the outlaw and nodded his thanks. The man was a stranger to him—young, rangy, dressed like a cowboy with the deeply tanned face and hands of a man who spent most of his time working outdoors.

He smiled faintly and returned Smoke's nod. Then he had to retreat into the alcove as a bullet whistled past his head and shattered a window in the building. The remaining outlaws raked the area around Smoke and the young stranger with a fierce volley.

Rapid, pounding footsteps on the opposite boardwalk drew Smoke's attention. Taking a chance, he looked in that direction and saw his friend Monte Carson, Big Rock's sheriff, running toward the train station. Monte had a shotgun in his hands and looked like he was trying to get close enough to the outlaws to use it.

One of the masked men must have noticed his approach. Monte ducked as a bullet hummed close to his head and jumped off the boardwalk to land behind a parked buggy.

The horse harnessed to the buggy suddenly screamed, reared up, and jerked away from the hitch rail where its reins were tied. The reins pulled loose, and as the horse's front hooves came back down on the ground, it lunged ahead in a wild run, hauling the buggy behind it.

Smoke figured one of the slugs flying through the air had creased the animal, and the pain had spooked it into bolting. Whatever the reason, the result was the same.

Monte Carson was left out in the open, an easy target for outlaw lead.

Smoke had just reloaded his Colts again; he had a full wheel in each gun. To give Monte a chance to reach some other cover, Smoke surged to his feet and blasted away with both irons. Splinters flew from the body of the wagon the outlaws were using as a shield.

The stranger who had helped Smoke earlier joined in, as well. He stepped out of the alcove and emptied his gun toward the outlaws.

Either he or Smoke scored a hit. One of the duster-clad men reeled out from behind the wagon and collapsed, pitching limply to the ground and lying there in a crumpled, motionless heap mutely eloquent of death.

That left three men, and one of them might be wounded. The odds were even already and soon could be stacked high against the outlaws as more of the townspeople responded to the shooting. Many frontier settlers, even the ones who lived in towns such as Big Rock, owned guns and didn't mind pitching in on the side of law and order whenever trouble cropped up.

From the corner of his eye, Smoke saw Monte bound onto the boardwalk again and charge ahead until he reached an alley. The lawman ducked into that opening, used the corner of the next building as cover, and loosed both barrels at the outlaws. He ducked back, broke the shotgun open, and thumbed fresh shells into it.

Smoke stretched out behind the water trough and began reloading again. The stranger was doing the same thing in the nearby alcove.

This created a momentary lull in the firing, and the masked lawbreakers decided to try to take advantage of it.

They burst out from behind the wagon and made another dash for their horses, shooting wildly as they sprinted toward the animals.

If they had had another couple of seconds, they might have made it, but the constant crash of gunfire made their mounts nervous enough that the horses danced away when the outlaws reached for them.

Smoke came up on a knee again with his freshly reloaded Colts in his hands. The revolvers boomed and bucked as he opened fire.

A few yards away, the stranger joined in once more, too, and across the street, Monte Carson got in on the fight with a thunderous roar from the shotgun he wielded.

Two of the outlaws went down, driven off their feet by the smashing impact of buckshot and bullets. The third man was able to jerk his horse's reins loose from the hitch rail and get his foot in the stirrup, but as he tried to pull himself into the saddle, bullets from Smoke and the stranger tore through him. He cried out and fell backward, away from the horse.

His foot hung in the stirrup, and as the animal gave in to its panic and stampeded away from the station, it dragged the unfortunate owlhoot. The man bounced against the ground for a good hundred yards along the street before his foot finally slipped from the stirrup, leaving him lying there, motionless.

Smoke still had a couple of rounds in both Colts. He kept the guns trained on the outlaws who had fallen in front of the depot as he stalked toward them. He heard footsteps nearby and a glance to the side revealed that the man who had helped him was joining him to check on the owlhoots.

At the same time, Monte Carson set the shotgun aside, drew his revolver, and trotted down the street toward the man who'd been dragged by his horse.

It didn't take Smoke and his companion long to confirm that the four men at this end of the street were dead. Satisfied that they were no longer a threat, Smoke pouched his left-hand iron and began replacing the expended shells in the cylinder of the other gun.

As he did that, his fingers efficiently accomplishing the task he had carried out thousands of times, he nodded to the young man and said, "I'm much obliged to you for your help, amigo. That first fella might have gotten me if you hadn't taken care of him."

A rakish grin spread across the young man's face.

"No, I reckon you'd have drilled him a second or two later if I hadn't," he said. "Those varmints weren't any match for Smoke Jensen."

"You know who I am?" Smoke said.

"I've seen your picture in *Harper's Illustrated Weekly.* I've read some of those dime novels about you, too, but to be honest, the way they draw you on those yellow covers doesn't look a whole heap like you."

Smoke had to laugh at that, as he slid the freshly reloaded Colt back into leather.

"There's not much about those dime novels that's accurate," he said as he began refilling the cylinder of the other gun. "I sometimes think the publishers must find the fellas who write them in one of those homes for the feeble-minded."

"Yeah, after reading about you in those yarns, it seems like you ought to be ten feet tall, at least."

In truth, Smoke was only medium height. Maybe a tad more, but not much. His shoulders were exceptionally broad, but that was really his only distinguishing physical characteristic. He had a shock of ash blond hair, a keen, penetrating gaze, and faint lines around his eyes that came from living much of his life outdoors and in danger, which meant he had to keep a careful lookout around him at all times.

There were also lines at the corners of his mouth showing that he was quick to smile and had a ready laugh.

Folks sometimes talked about a man being comfortable in his own skin. Smoke Jensen was just about as comfortable in his own skin as a man could get.

But he didn't look like a man who had a reputation as one of the fastest guns—maybe *the* fastest gun—west of the Mississippi or anywhere else. In the little more than a dozen years since he and his father had headed west from the Jensen family's hardscrabble farm in the Missouri Ozarks, numerous legends had grown up around Smoke.

He had been a wanted outlaw for a time, the charges against him false ones framed on him by enemies. He had been a deadly avenger, settling the score for the murders of his brother, his father, and most of all, his young wife and their infant son. He had been a lawman, albeit a somewhat reluctant one, wearing a star to help him in his quest for justice.

But in recent years, he'd been content to be a rancher, establishing the Sugarloaf spread with his second wife, Sally, as well as being one of the founders of the town of Big Rock. At heart, he was a peaceable man, and it would have been fine with Smoke if trouble took another trail and left him alone. Sometimes it did for a while—but it seemed as if those intervals of peace and quiet never lasted long.

Monte Carson walked up the street to join Smoke and the stranger. Monte had the shotgun open and tucked under his arm.

Smoke nodded to the double-barreled weapon and said, "I reckon you won't be needing that anymore."

"Not right now, anyway," Monte agreed. "That fella down the street is as dead as he can be. I'm assuming the others are, too?"

"I'm afraid so," Smoke said. "I wonder what they were after in the depot."

"Don't know, but I intend to find out." Monte looked at the stranger. "Before I do, though . . . Who might you be, mister? I like to keep track of who's in my town, and I don't believe we've met."

"I just rode in a little while ago," the man said. "Name's McKinley. Dean McKinley."

"Didn't I see you trading shots with those outlaws?"

Smoke said, "Dean here saved my bacon by taking a hand when he did."

"Mr. Jensen exaggerates how much I did," McKinley said, "but I'm glad I was able to help out."

"What brings you to Big Rock, McKinley?" Monte asked.

"An old dun horse," McKinley replied with a smile. Before the lawman could take offense at the answer, he went on, "I'm riding the chuck line, Sheriff. Just looking for a job."

"Ranch work?" Smoke asked.

"All I've been doing for the past eight years."

"How old were you when you started? Twelve?"

"Fourteen," McKinley said.

Smoke inclined his head toward Longmont's.

"Come on with me," he invited. "We'll get a cup of coffee and jaw for a spell. It's on me."

"Now *I'm* obliged to *you*," McKinley said.

Monte started toward the train station. Smoke told him, "Stop by Louis's on the way back to your office, Monte."

The sheriff lifted a hand in acknowledgment of the request.

Now that the shooting was over, the citizens had emerged from their temporary hiding places and were gathering to stare at the bodies of the dead outlaws. The women didn't get too close, and they struggled to hold back the youngsters who wanted to take a good look at the bloody corpses. A hum of excited conversation came from the men. Anything that broke the monotony of day-to-day life was welcome in frontier communities—even if it came with the price of some bullets flying around.

When Smoke and Dean McKinley entered Longmont's, Smoke led the way across the room toward the rear table where the proprietor always sat. Nattily dressed and sleekly handsome, Louis Longmont had a dual reputation as a gambler and a gunfighter. He was also one of Smoke's oldest friends.

Smoke signaled to the bartender to bring coffee for him and McKinley. Louis already had a cup in front of him with tendrils of steam rising from the dark black liquid.

"I'm surprised we didn't see you out there on the street once the guns started going off," Smoke said as he sat down and motioned McKinley into one of the other empty chairs. "You're usually as dependable as an old firehorse hearing the alarm bell."

"I was indisposed," Louis said. "Truthfully, I still am, a bit."

Smoke grinned. "You're hungover!"

"I received a shipment of especially fine wine," Louis explained. "You wouldn't expect me to serve something I hadn't sampled myself, would you?"

"Oh, of course not," Smoke said, still smiling.

"And I had a lady friend who, ah, helped me sample it," Louis added. He waved an elegantly manicured hand. "Besides, I'd seen you through the window a short time earlier. I knew you were out there and would handle the situation, whatever it might be."

"Yeah, I was about to come in here when the shooting started. Figured I'd have a cup of coffee with you before I went on down to the train station—which, as it happens, is where the trouble seems to have started."

Quickly, Smoke filled Louis in on what had happened.

"I still have business down there," he concluded, "but it can wait until Monte gets through talking to them."

"You have something coming in on the train that arrived a short time ago?" Louis asked.

"Nope. I need to check and see if there's a telegram waiting for me and send a reply if there is."

Louis nodded but didn't press Smoke for further explanation. Instead, he looked across the table at McKinley and asked Smoke, "Who's your friend?"

McKinley extended his hand, and said, "Dean McKinley, Mr. Longmont. It's a real pleasure to meet you."

Louis clasped the young range rider's hand. "You know who I am?"

"He's read the dime novels," Smoke said dryly.

McKinley laughed and reached toward the hip pocket on his jeans.

"That's right," he said as he pulled out a thin yellow-backed book that he had folded in half so it would fit in his pocket. "Just bought one I haven't read before. That's what I was doing when the shooting started. Sorry, Mr. Jensen, but it's not one that has you in it."

"That's all right, I promise you," Smoke told him.

The bartender arrived with coffee, setting the cups in front of Smoke and the young cowboy. McKinley took an eager sip and then looked surprised.

"What's that taste in it?" he asked.

"Chicory," Louis said. "Very popular in the Cajun country where I'm from."

"Well, it's good, that's for sure."

Smoke said, "It's probably not too late in the morning to get the cook to rustle up some flapjacks and bacon, if you're hungry, Dean."

"Well, come to think of it, I haven't eaten anything yet this morning, and I *am* a mite short on funds . . ."

"And yet you just bought a dime novel," Louis pointed out.

"A fella's mind gets hungry, just like his belly."

Smoke laughed and clapped a hand on the young man's shoulder.

"Let's get you a good breakfast," he said, "and then there's something else I want to talk over with you."

Chapter 2

Dean McKinley had quite an appetite, which came as no surprise to Smoke. Despite being called chuck line riders, young cowboys on the drift, looking for a job, often went a long time between meals.

McKinley had polished off a big stack of flapjacks with butter and syrup, and was just finishing the plate of bacon that came with it, when Monte Carson came into Longmont's and headed for Louis's table.

Monte raised a finger to the bartender, who knew that meant to bring him a cup of coffee. He pulled out an empty chair at the table and thumbed his hat back as he sat down.

"The bank was sending a bunch of old bills back to the mint in Philadelphia to be taken out of circulation," he said. "Until then, though, they would still spend just fine, and those boys got wind of it somehow and decided to latch on to them."

"Doesn't the bank usually notify you when an unusual amount of currency will be coming or going?" Louis asked.

Monte nodded. "That's right. This was just a misunderstanding. The bank president thought one of the tellers had told me about it, and the teller thought the president had. Like that old saying about the right hand not knowing what the left hand is doing."

"Or not doing, in this case," Smoke said with a smile.

"Yeah. But then it was all for nothing, because the shipment wasn't ready to go when the eastbound rolled in this morning, and they're going to have to postpone it until the day after tomorrow. So those varmints went in there figuring to grab themselves a small fortune and came out empty-handed."

Louis said, "But now you'll be prepared to make sure there's no trouble when the shipment does go out."

"That's right," Monte said. He nodded his thanks to the bartender as the man placed a cup of coffee in front of him. After taking a sip, the sheriff looked across the table at Dean McKinley. "Judging by those empty plates in front of you, young fella, I'd say you had yourself a good surrounding just now."

"I bought breakfast for Dean," Smoke said. "Seemed to me like he earned it."

"Oh, I'm not disputing that. I saw the way he pitched in against those outlaws." Monte paused for a moment as he regarded McKinley, then went on. "You know, most lawmen would consider it a mite suspicious that you rode into town the same morning as a gang of owlhoots tried to steal a money shipment."

McKinley leaned back in his chair and his eyes widened. "Sheriff, you're not saying you think I had anything to do with those lawbreakers, are you?"

"Dean gunned down a couple of them," Smoke pointed out.

Monte shrugged. "Outlaws have turned on their own plenty of times, for lots of different reasons."

McKinley's face flushed. His tawny eyebrows drew down in a scowl.

Monte lifted a hand to forestall the young cowboy's angry reaction.

"Now, let me be clear. I'm not saying that's what happened here. But the thought occurred to me, and I'm not going to lie about it."

McKinley still didn't look happy, but his voice was calm and controlled as he said, "I don't suppose I can fault you for that, Sheriff. A lawman's job is just naturally to be suspicious, I reckon. But for what it's worth, and you can believe me or not, I never laid eyes on any of those varmints until I was trading gunshots with them."

When he was finished, silence hung over the table for several heartbeats before Monte Carson nodded.

"For what it's worth, I do believe you," he said.

"So do I," Smoke added.

Monte smiled faintly. "And if I had any lingering doubts, Smoke speaking up for you would take care of them. I don't figure I've ever met a better judge of character than him."

The comments appeared to mollify McKinley. He nodded and said, "I appreciate that, sir. I really do. And Mr. Jensen, having you stick up for me is a real honor." He smiled. "I've read about you, too, Sheriff, so I'm mighty pleased you don't think I'm an owlhoot."

"Read about me? What are you—" Monte stopped short and rolled his eyes a little. "You've read some of those ridiculous dime novels they've started writing about Smoke and his friends, haven't you?"

"As far as I know, I've read all of them," McKinley said. "There aren't that many so far, but they come out pretty regular-like."

"Well, don't put too much stock in them. Those old boys who write them have—ah, been known to exaggerate."

Smoke grinned and said, "That's what I've been telling him." He grew more serious as he went on. "About that other thing I want to discuss with you, Dean. You know I have a ranch not far from here?"

McKinley nodded. "Sure."

"It's a big place, and I can always use another hand. How about it?"

The young man's eyes widened. "You mean I could ride for Smoke Jensen's Sugarloaf Ranch? That's what you're asking me to do?"

"You said you were looking for a riding job."

"You don't have to make that offer just because of what happened this morning," McKinley said. "I would have taken a hand against those outlaws, anyway, once I saw the way they were throwing lead around all over the street. Somebody had to stop 'em before they hurt a woman or a kid. Shoot, when I stepped out of that alcove and drew down on them, I didn't even know who you were, Mr. Jensen. I hadn't gotten a good look at you yet."

"I'm not trying to pay you back for that," Smoke said. "I consider it just a lucky turn of events that put us together. I can use a hand, and you can use a job. That's all it amounts to."

"In that case"—McKinley extended his hand—"I'll be mighty pleased and honored to ride for your brand, Mr. Jensen."

Smoke shook hands with him and added, "My foreman, Pearlie Fontaine, will have to agree, but I don't anticipate any trouble there. Pearlie is a pretty keen judge of character himself."

The two of them finished their coffee, then Smoke said, "I'll walk on down to the station and take care of my business there. If you want to gather your gear and get your horse, Dean, we can meet back here in a little while and ride out to the Sugarloaf together."

"There's no gathering to do," McKinley replied. "Everything I own is in my saddlebags and my war bag, and they're still on my horse. I hadn't gotten around to looking for a place to stay and a stable for him. So I'm ready to go whenever you are, Mr. Jensen."

"Then you can walk down to the station with me. And call me Smoke. Anybody I've fought beside, shoulder to shoulder, has earned that."

"It'd be my pleasure, Mr.—I mean, Smoke."

They said their farewells to Monte and Louis, and left the restaurant. By now, the undertaker and his assistants had loaded up the bodies of the fallen outlaws and taken them off to be prepared for burial. The gang's horses had been rounded up and corralled at the livery stable. They would be sold, along with whatever tack was on them, to pay for planting their former owners.

The gun smoke had drifted away, and life in Big Rock was back to normal. Smoke returned the friendly nods of numerous citizens as he and Dean McKinley walked toward the railroad station.

"Most folks seem to know you," McKinley commented.

"Well, I've been in these parts since before Big Rock was a town," Smoke said. "There used to be another settlement not far from here called Fontana. It started out as a nice enough place, I guess, but it turned into an outlaw town after a while, when a man who got too greedy moved in and brought a bunch of hired gunslicks with him."

"I think I read about that in one of those dime novels," McKinley said. "The way I remember it, all the honest folks in Fontana moved over here when you and some other fellas founded Big Rock. And Fontana sort of dried up and blew away—after a bunch of shooting between you and those hired killers."

Smoke nodded and said, "It was quite a ruckus, all right. Seems like a long time ago now, but it really wasn't. Reckon it's just that a lot of things have happened between then and now. The railroad coming in and the town growing so much, and I've been busy building up the Sugarloaf. We've gone in for raising horses, too, as well as cattle. In fact, that has to do with the business that brought me to Big Rock this morning. I'm expecting a telegram from the army."

"From the army?" McKinley repeated.

"Yes, from a colonel named Griffin, in particular. He's the

commanding officer at Fort Craig, down in New Mexico Territory. He and I have been negotiating a deal for the Sugarloaf to provide a herd of horses that the cavalry at the fort can use as remounts. If it goes well—if they're satisfied with the horses and I'm satisfied with the price—it could be an ongoing arrangement."

"Sounds like a good deal, all right," McKinley agreed.

"I hope it works out that way, but we'll have to wait and see."

They entered the station, and Smoke led the way across the lobby to the Western Union office. The telegrapher, a burly rusty-haired man, sat at the key and smiled through the wicket.

"I was about to whistle for the boy and send him to find you, Smoke," he said. "I have a telegram for you. Came in just before all the trouble started."

"I was hoping it might have, Lester," Smoke said.

The man sorted through a small stack of yellow telegraph flimsies, found the one he was looking for, and slid it across the counter to Smoke, who needed only a moment to scan the words printed on it before he smiled in reaction to what he read.

"Will there be an answer?" the telegrapher asked.

"Yep. Tell the colonel that the price is agreeable and he can take delivery of the horses"—Smoke paused to figure in his head for a minute—"three weeks from today. Give or take a couple of days."

The telegrapher printed the message on a form, figured the price, and picked up the coin Smoke put on the counter to pay for it. Then his finger moved on the telegraph key with smooth, rapid efficiency to send the message.

Smoke tucked the flimsy with Colonel Griffin's message in his shirt pocket and left the station with McKinley. The cowboy said, "I guess you got your price."

"The amount the war department approved wasn't quite as

much as what I asked for, but it was all I really expected to get," Smoke said. "There's always got to be a little haggling when you're dealing with the government."

"Will the cavalry come to the Sugarloaf to pick up the horses?"

"No, that was part of the deal Colonel Griffin was pretty firm on. He says he can't spare the men to do that, so I'm going to drive the herd to Socorro, a town on the Rio Grande not far from the fort, and they'll take delivery there." Smoke shrugged. "It would have been better if they'd come here to get the horses, of course, but to tell you the truth, I didn't put up much of an argument. It's been a while since I've been anywhere, and my feet get a little itchy when they stay in one place for too long. So, I don't really mind the drive." He paused. "I'm not sure how Sally's going to feel about it, though."

Sally Reynolds was a beautiful dark-haired young woman from a wealthy family in New England. With her background, she could have lived a life of leisure back East, but ambition and the desire to accomplish something in the world on her own had led her to become a teacher.

She had wound up in the raw frontier settlement of Bury, Idaho, where she had taught the children of storekeepers, farmers, and ranchers, and scandalized the community by befriending soiled doves and saloon girls.

The scandal had grown when she had met and fallen in love with a young gunfighter named Smoke Jensen, who had a tragic score to settle with the evil men who ran things in those parts.

Bury wound up burned to the ground, the innocent folks who lived there having fled from the apocalyptic battle between Smoke and his enemies. And Sally Reynolds wound up Sally Jensen, very happily married to Smoke ever since. They had traveled together to an untamed valley at the edge of the Rockies in Colorado and transformed it into one of the best ranches in the state—or anywhere else on the frontier, for that matter.

Several years of peace, anonymity, and hard work had ended with the arrival of unchecked greed in the person of Tilden Franklin. When the dust from that epic clash settled, Smoke had two new friends and staunch allies in Monte Carson and Pearlie Fontaine, hired guns who had come to the area in Franklin's employ but quickly discovered they were fighting on the wrong side. In the years since then, the settlement of Big Rock and the spread known as the Sugarloaf both had grown prosperous.

Smoke and Dean McKinley were riding on Sugarloaf range for quite a while before they came in sight of the ranch headquarters. Smoke and Sally had lived in a log cabin when they started the spread, but these days, the main house was an impressive two-story structure of whitewashed lumber with a nice gallery along the front.

The bunkhouse was built of logs but was large, sturdy, and comfortable. The big barn, several storage sheds, and a number of corrals were all very well kept. Pearlie, who worked as Smoke's foreman these days, wouldn't allow anything else. He had a top-notch crew under his command, and he didn't let them slack off in any of their tasks.

McKinley looked around as they rode in, his face revealing how impressed he was by what he saw.

"This is just about the nicest place I've ever worked, Smoke," he said. "Most of the other spreads were just greasy-sack outfits where I was the only hired hand—or me and one other hombre."

"I've been lucky," Smoke said.

"More like hard work than luck, I'm guessing."

Smoke chuckled. "There have been plenty of days when we've worked from can to can't, that's true. The effort is worth it, though, when you're building something good."

Pearlie emerged from the barn, obviously having heard their horses approaching. The lean, weathered foreman cast a wary, speculative eye on the stranger riding beside Smoke. He didn't say anything, though.

Smoke reined in. McKinley followed suit. Smoke rested both hands on the saddle horn, leaned forward, and said, "Pearlie, meet Dean McKinley. Dean, this is Pearlie Fontaine, my foreman."

McKinley nodded. "Mighty pleased to meet you, Mr. Fontaine."

"Likewise, maybe," Pearlie said. With a true Westerner's unflagging hospitality, he reached up and shook hands with the young cowboy. "What brings you to the Sugarloaf?"

"I did," Smoke said. "I asked Dean to ride for our brand. But I realize that's stepping on your toes a mite, Pearlie, so if you object—"

Pearlie stopped him with a snort. "Like I'd ever overrule you about a decision regardin' the runnin' of this ranch. Even if you didn't own the place, Smoke, you know I trust your judgment."

"Well, I trust you to let me know if I ever run off the rails."

"Sure, no doubt about that, but that ain't likely to happen."

Smoke and McKinley dismounted. Pearlie went on, "You fellas ran into each other in town, I reckon?"

"Yeah, and there was gun smoke in the air," Smoke said. Pearlie listened with great interest as Smoke described the botched holdup at the train station and the bloody aftermath.

When Smoke was finished, Pearlie nodded to McKinley and said, "Smoke done the right thing askin' you to work for the Sugarloaf, son. You get to know what a fella's made of right quick when there's bullets flyin' around like that." He reached for the reins. "I'll tend to the horses while you go introduce Dean to Miss Sally."

"Thanks," Smoke nodded. He inclined his head toward the house as an indication that McKinley should come with him.

As they walked toward the house, McKinley said quietly, "He's the foreman, and yet he's going to unsaddle and take care of those horses personally?"

"Sure," Smoke replied without hesitation. "Everybody works on the Sugarloaf, and nobody is better than anybody else. That would be a good thing for you to remember."

"Yes, sir, I sure will."

They found Sally in the kitchen, her sleeves rolled up, her forearms dusted with flour, and her hands in a big bowl in which she was mixing bread dough. She looked over her shoulder, blew back a strand of dark hair that had fallen over her forehead, and said, "Good gracious, Smoke, try to give me some warning the next time you bring home company!"

McKinley snatched his hat off, held it in front of him, and looked embarrassed as a pink flush spread over his tanned features.

"Begging your pardon, ma'am, but I don't reckon I'm company," he said.

"Dean's right," Smoke said. "Meet the newest member of the Sugarloaf crew, Sally. This is Dean McKinley. Dean, my wife, Mrs. Jensen."

Sally wiped her hands on a dish towel and shook hands with McKinley. "You don't have to worry about that Mrs. Jensen business," she told him. "The men all call me Miss Sally, and I expect you will, too."

"Yes, ma'am, Miss Sally."

"There's good news, Sally," Smoke said. "I got that telegram from Colonel Griffin I was hoping to see. We've struck a deal for the horses."

She put a hand on his arm. "That's wonderful." Then a slightly crestfallen look came over her face. "But that means you'll have to go to New Mexico, doesn't it? You said that if you made a deal, the army would expect you to deliver the horses to them, instead of coming and getting them themselves."

"That's right, but I'm hoping if they're satisfied and want to continue the arrangement, they'll come here to pick them up. Once they see the quality of the animals we're raising, I think there's a good chance of that."

"I hope so. I don't like it when you're gone, especially when you can't take me with you!"

"I never said you couldn't come along," Smoke told her, "but it'll be a long, hard drive. It'll probably take a full two weeks."

"And if I leave, there won't be anyone to take over the school in town temporarily while Miss Herring is gone next week."

"You miss teaching, don't you?" Smoke asked, seemingly having forgotten that McKinley was still standing there, hat in hand.

"I do," Sally admitted, "but I can't think of anywhere that married women are allowed to be teachers, except on a temporary basis in situations like this one." She smiled as her hand tightened on Smoke's arm. "But that's all right. I'd rather be married to you than teach."

McKinley cleared his throat and said, "Maybe someday they'll let ladies do both. Seems like it shouldn't be a problem."

"I agree with you, Dean."

To Smoke, McKinley said, "Reckon I'd better head on out to the bunkhouse and stake my claim on an empty bunk."

"There should be several," Smoke told him. "I like for the men to have plenty of room."

McKinley nodded again to Sally and said, "It sure is a pleasure meeting you, ma'am."

"Do you like bear sign?" she asked.

"Bear sign? You mean those little round cakes you fry up? Ma'am, I don't think there's a cowboy anywhere who doesn't like bear sign!"

She laughed and said, "Then I believe you're going to be happy here on the Sugarloaf, Dean."

CHAPTER 3

Sally's prediction proved to be true: Dean McKinley was as happy riding for the Sugarloaf as he had ever been during his career as a cowboy.

It wasn't just because of the delicious bear sign or the fact that Sally was an all-around superb cook who fed the men very well, either. Dean worked as hard as he ever had in his life, from dawn to dusk, but he worked alongside friendly, competent men, for bosses, in Smoke and Pearlie, who were demanding but fair.

Not only that, but there was also a genuine feeling of appreciation for what the crew accomplished. Neither Smoke nor Pearlie was the sort of man to throw around compliments, but when you'd done a job and they gave you a nod of satisfaction, you knew they meant it.

It wasn't as if the spreads where Dean had worked in the past were bad places, either. He'd been content for the most part. But there was just something different about the Sugarloaf . . .

Most of the next week after Smoke and Dean met in Big Rock was spent rounding up the horse herd that would make the five-hundred-mile trip to Socorro, down in New Mexico Territory. The herd had been somewhat loosely gathered to start with, but the horses had to be corralled and have road brands slapped on them. Once the army had taken possession of them, they would be branded as property of the United States Army.

There were also some stragglers Smoke wanted rounded up and added to the herd. These horses were more of a challenge, because they had drifted off to the upper reaches of Sugarloaf range and were a tad wild, according to Pearlie.

Dean spent several days as part of the group scouring the foothills and chousing those horses back toward headquarters. Once they were in the corrals, several men took over the chore of gentling them, making sure they were cooperative enough to take along on the drive.

It was a busy time. Dean stretched out on his bunk every night with a feeling of aching weariness in his body, but also with a sense of satisfaction with the job he had gotten done that day.

That was something he hadn't really experienced since his folks died when he was fourteen years old. He had been focused on sheer survival more than anything else.

He was riding with Pearlie in one of those high pastures when the foreman said, "You can tell me to go climb a stump if you want to, kid, since it ain't none of my business, but I was wonderin' where you hail from. You don't sound like a Texan, or somebody from down south like Georgia or Mississippi."

"I don't mind talking about it, Pearlie," Dean said. "I was born and raised over in Kansas. My folks had a farm in the eastern part of the state."

"Any brothers and sisters?"

"Nope. I'm the only child." Dean made a face. "That seemed to be the source of a few hard feelings between my ma and pa, but I don't see how that was really my fault."

Pearlie snorted. "Yeah, it don't seem like you'd have any say in the matter."

"Anyway, it wasn't much of a farm, but they hung on to it and kept trying to make it pay all through the war. Those were hard days. I'm just old enough to remember the Jayhawkers coming through and raising Cain. My pa didn't take either side. He just wanted to be left alone to do his work. Seems like a reasonable attitude to me, but some folks just can't stand to leave folks alone."

Pearlie blew out a breath and said, "You're sure as blazes right about that! A whole heap of the trouble in this ol' world comes about because of folks who can't abide anybody else not thinkin' like they do."

"We made it through the war, though," Dean continued, "and things went on like they were for a few more years—always a struggle but always getting by somehow. Then they both got sick with a fever and died. Wasn't a thing in the world I could do about it. Or anybody else, either."

"Mighty tough break," Pearlie said with a shake of his head. "What'd you do?"

"The preacher at the church in the little town not far off took me in for a little while, but only long enough for him to write to my uncle—my ma's brother—who had a livery stable in Abilene. He said I could live with him, so the church paid my fare on the train to get there. It didn't amount to much." Dean paused and drew in a breath. "When I got there, though, I wished they hadn't gone to the trouble. Turned out my uncle just wanted a stable hand he wouldn't have to pay."

"You told Smoke you'd been cowboyin' since your folks died. You didn't say nothin' about workin' in a livery stable."

"That's because I was there for such a short time I tend to disremember it."

That was stretching the truth a mite, Dean mused to himself. He didn't allow himself to spend time dwelling on it, but he hadn't forgotten how his uncle had taken a doubled-up rope to his back more than once, whenever Dean did something that didn't quite suit him.

"My uncle and I didn't get along too well. He didn't think I was a very good worker."

"Well, that's hard for me to believe," Pearlie declared. "I ain't seen you slack off the least bit since you been ridin' for the Sugarloaf, and you're dang near a top hand when it comes to ridin' and ropin' and handlin' stock."

"I appreciate you saying that, Pearlie, I really do," Dean said. "I fit in here better than I ever did back in Abilene." He grinned and waved a hand at the spectacular scenery around them. "Riding this range is a whole heap better than mucking out stalls!"

Pearlie chuckled and said, "Yeah, I reckon I can see how it would be."

"Since I was working in a stable, I got to know some of the cowboys who'd come up the trail from Texas with the cattle drives back in those days. We had an old horse on the farm, so I knew how to ride. I left the stable and tagged along with some fellas who were going back to Texas. A couple of them weren't much older than me, and I'd made friends with them."

"What'd you do for a mount?" Pearlie asked.

"My uncle, uh, loaned me one."

The two men rode along in silence for a moment. Then Pearlie said, "So you stole a horse from your uncle, ran away from the stable, and lit a shuck for Texas with a bunch of wild cowboys."

"I wouldn't call it—" Dean began hastily.

Pearlie held up a hand to stop him. "No, no, don't waste your breath denyin' it, son. Just answer me this: Did you have a good reason for doin' what you did?"

Dean thought again about that rope lashing across his back, knocking him to his knees and filling him with pain, and he said, "Yes, sir. As far as I'm concerned, I sure did."

Pearlie nodded slowly and then said, “You may not know this about me, but I’ve done a few things in my life I ain’t all that proud of. Nearly ever’body does, even if sometimes it’s mostly by accident and you’re sorry for it from then on.”

“I’m not sorry,” Dean said.

“I ain’t askin’ if you are.” Pearlie scratched his jaw. “How long we been ridin’ this mornin’?”

The question surprised Dean. “I’m not sure. An hour or so?”

“Look over your shoulder.”

Dean did so, but he didn’t see anything unusual.

“Reckon you can go back and fix it so we didn’t cover any o’ the ground we covered in the past hour?”

“You know I can’t,” Dean said. “Once you’ve ridden over a trail, it’s done.”

Pearlie pointed ahead of them. “Then you’d be spendin’ your time better to look up yonder, wouldn’t you?”

For a moment, Dean didn’t say anything. Then he grinned and told Pearlie, “I can’t argue with that. But there’s one more thing I want to tell you.”

“Go ahead.”

“When I got to Texas, I found a job working on a ranch west of Fort Worth, and when the owner sent a herd up the trail to Abilene, I was part of the bunch that went along. We got there and the trail boss paid us off. The crew scattered to spend those wages on liquor, cards, and women.”

“That’s usually the way it works,” Pearlie said dryly.

Dean said, “I went back to my uncle’s livery stable and slapped those gold eagles in his palm. It was more than that horse I took was worth, but doing that was worth it to me. The son of a gun did some blustering and said he was going to call the law on me, anyway, but then he changed his mind and decided we were square.”

"Let me guess," Pearlie drawled. "You'd grown a mite since he'd seen you last."

"Six inches and forty pounds," Dean said. "I was packing iron, too, because I hadn't gotten around to checking my gun yet with the marshal, Bear River Tom Smith, even though we were supposed to when we came into town. But I never made a move for it. My uncle knew it was there, though."

"Reckon that was the last time you saw your uncle?"

"Yep. I worked on a few more drives, but I found out I like regular ranch work better." Dean laughed. "Eating dust for hundreds of miles isn't very appetizing, and somehow I always got stuck riding drag."

"And yet now you're goin' on a trail drive all the way to Socorro. Horses instead o' cattle, mind you, but there'll still be plenty of dust to eat, and I reckon you'll get your share."

Dean sat up straighter in the saddle. "What do you mean by that, Pearlie?" he asked. "Smoke hasn't said anything to me about going along on the trip. I figured that since I've only been working on the Sugarloaf a little while, he'd never pick me for something like that."

"Smoke keeps his own counsel," Pearlie said. "But I know that before he decides on who goes and who stays, he'll ask me what I think. Part of the way, that drive will be followin' the Rio Grande, you know."

"Yeah . . ." Dean said, unsure what the foreman meant by that.

Pearlie looked over at him, nodded, and said, "So I'll tell him I think you'll do to ride the river with, son."

A couple of days after that, Smoke assembled the men in front of the house and pointed one by one to the twelve hands who would be going along on the drive. The other ten members of the crew would remain on the Sugarloaf and tend to the work that would continue there.

As Pearlie had predicted, Dean McKinley was one of the men Smoke picked to go with him to Socorro.

Things moved quickly from that point. The ranch owned a chuck wagon, and the cook Smoke had hired to drive it arrived that same day, bringing a wagonload of supplies from the mercantile in Big Rock to stock it. Once the barrels, bags, and crates of provisions had been transferred over to the chuck wagon, the driver who had come out with the cook took the store's wagon back to town.

The cook was a bald, leathery old-timer named Arbogast. Dean never heard his first name, not then or later. The man was so scrawny it seemed unlikely, looking at him, that he would be much of a cook, but Pearlie assured the young cowboy that wasn't the case.

In fact, the foreman licked his lips in anticipation and said, "Arbogast has handled chuck wagons for several spreads around here and worked for quite a few down in Texas, too. I ain't sayin' he's as good a cook as Miss Sally, mind you, because hardly anybody is, but Arbogast won't let you go hungry, and his grub'll stick to your ribs. That's all you can ask on a trail drive."

In addition to the twelve cowboys, Smoke had hired a young man from Big Rock named Perry Severs to be the wrangler and handle the remuda. Perry had been a hostler in the livery stable and had a good way about him when it came to working with horses.

Somewhat to Dean's disappointment, Pearlie was going to remain at the ranch. Somebody had to be in charge here at the Sugarloaf while Smoke was gone on a trip that was expected to take at least a month. Dean got along well with Pearlie and would miss the foreman, but he understood why Smoke wanted Pearlie to remain behind.

With the road branding completed and the chuck wagon stocked and ready to roll, all the hands who were going on the journey got a good night's sleep and turned out of their bunks early on the morning of departure, well before the sun was up. An air of excitement filled the bunkhouse's big main room as the men dressed. Plenty of talk and laughter went back and forth among them.

They flocked to the house for a last breakfast at the big dining table. Sally had been up even earlier, preparing the sort of meal that the men would remember with fondness all the way to New Mexico Territory and back. They consumed scores of flapjacks and biscuits, mounds of hashed brown potatoes, tall stacks of thick ham slices, an equal number of fried steaks, and enough eggs to have kept a whole flock of chickens busy for a while. To wash it down, they guzzled gallons of cold buttermilk and hot black coffee.

Some of the men were groaning when they pushed back from the table, but they would work that fullness off—and then some—as the day went on.

The sun still wasn't up when breakfast was finished, but the sky in the east had grown considerably lighter. Cowboys streamed from the house to the barn to saddle the mounts they would use today. Perry Severs headed for the big corral where the remuda was kept.

In a large pasture south of the ranch headquarters, the three hundred horses destined for Fort Craig grazed peacefully, watched over by four hands who had pulled nighthawk duty.

Arbogast pulled his gaunt frame up onto the driver's seat of the chuck wagon and took the reins. He flapped them against the backs of the horses already hitched to the vehicle and got them moving. The chuck wagon rolled out in the predawn grayness. Arbogast would travel in front of the drive all day, selecting a good campground late in the afternoon and then letting the others catch up to him while he prepared the evening meal.

All the men would have to eat in the middle of the day were

biscuits and bacon left over from breakfast, but that would be enough.

Dean led his saddled dun out of the barn. He would ride his personal horse this first day. He had two more mounts belonging to the Sugarloaf assigned to him in the remuda, a sturdy chestnut and a bay with a blaze face and a bit of an attitude. Dean figured he would get along fine with the bay, though.

Some of the men had already headed out to the pasture where the herd was waiting. Dean had swung up into the saddle and was about to do that himself when he spotted Pearlie on the porch of the main house. The foreman waved him over.

Dean walked the dun up to the porch. Pearlie leaned on the railing and said, "I just wanted to wish you good luck, kid. Keep an eye on Smoke, and follow his lead. Do what he says, and you won't never go wrong."

"That's exactly what I intend to do," Dean replied. He gave in to impulse and went on, "I wish you were coming with us, Pearlie."

"I do, too, son. I do, too. It's been a while since I been to New Mexico Territory. There's some pretty country down there, and I wouldn't mind seein' it again." The older man grinned. "And if there's one thing you can count on, it's that anytime Smoke goes somewhere, there's bound to be some excitement along the way. I envy you that."

"You really think so?"

"Well, if history's anything to go by—"

Before Pearlie could say anything else, Smoke and Sally emerged from the house. Smoke's arm was clasped around his wife's shoulders, and she was pressed close against his side. Clearly, the two of them hated to be parted; anybody with eyes could see that.

However, Smoke had a job to do, and he wasn't one to allow sentiment to interfere with that. He gave Sally a squeeze and stepped away from her.

The two of them must have already said their real goodbyes, Dean thought.

"Ready to go, Dean?" Smoke asked.

"Yes, sir, Smoke," the young cowboy replied, with genuine enthusiasm. "Can't wait."

"You don't have to," Smoke said. One of the men who was staying behind led up Smoke's favorite horse, Drifter, saddled and ready to ride. Smoke went down the steps, took the reins, and swung lithely into the saddle.

"We'll be back in about a month, if all goes well," he went on. With a smile, he added, "When you're dealing with the government, you never really know how long things are going to take."

"That's because government's an unnatural institution," Pearlie said. "One o' them, what do you call 'em, necessary evils."

Sally said, "I think you're exaggerating a bit, Pearlie. Government isn't that bad."

"No offense, Miss Sally, but you growed up back East where things are tamed down. It ain't like that out here."

"I've been out on the frontier long enough to know what it's like," she reminded him, "and I can see why sometimes government might be a burden to people who like to . . ." She searched for the words.

"Stomp their own snakes?" Pearlie suggested.

"Exactly!"

Smoke said, "I hope we don't have to stomp any snakes on this trip, but if we do, we'll take care of it." He looked over at the young range rider beside him. "Isn't that right, Dean?"

"You can bet a hat on that!" Dean responded.

Smoke lifted a hand, said quietly to Sally, "We'll be back," and wheeled Drifter around. He nudged the big horse into motion. Dean fell in alongside him on the dun.

As they rode toward the pasture where the herd was waiting along with the other men who were going along on the drive,

Dean asked, "Do you really think we can go all the way to New Mexico Territory and back without running into any trouble, Smoke?"

"Well, it doesn't seem too likely," Smoke said. Off to their left, the reddish-gold orb of the sun was about to poke its face over the horizon. "But I suppose we'll find out."

Chapter 4

Smoke wasn't the sort of man who minded admitting that he was surprised, and surprise was the emotion he felt at what he, his men, and the horse herd encountered on the way to Socorro.

Nothing. Well, nothing really to speak of.

Or rather, they saw plenty of spectacularly beautiful scenery as they traveled southward with the rolling grasslands of eastern Colorado on their left and the magnificent Front Range of the Rockies rearing toward the heavens on their right. Eventually, the Sangre de Cristos curved in from the west and loomed in front of them, to the naked eye blocking their path until they came to the dizzying drop of Raton Pass. Getting the herd down through the pass was hard, sweaty, nerve-racking work, but Smoke and the men from the Sugarloaf managed without losing a single animal.

On the flatlands again, angling southwest along the bulge of the mountains, a storm moved in unexpectedly one night, dumping torrential rain on men and horses alike.

The worst of it, though, was the lightning that accompanied the rain, jagged fingers of fire that clawed through the ebony sky and sent bolts of pure destruction slamming down to the earth around the herd.

No one slept that night, and it took a supreme effort from the men, including Perry Severs and Arbogast, to prevent the herd from stampeding and scattering all over creation.

When the storm finally moved on just as day was breaking, Smoke told the men they would stay right where they were and rest for twenty-four hours after that ordeal. That delay would also allow the perennially thirsty ground to suck up the moisture so it would no longer be a sea of mud.

The mountains petered out and the herd jogged west, into the valley of the Rio Grande, then swung south with Albuquerque and the Manzano Mountains ahead and to the west.

More than a week had passed since they had left the Sugarloaf. Arbogast drove the chuck wagon into Albuquerque to replenish their supplies, a couple of men going with him just to make sure that the cook didn't run into any trouble. Smoke held up the herd again for half a day to give Arbogast time to rejoin them, which he did, with the report that nothing unusual had happened while he was in town.

The lack of trouble began to nag at Smoke. He wasn't used to that.

He began to wonder if destiny was saving up some bad luck for him.

When the drive resumed, they crossed the Rio Grande at the Atrisco Ford, south of the settlement. The river was fairly broad here but shallow, and the banks were wooded and easy for the horses to handle, unlike the towering, rocky gorges through which the stream snaked in much of the territory.

Smoke sat his horse on the western bank and watched the herd come across. They had lost some weight during the long days of the journey, he noted, but not a significant amount. They would recover quickly once they were being fed army fodder every day at Fort Craig.

The men were beginning to look a bit haggard and drawn, as well. Despite the fact that the drive had been relatively easy, it still took a lot of hard work to move three hundred horses more than five hundred miles.

But they would have a break when they reached Socorro and turned the herd over to the army. Unlike a cattle drive, where the men were paid off when the herd reached the railhead and could either return to the home ranch or do whatever they wanted, these cowboys were all regular members of the Sugarloaf crew. Smoke wouldn't force any of them to return to the ranch with him, but he anticipated that they all would. He would give them some of their wages when they reached Socorro, so they could celebrate the end of the drive, but not enough to have a big blowout and get themselves in trouble.

Dean McKinley was one of the last men to cross the river. As he rode ashore, he looked as tired as the rest of them, but he summoned up a smile and told Smoke, "This is the first time I've been west of the Rio Grande."

"There's still a lot of country between here and the Pacific Ocean," Smoke told him.

"I know, and I'd sure like to see some of it, one of these days. Right now, though, we've still got a herd of horses to deliver to the army."

Smoke returned the young cowboy's grin and waved him on.

The herd had to swing well west of the river as it dropped into a deeper and wider canyon, but they stayed within the valley formed by the Rio Grande in ages past. From time to time, the trail was close enough to the rim for Smoke to peer down the steep, rugged slope to the silvery stream flowing far below. He had been here before, but it was a sight that never failed to impress him.

For a couple of days, the trail wound through some small hills with a mountain range lying to the west coming steadily closer. Smoke knew those were the Magdalena Mountains and that they lay a short distance southwest of Socorro. That meant they weren't far from their destination.

That thought quickened his pulse a little. He was eager to conclude his business with the army so that he could get home to his wife.

Socorro had been a settlement for hundreds of years, first an Indian village, then an actual town established when the Spaniards began moving up here from Mexico. These days it was a bustling trading center, the southernmost settlement before the desert known as the Jornada del Muerto—Journey of the Dead Man—began. Fort Craig itself, Smoke knew, lay at the northern tip of that arid wasteland.

It was the middle of the afternoon, fifteen days after leaving the Sugarloaf, that they came in sight of Socorro, sprawled on the western bank of the Rio Grande as the river made a curve to the west. As an old Spanish settlement, many of its buildings were adobe, some were constructed of massive sandstone blocks, and in the nearly three decades since New Mexico had become a United States territory, quite a few frame structures had gone up, built with lumber from trees in the nearby mountains. The population was a lively mixture of white, Mexican, and Indian.

Smoke called a halt on some grassland just north of the settlement. Until he had a chance to talk to the army representative meeting him here and find out what the man wanted done with the horses, this was as good a place as any to keep them contained.

His second-in-command on this drive was an experienced cowboy named Vic Russell. He waved Russell over and told him, "I'll ride on into Socorro and see if I can find Colonel Griffin or, more likely, one of his junior officers who got sent up here to take possession of the herd."

"You want us to keep them grazing here, Smoke?" Russell asked.

"That's right. Take them down to the river, one small bunch at a time, and let them drink. It's good that they're not too thirsty. They'll be easier to control that way."

Russell nodded in understanding. "You want anybody to go into town with you?"

"No, that shouldn't be necessary," Smoke replied with a shake of his head. "I'm not expecting any trouble."

"Trouble's got a way of croppin' up when you least expect it," Russell said. "Although it sure hasn't on this trip, has it?"

"Not really."

The lanky cowboy thumbed his hat back and said, "In a way, that's a mite worrisome, ain't it, Smoke?"

Smoke grinned. "That crossed my mind, but I'm trying not to think about it."

He lifted a hand in farewell to the men and turned his horse toward the settlement. It wasn't long before he was reining to a stop in front of the Grand Central Hotel, a two-story wooden structure with an impressive balcony above the entrance.

Across the street was a broad, well-kept plaza enclosed by a picket fence, and on the far side of the plaza rose a distinguished old Spanish mission with a bell tower. Smoke tied his horse to an iron hitching post at the end of a long water trough in front of the hotel.

The Grand Central didn't have a porch or a boardwalk, just a single step that led up to the double doors. Smoke paused outside the doors and took off his hat, then used it to swipe some of the trail dust off his clothes. He put the hat back on, went inside, and headed across a nicely furnished lobby with potted palms and comfortable-looking armchairs.

"What can I do for you, sir?" a middle-aged clerk behind the desk asked. "Do you need a room?"

"No, thanks," Smoke said. "I might later, but right now I'm supposed to meet someone here. An army officer—"

The sudden rattle of a newspaper being closed and folded made Smoke glance over his shoulder. A man who had been sitting in one of the armchairs with the paper in front of him was now getting to his feet. Smoke noted the man's uniform and realized he should have noticed the yellow stripe down the sides of the blue trouser legs, which were all that had been visible of him behind the paper.

The man tucked the newspaper under his left arm and strode purposefully toward Smoke. "Mr. Jensen?" he asked.

"That's right." Smoke saw the two small linked silver bars on the shoulders of the man's uniform jacket and the crossed sabers insignia pinned to his collar. This fellow was a captain, not Colonel Andrew Griffin himself, which came as no surprise to Smoke. He had suspected that the commander of Fort Craig would send a junior officer in his place.

"Captain Philip Litchfield," the man said, introducing himself as he extended his hand. He was in his early thirties, medium-sized, with sleek, dark hair and a narrow mustache. As they shook, he added, with a slight tone of reproach in his voice, "I've been expecting you for the past couple of days."

If Litchfield was expecting an apology because he'd had to wait, he wasn't going to get it. Driving three hundred horses that far wasn't an exact science. But Smoke did say, by way of explanation, "We got held up for a day by a bad rainstorm."

"I see. They're rare in this part of the country, but when one does blow up, it can be quite violent." Litchfield smiled. "I'm glad you're here. Welcome to New Mexico Territory. You have the horses you and Colonel Griffin agreed upon?"

"I do," Smoke said. "Didn't lose a one of them on the way down here."

Litchfield looked impressed. "That's quite an accomplishment."

"Luck and hard work. That'll take care of most problems."

"Indeed."

The captain's bearing was stiff and formal, and Smoke had the feeling he would be a hard hombre to warm up to. But that didn't matter, he reminded himself. He was just here to sell some horses, not to make friends.

"Where are the animals?" Litchfield went on.

"They're grazing north of town. If there's somewhere you want us to put them, or if you want us to just turn them over to the men you brought with you—"

Litchfield's sudden frown made Smoke come to a stop. The captain said, "I'm afraid there's been a misunderstanding, Mr. Jensen. You're not turning the horses over to me here in Socorro. I and the troopers I brought with me will be providing an escort for you as you take the animals on to the fort and make the official delivery there."

Irritation at this unexpected change in plans welled up inside Smoke, but he kept it under control as he asked, "How far is it from here to the fort?"

"A bit more than forty miles."

"We can do that in a day if we push the horses hard, but it might be better to take a day and a half for the trip." Smoke shrugged. "I didn't think that was the deal, but after we've come this far, I don't suppose another forty miles makes much difference. As late in the day as it is, it makes more sense to wait and get a fresh start in the morning."

The dubious look that appeared on Litchfield's face warned Smoke that the officer had something else to say.

Smoke controlled his growing impatience and asked, "What is it, Captain?"

"You'll need to corral the animals here in Socorro and wait for an army veterinarian to examine them and give them a clean bill of health before they're taken on to the fort."

"I have three hundred horses, Captain. Are there that many empty corrals in town?"

"No, but I've made arrangements to use two of them. You can put fifty horses in each corral. Bring them in a hundred at a time, and once the doctor has examined them, they can be moved to an area south of town so they won't be able to mingle with the unexamined animals."

Smoke felt like yanking his hat off and scrubbing a hand over his face in frustration, but he suppressed the impulse. "You have one horse doctor?"

"That's correct. Captain Samuel Brant. He's an experienced veterinarian and quite good at his job."

"How long do you figure this process will take?"

"Captain Brant will be very thorough in his examinations, of course, but I don't think the whole thing will require more than four days."

"We've been gone from home for more than two weeks already, Captain," Smoke pointed out.

Litchfield stiffened. "The army has its own way of doing things, sir, and anyone doing business with the army is well advised to become accustomed to that."

"Of course," Smoke allowed. "Where are those corrals you mentioned?"

Litchfield told him how to find the corrals.

"I reckon there's time to bring in the first batch of horses today, so the doctor can get started checking them first thing in the morning," Smoke said. "Will that be all right?"

"That's fine." Litchfield smiled thinly, but his pale blue eyes remained as cool as chips of ice. "I can provide guards to watch over the animals during the night, if you'd like."

"That would be good. Once my men have the horses in the corrals, I'd like for them to have a break. They've been working hard."

"I'm sure they have. You'll find that Socorro is a hospitable place. The last bit of hospitality you'll find in quite a distance, in fact. South of the fort is the Jornada del Muerto—and it's not hospitable at all."

When Smoke got back to the herd after bidding farewell to Captain Litchfield for the time being, the men were just as surprised as he had been to hear that the drive wasn't over after all.

"You mean we have to just sit and wait while some army horse doctor pokes and prods every one of those critters?" one of the men asked.

"I'm afraid so," Smoke said. "In a way, I can understand why they're doing it like this. The army wants to make sure it's getting good value for its money."

"That means they don't trust you," another cowboy put in. "That's a dang insult!"

Mutters of sullen agreement came from several of the others.

Smoke shook his head to quiet them and said, "No, it's fine. With a big chunk of the horses corralled, it won't take all of you to watch them."

That comment perked them up immediately. Vic Russell said, "You mean we'll be able to go into town?"

"Not all at once, but there ought to be enough time for everybody to pay a visit to Socorro."

"I like the sound of that," a man called.

"Do they have saloons there?" another asked.

Smoke laughed. "Plenty, from what I saw." He picked out half a dozen men to drive a hundred of the horses to the corrals. The other six men would keep watch on the remainder of the herd.

By the time they had cut out a third of the animals, driven them to the enclosures on the edge of town, split them into two groups, and gotten them securely behind the fences, dusk had begun to settle down over Socorro and the mountains that rose in the distance.

As Smoke swung the corral gate closed, he said to his men, "Four of you can stay here in town tonight. The other two head back out to where the herd's bedded down. You can draw lots to figure out who stays and who goes, or figure it out some other way among yourselves."

The men huddled together for a couple of minutes, and then Dean McKinley and three others approached Smoke.

"We're stayin'," Carl Moore told Smoke. The other two men, along with McKinley, were Alvie Rogers and Walt Pogue.

Smoke had already taken some gold eagles from the money belt he wore. He gave two coins to each of the men.

"I don't want to have to get anybody out of jail in the morning," he warned them. "So have a good time, blow off some steam, but stay out of trouble. *Sabe?*"

The men nodded that they understood.

"If you need me, I'm going to be at the Grand Central Hotel," Smoke went on. He didn't want the men to think that he was putting on airs, so he added, "That's where Captain Litchfield is staying, along with that army veterinarian, and I want to make sure they don't waste any time getting this job finished up."

The two men going back to the herd mounted up and rode out of Socorro. McKinley, Moore, Rogers, and Pogue led their horses off to the livery stable where Smoke had made arrangements already when he left his own horse there.

Smoke turned his steps toward the hotel. It was getting on toward suppertime, and the Grand Central had a dining room. He figured the easiest thing would be to eat there.

He was walking south along Manzanares Avenue when he noticed a small group of riders moving toward him. One man was in the lead, atop a fine-looking black horse, with three men trailing a short distance behind him.

The man in front was young and handsome, dressed in tight, embroidered trousers, a short, tight jacket, and a white shirt. His flat-crowned black hat had a band formed of silver conchas. His saddle was adorned with silver decorations, as well.

The other men wore rough range clothes and gray felt sombreros that identified them as Mexican vaqueros. The handsome young man was probably their boss, or the son of their boss.

He reached into his shirt pocket, took out a thin, black cigarillo, and snapped a lucifer to life with his thumbnail to set fire to the gasper. The look he gave to Smoke as he rode past with the cigarillo clenched at a jaunty angle between his teeth was pure arrogance personified.

The three vaqueros paid no attention to Smoke.

The four riders were all past him when he heard someone coming up quickly behind him. He looked over his shoulder and saw Dean McKinley catching up to him.

"Anything wrong, Dean?" Smoke asked as the young cowboy walked up.

"No, sir, not that I know of. It's just that Carl and Alvie and Walt found themselves a saloon they wanted to visit, and I decided not to go along."

Smoke smiled. "You didn't want a nice cold beer?"

McKinley hesitated; then, with the air of someone admitting a shameful secret, he said, "I never have been much of one for beer and whiskey. I'd rather have a good cup of coffee any day, or a glass of cold lemonade. And after they'd had some drinks, they figured on hunting up a poker game, and to be honest with you, Smoke, I'm the worst poker player to ever pick up a hand of cards."

Smoke laughed. "That doesn't leave much for a saloon to offer except—"

"Oh, I know about the gals who work in places like that. They sort of make me nervous."

"So what do you figure on doing while you're in town?"

"I thought I'd see if I could rustle up a good meal and a comfortable place to get a good night's sleep."

"You're a practical young man, Dean," Smoke said. "Come with me. We'll see if we can get you a room in the hotel, and we can have supper in the dining room."

McKinley looked surprised. "Really? That's mighty nice of you, Smoke."

"When I was in there earlier, I think I saw a counter where they have some dime novels for sale, along with cigars and candy."

A big grin spread across the young cowboy's face. "Maybe I can find one I haven't read before."

They walked on to the hotel as darkness fell. The streets were still busy with people moving around on foot and quite a few riders, as well as buggies and wagons rolling along here and there.

Then a flash of quick movement caught Smoke's eye, as it always did because somebody moving fast often meant danger of some sort.

However, in this case the threat wasn't directed at Smoke. A well-dressed woman was walking hurriedly along the street ahead of them, and several roughly clad men appeared to be following her. The way she kept glancing back over her shoulder told Smoke she was aware of them, and her rapid footsteps seemed to indicate that she was afraid of the men.

Her worry was justified, too, because one of them suddenly called to her, "Hey, lady, wait up! We just want to talk to you. Ain't no need to be scared of us."

The woman didn't respond. In fact, she picked up her pace even more, almost breaking into a run.

The man who had spoken to her cursed and lunged after her, reaching out toward her. His hand clamped around her upper right arm from behind and jerked her to a stop as she gave a frightened exclamation.

Smoke and Dean McKinley had both come to an abrupt halt as they watched this unexpected drama. As the man who had grabbed the woman hauled her around and took hold of her other arm as well, McKinley said quietly, "Smoke, I know you told us to stay out of trouble, but I don't reckon I'm going to be able to."

CHAPTER 5

"I'm glad to hear you say that, Dean," Smoke told him, "because I'm about to break my own rule, and I'd feel mighty foolish if I did that by myself."

He didn't waste any more time. He strode toward the woman and the four men now crowding around her and ordered sharply, "Let that lady go right now."

The one holding the woman maintained his grip on her. The other three turned quickly toward Smoke and McKinley, arranging themselves in a line to block their path.

"Go on about your business, mister," one of them growled. "You don't want to be stickin' your nose in somethin' that ain't none of your affair."

"I'm making it my affair," Smoke said in a flat, level voice as he came to a stop with McKinley beside him. "I won't stand by and see a lady treated in such a rough fashion."

"How do you know she's a lady?" another of the trio demanded. "She's out walkin' the street after dark, ain't she? Seems to me she's likely a whole other sort o' gal!"

The woman's gasp told Smoke how offended she was by that suggestion.

"Do you know who I am?" she asked.

The man who had hold of her arms shoved her behind him as he turned to face Smoke and McKinley.

"No, and I don't care," he rasped. "Just some soiled dove, not worth fightin' over." He stepped forward. "But a couple of two-bit saddle tramps tellin' Watt Calder what to do? That gets 'em a beatin'!"

With that, the man charged Smoke and swung a hamlike fist at his head. One of the other men yelled, "Get him, Watt! Tear him to pieces!"

Calder was big but slow. Smoke had no trouble ducking aside from the ponderous punch. As Calder's fist sailed past his head, Smoke stepped in and hooked a hard right into the man's ample belly.

Calder gasped and bent forward as Smoke's fist sunk to the wrist in his soft midsection. That put his bearded chin in perfect position for the left uppercut that Smoke threw.

The blow landed solidly. Calder's teeth clicked together and his head rocked back. Smoke moved back a half step to give himself some room and looped a right to Calder's jaw. That punch sent the big man staggering backward.

Smoke struck with such speed that the fight had lasted only a couple of heartbeats so far. Calder's companions, evidently expecting him to triumph with ease, stood rooted to the ground and stared as Smoke manhandled their friend.

That shock didn't last long, however. They yelled curses and charged as Calder stumbled backward toward them.

Calder's feet got tangled up with those of one of the men, and they both went down. The other two avoided that collision and kept coming.

Dean McKinley met them head-on. He launched a straight right that slammed into the first man's face and flattened his nose, stopping him in his tracks.

The second man tackled McKinley and drove him off his

feet. They crashed to the ground with McKinley on the bottom. The man rammed a knee into his stomach and pinned him to the ground, then reared up and began raining down punches at the young cowboy's head.

Smoke cast a glance at Calder and the other man and saw they were still tangled up on the ground. He stepped behind the man hammering fists at McKinley and grabbed him around the neck. Smoke hauled the man up and back, away from McKinley. The hombre thrashed around, but Smoke's forearm was locked across his throat like an iron bar. In a minute or so, the man slumped, passing out from lack of air. Smoke released his grip and let the fella crumple to the dirt.

Calder was back on his feet, and so was the man who had fallen down with him. The third man, the bottom half of his face dark with blood welling from his broken nose, was with them as they came at Smoke again.

Groggy from the punishment he had absorbed, McKinley pushed himself up and grabbed one of the men around the knees. The man toppled forward. McKinley scrambled after him, grabbed his hair from behind, and ground his face into the dirt.

Smoke stood toe-to-toe with the other two, slugging it out with them as he ducked and weaved. He was able to avoid some of their blows, but enough of the punches got through that Smoke was rocked back on his feet.

He caught his balance, jerked his head out of the way of a flying fist, and counterattacked. He hit Watt Calder hard enough in the solar plexus to knock the breath out of the man. That stopped Calder for a second, and Smoke seized that opportunity to grab the other man's arm, pivot, and heave. The wrestling throw had the man flying through the air with a startled yell that ended abruptly when he crashed down on his back.

Calder was the only opponent still on his feet. McKinley surged up and cocked his fists, ready to strike, and Smoke was closing in on the big man at the same time.

Neither of them had the chance to throw another punch. With a resounding crash of crockery, someone broke a heavy pitcher over Calder's head from behind. It didn't seem like enough of a blow to put Calder down, but evidently, on top of the punishment he had received already, it was enough. His legs buckled, he dropped to his knees, and then he pitched forward on his face like a falling tree.

Neither Smoke nor McKinley was expecting to see what they saw then. Standing where Calder had been was a very attractive young woman with a mass of auburn hair falling in waves around her head and over her shoulders. In the slim fingers of one hand, she still held the handle of the pitcher she had busted over Calder's thick skull.

"That'll teach you to molest my aunt, you—you reprobate!" she said, as she glared down at Calder's recumbent form.

The other woman was standing back a few feet. Smoke could see now that she was older, in her late thirties, perhaps, with dark hair. She was pretty, too, but not as eye-catching as the auburn-haired younger woman, who looked at Smoke and McKinley, and asked, "Are you gentlemen all right?"

"Yes, miss, I think so," Smoke replied.

"Fine and dandy," McKinley added, although some puffy bruises were already starting to show on his face from the punches that had landed there.

The young woman looked at the broken pitcher handle in her hand, rolled her eyes, and tossed it aside. She stepped around Calder and came up to Smoke. With a smile, she rested her fingertips on his arm and said, "Thank you so much for stepping in when you did, Mr. . . . ?"

"Jensen," he said. "Smoke Jensen." He nodded toward his companion. "This is Dean McKinley."

The young woman flashed her smile at the cowboy. "And thank you, too, Mr. McKinley. I think you're both just so gallant and brave, coming to the defense of a helpless woman that way."

"I wasn't exactly helpless, Virginia," the older woman said in a crisp tone. As if to confirm her statement, she reached into the small bag she carried and brought out a small pistol. The silvery finish on the little gun sparkled in the light that spilled through the open door of the hotel behind her.

"I know that, Aunt Dorothy, but you have to admit, it was very courageous for Mr. Jensen and Mr. McKinley to intervene against such overwhelming odds."

"They only outnumbered us two to one," Smoke said. "That's not so overwhelming."

"Especially since this is Smoke Jensen, miss," McKinley put in, as if expecting her to know who Smoke was.

A look of recognition appeared on Virginia's face. "Mr. Jensen!" she said. "I recognize the name now. You're the man Captain Litchfield came here to meet, the one with the horses."

"That's right," Smoke said. "You're acquainted with the captain?"

Before Virginia could answer, the officer himself appeared, hurrying out of the hotel.

"Virginia," he said. "I just heard there was some trouble out here. Are you and Mrs. Bacon all right?"

"We're fine, Philip," Virginia said. "Thanks to Mr. Jensen and Mr. McKinley."

She still had her hand resting on Smoke's arm as she turned toward Litchfield, and Smoke saw the way the man's eyes narrowed when he took note of that fact.

"Some terrible men accosted Aunt Dorothy," Virginia went on, "but our new friends leaped to her defense even though they were outnumbered. That didn't seem to matter, though. They disposed of the scoundrels in short order."

"Shoot, miss," McKinley said, "we just softened them up a mite. You're the one who finished off the big varmint and put an end to the fight."

"What do you mean by that?" Litchfield snapped. "Virginia, if you put yourself in danger, your father will—"

"My father will huff and growl like the surly old bear he is," Virginia interrupted. "Don't worry, Philip. I'll make sure he understands that none of this was your doing."

The older woman—Aunt Dorothy, Virginia had called her, and Mrs. Bacon, according to Litchfield—said, "If any one of us is to blame for this unfortunate business, it's me, Captain. I had walked down the street to the store and didn't realize the hour had gotten so late. It was already dark when I started back to the hotel. Those men"—she scowled at Calder and his friends, who were starting to groan and stir around—"evidently took that as an invitation to follow me and make rude comments."

"I'll have them thrown in jail," Litchfield said coldly. "I'll send a trooper to find the sheriff—"

"There's no need for that," Dorothy Bacon said. "This unpleasant business is over. Let's leave it that way."

Litchfield looked like he wanted to argue, but he gave her a curt nod and said, "Very well, ma'am, whatever you wish."

"What I wish is to go up to the room and rest."

Virginia finally stepped away from Smoke, but not before giving him another big smile. She went over to her aunt and linked arms with her.

"Come along, Aunt Dorothy. I'll go up with you. We'll have supper sent up, so that you can go ahead and get comfortable."

"That sounds very good," Dorothy agreed.

Frowning, Litchfield said, "I thought you and I were going to have supper together, Virginia."

"There'll be time enough for that another evening," she

said. "Didn't you tell me it was going to be several more days before we start for the fort with Mr. Jensen's horses?"

"You're going to the fort, miss?" Smoke asked before Litchfield could say anything.

"Yes, of course," she said. "I pay occasional visits to my father, and since Captain Litchfield and a detail of troopers were already going to be here in Socorro, it made sense for them to accompany Aunt Dorothy and me back to the fort."

"And your father is . . . ?"

Smoke had a pretty good idea he already knew the answer to that.

"Colonel Andrew Griffin, naturally," she said.

She led her aunt into the hotel, but as they stepped through the doorway, she looked back over her shoulder and favored Smoke with another dazzling smile.

Litchfield's jaw was tight, and his eyes glittered with annoyance. He followed the two women into the Grand Central.

"So that was the colonel's daughter," McKinley said. "She acted like she was mighty impressed with you, Smoke."

"She was just trying to make Litchfield jealous," Smoke said. "You could tell that."

"Maybe so, but she was enjoying it, too. And she looked mighty pleased with herself when she walloped the big ox over the head. Seems like the high-spirited type."

"Don't forget, I've already got an even prettier one of those at home. Let's go get that supper we were bound for."

They stopped at the desk, where Smoke got a room for the night for McKinley, paying for it himself and not allowing the young cowboy to do so. Then they went into the dining room, which was still fairly busy.

Spotting Captain Philip Litchfield sitting at a table by himself, Smoke motioned for McKinley to follow him and walked over to it.

"Mind if we join you, Captain," he asked, "seeing as you don't have a dinner companion after all?"

Smoke knew that was sort of rubbing Litchfield's nose in Virginia's decision not to dine with him, but much about Litchfield's attitude had rubbed him the wrong way.

Besides, he wanted to know more about what would be waiting for them at Fort Craig, and Litchfield was the best source of that information.

Litchfield looked irritated for a second, but then he shrugged and said, "Of course. Please sit down." He forced a smile onto his face. "I'd be happy for you to join me."

Maybe he considered himself an officer and a gentleman and was trying to live up to that second part, Smoke thought as he and McKinley took seats at the table. Litchfield had a cup of coffee in front of him but no food yet.

A buxom middle-aged waitress wasted no time in coming over and asking if the two newcomers wanted coffee. Smoke and McKinley answered in the affirmative, then ordered the special of the day, which was fried steak, potatoes, greens, and apple pie with cream.

"Have you eaten here before, Captain?" Smoke asked, when the waitress was gone. "How's the food?"

"Adequate. Well prepared but nothing special." Litchfield grunted. "But superior to army chow, I'd say."

Something about the captain's voice struck Smoke as familiar, and after a moment he realized what it was.

"You're from back East somewhere, aren't you? Vermont, maybe?"

Litchfield's dark eyebrows rose in surprise. "How did you know that?"

"My wife's family is from New England. I've spent some

time in that area. Not much, but enough to recognize your accent."

"A military man moves around enough that accents get dulled, but I suppose some of it always remains." Litchfield sipped his coffee. He seemed to have relaxed a little and was acting a bit less like a stuffed shirt. "You're a married man, Jensen?"

"I am."

"You should tell Miss Griffin that, otherwise she's liable to continue fluttering around you like a butterfly." Litchfield cocked a single eyebrow this time. "Unless, of course, you enjoy such behavior from a young woman."

"Don't worry, Captain, I'm happily married and intend to stay that way."

Litchfield shook his head. "It's none of my affair. Miss Griffin behaves as she pleases. It's up to her aunt, Mrs. Bacon, to see that she doesn't do anything improper."

"Do the two of them live here in Socorro?" Smoke asked.

"Mrs. Bacon does. She has a permanent suite here in the hotel that the colonel arranged for her. He's her only living relative, so he brought her out here from Saint Louis when her husband passed away. I believe he thought she would be a good influence on Virginia." Litchfield took another sip of coffee. "Virginia's mother died when she was very young. It has to have been quite difficult for the colonel, raising a daughter without a mother on a series of army posts."

"I can imagine," Smoke said.

Litchfield frowned. "I shouldn't be gossiping like this. It's quite unseemly."

"We'll change the subject then. What's Colonel Griffin like?"

"A top-notch officer. Absolutely fine. It's a privilege to serve under his command."

"Of course, you couldn't very well say anything else, could you?" Smoke observed.

The frown on Litchfield's face turned into a scowl. "It's the truth, sir," he said.

"I don't doubt it," Smoke assured him. "My dealings with Colonel Griffin have all been by letter and telegraph, but he strikes me as a no-nonsense sort, very straightforward. A man like that makes a good commanding officer, from what I've seen."

"Were you in the army?" Litchfield asked.

"No, but I've been around quite a few military men."

"It's not the same thing, but you're correct about Colonel Griffin. He's a fine commander."

Their food arrived then, Litchfield's as well as the orders for Smoke and McKinley, and they dug in. There wasn't much conversation until they were finishing up the meal, when Smoke asked, "What's the country like between here and the fort?"

"Very much like what you came through for the last hundred miles getting here," Litchfield said. "It's decent ranch land, and there's some farming along the river, but it's really not much good for anything else. South of the fort, of course, it's a different story."

"How do you mean?"

"The Jornada del Muerto isn't good for *anything*."

Smoke nodded at that blunt declaration. "I've passed through there, and that's the way I remember it, too. It's the sort of country you want to get through and put behind you as quickly as you can."

"It's still used as a wagon route up from the border, and because of that, we have to send patrols into the desert at times." Litchfield leaned back in his chair. "The Apaches in this region are all supposed to be contained on the reservation at Fort Stanton, but discontent runs high among the savages there, and some of them break out to go raiding fairly often. When they do, we have to help round them up and put a stop to their depredations. The desert is as hard on horses as it is on men. That's why we need a steady supply of remounts."

McKinley said, "How about the men? Don't you need replacements for those, too?"

Litchfield waved off the suggestion. "Most of our troopers are buffalo soldiers. They're hardier than the horses."

"Buffalo soldiers?" McKinley repeated.

"Black troops," Smoke told him. "The Indians gave them that name because their hair's dark and curly like a buffalo's."

Litchfield nodded. "Yes, the Ninth Cavalry is posted at Fort Craig, along with a couple of Black infantry companies. I don't have anything to do with those foot soldiers, though."

He sounded like he disapproved of those companies because they were infantry, not because they were Black, Smoke thought. That was a pretty common attitude among cavalry officers, no matter what races were involved.

"I hope things work out so that I'll be able to supply you with the horses you need," Smoke said. "Your veterinarian will confirm that they're all in good shape, and I think Colonel Griffin will be pleased when he sees what fine mounts they are."

"Well, time will tell about that, I suppose." Litchfield glanced toward the entrance between the hotel lobby and the dining room, then lifted his head and straightened in his chair. Smoke followed the direction of the officer's gaze and saw that Virginia Griffin had just come into the room.

CHAPTER 6

Virginia spotted the three men at the table and started toward them, wearing her usual dazzling smile.

"I hoped I would find you here," she said, as she came up behind Smoke and rested a hand on his shoulder. The words seemed to be addressed to all three men, but the way she touched him made the comment more personal.

Litchfield got to his feet, and so did Smoke and McKinley. That forced Virginia to drop her hand.

"How is your aunt?" Litchfield asked.

"She's fine. She had a glass of wine with supper and dropped right off to sleep afterward."

"Would you care to join us?" the captain invited. "I can have them bring you a cup of tea or coffee."

"Tea would be nice," Virginia said. She stood beside an empty chair and seemed to be waiting for Smoke to pull it out for her, but he didn't make a move to do so even though his sense of chivalry made him want to.

McKinley and Litchfield started around the table at the same time, but McKinley got there first and held the chair, prompting a quick glare from Litchfield.

"Let me get that for you, Miss Griffin," McKinley said.

"Thank you, Mr. McKinley."

"Shoot, you can call me Dean," he said, as he slid the chair under her while she sat down.

"That's a bit informal, don't you think?" Litchfield said stiffly. "The two of you have just met."

"Oh, I've never been the formal sort," McKinley said with a grin.

Virginia ignored that exchange and looked at Smoke as the three men resumed their seats. "What have you gentlemen been discussing?"

Before Smoke could answer, Litchfield said, "Jensen's been telling me that his wife is from the New England region, too. He even recognized my accent as coming from Vermont."

Virginia still smiled sweetly, but a slight edge crept into her voice as she said, "Your wife, Mr. Jensen?"

"That's right," Smoke said. "Her name is Sally."

Litchfield asked, "Do you have any children?"

"Not yet, but I'm sure we will, one of these days."

"Yes, I hope so," Virginia murmured, but she didn't sound too sincere about the sentiment. Smoke could almost see the wheels of her brain turning rapidly. Given this new information, she was going to have to change her approach.

She did that smoothly, with only a moment's hesitation before she turned to McKinley and asked, "What about you, Mr. McKinley? Are you married?"

He shook his head. "No, ma'am, I'm not. Reckon I've been too busy working to worry about romancing some gal."

"That's a shame. A man as handsome as you are ought to take some time away from work for the softer things in life."

"I agree with you, Miss Griffin. So far, it just hasn't worked out that way."

"That's one of the good things about life. Things can always change. And I don't believe it would be too improper or informal for you to call me Virginia . . . Dean."

Litchfield was seething again, Smoke noted. He didn't know

whether to laugh out loud at the captain's discomfiture or tell McKinley to behave himself. Although Litchfield hadn't acted quite so pompous and arrogant during supper, Smoke still didn't particularly like the man, so he decided it would be all right to let Litchfield stew a little.

Besides, in a few days, he and McKinley and the other men from the Sugarloaf would be headed north on their way home, and McKinley and Virginia would never see each other again. Virginia could go right back to teasing Litchfield mercilessly—and Smoke had no doubt that was exactly what she would do.

McKinley said, "I hear you and your aunt are going to be traveling to the fort with us, Virginia."

"That's right. I'm not fond of Fort Craig, to be honest—it's such a dusty and desolate place—but I am looking forward to seeing my father, of course. I miss him, and I'm sure he misses me. I really do prefer staying here in town, though, at least most of the time." She laughed. "Of course, Socorro is a bit on the dusty side, too! But at least there are places to shop and people around who aren't savage Indians or ruthless bandits."

"Bandits?" Smoke repeated. Litchfield had mentioned Apache raiding parties, but he hadn't said anything about bandits.

Litchfield did so now, leaning forward and saying, "There's a gang of them led by a man known as the Desert Wolf. Lobo del Desierto, the Mexicans call him. He came across the border and has rampaged through the southern half of the territory for several months, venturing as far east as El Paso and as far west as southeastern Arizona. It's rumored that he has a hideout somewhere in the badlands of the Jornada del Muerto, but no one knows for sure, just as no one knows who he really is. The man's a blasted phantom!"

"I think a lot of that is just a story," Virginia said dismissively. "No man could be as terrible as people make out the Desert Wolf to be."

Smoke said, "I wouldn't be so sure about that, Miss Griffin.

I've run into some mighty bad hombres in my time." He looked at Litchfield. "Is there any chance this Lobo fella might come after those horses between here and the fort?"

"You can never rule out anything where the Desert Wolf is concerned," Litchfield said, "but between your men and the dozen troopers I have with me, we'll be a large, well-armed force. I think even a desperado like the Wolf will have more sense than to attack us."

McKinley said, "I hope so. I'd hate to see a couple of ladies like Miss Griffin and her aunt in any danger."

"They'll be well protected, I assure you of that," Litchfield said.

They talked a while longer while Virginia sipped a cup of tea the waitress brought to her. She devoted most of her attention to McKinley, to Litchfield's continued, obvious annoyance.

Watching McKinley and Virginia flirt with each other, Smoke felt positively ancient, even though in reality he was only seven or eight years older than both of them. He supposed that going through the early losses and tragedies he had endured in his life, not to mention all the dangers he had survived along the way, had aged him more than the years could account for. And despite the fact that he and Sally had been married for less than five years, they loved each other so much it seemed like they had been together forever.

All in all, Smoke wouldn't trade what he had to be young again. Not hardly.

Finally, Virginia started to get to her feet. Litchfield and McKinley bolted out of their chairs. Litchfield reached her first this time and pulled out her chair for her as she stood.

"Thank you, Philip," she told him. "I believe I'll retire for the evening."

"I'll walk you to your room," he said.

"Thank you." She turned to McKinley and touched him lightly on the arm, just as she had touched Smoke earlier in the evening. "And thank you for your kindness and consideration, Dean, not to mention your enjoyable conversation."

"It was my pleasure, Miss Virginia," he told her. "I hope we get to talk some more."

"I'm sure we will. After all, we'll be here in Socorro for several more days, and then we'll be together on the trail to the fort."

"I'm looking forward to it."

Litchfield linked arms with her and walked her out of the dining room, which, by now, was mostly empty. Smoke and McKinley sat down again.

When Smoke chuckled, McKinley looked over at him and asked, "What's funny?"

"Watching that girl making you and Litchfield fall all over yourselves while she was running rings around both of you."

A sheepish grin spread over the young cowboy's face. "She does have kind of a flighty air about her, doesn't she? I knew she was just trying to get the captain's goat—mostly. I'd like to think she really does like me a little, though."

"I think she probably does," Smoke said, "but don't get your hopes up, Dean. A girl like her, a colonel's daughter raised on army posts, is more than likely going to wind up married to some officer."

McKinley snorted. "Like Litchfield? She can do better than him!"

"Maybe she will," Smoke said. "Just because she'll probably marry an officer doesn't mean it'll be him—even though it's pretty obvious he hopes she will."

"Well, I hope he's disappointed. And it's still going to be several days before we get to Fort Craig. You never know what's going to happen between now and then!"

Smoke was at the corral when Captain Samuel Brant showed up early the next morning to inspect the horses. Earlier in the day, Smoke had saddled up and gone exploring, finding a suitable spot to hold the horses that Brant had already passed. The army veterinarian was a stocky man with silver hair and a silver goatee, obviously someone with a great deal of experience. He shook hands with Smoke, then they stood at the fence and looked at the horses milling around inside the enclosure.

"Fine-looking animals, Mr. Jensen," Brant said. "I can tell they've traveled a good distance, but they appear to be the sort that will recover quickly from the trip."

"I think they will," Smoke agreed. "You'll find that they're healthy, too."

"Well, I'll have to be the judge of that, of course, but I'm not an unreasonable man, and I'll try not to hold things up for too long."

Brant got to work examining the horses. There was nothing Smoke could do but wait, so he left a couple of men at the corral in case the doctor needed anything and returned to the Grand Central Hotel.

Dean McKinley and Captain Philip Litchfield were both sitting in armchairs in the hotel lobby, eyeing each other warily. The auburn-haired reason for that wariness sat with her aunt on a divan between the two men.

Virginia Griffin kept up a sprightly conversation, switching her attention back and forth between McKinley and Litchfield. It was as blatant a display of emotional manipulation as Smoke had seen in a long time—and it appeared to be working splendidly as far as Virginia was concerned. She looked very satisfied with herself, and McKinley and Litchfield were both on edge as they tried to put on polite appearances.

Dorothy Bacon stood up when Smoke walked in and came across the lobby to join him. She smiled and said, "Mr. Jensen, would you do me the favor of strolling around town with me?" She glanced over her shoulder at her niece and lowered her voice as she added, "These young people are wearing me out."

"Ma'am, I'd be happy to take a walk with you," Smoke said, "but I reckon I'm about the same age as Captain Litchfield."

"Yes, but you seem more mature. And you're not being driven to distraction by Vingie."

"Is that what you call her?"

"A family nickname." She offered Smoke her arm. "Shall we?"

"Sure," Smoke said. He linked arms with the woman and they left the hotel.

"We'll walk around the plaza and over by the mission," Dorothy said. "It's early enough in the day that the air is still pleasant. It'll be as hot as blazes later, though."

"Yes, ma'am, I know. I've been to New Mexico before."

She laughed and said, "From what I've heard about you, Mr. Jensen, you've been all over the frontier. There are some very impressive stories about you."

"Most of those stories are a mite exaggerated," Smoke said, as they walked along the edge of the plaza. Although the hour was relatively early, the streets of Socorro were already busy. They would remain so until after the midday meal, Smoke knew, at which time most of the town's inhabitants would indulge in the old custom of taking a siesta.

"Even the most exaggerated stories often have a kernel of truth in them," Dorothy Bacon said. "And judging by the way you handled those ruffians yesterday evening, I suspect the ones about you aren't even all that exaggerated."

"I had help with those varmints."

"Yes, young Mr. McKinley."

"And your niece and that pitcher she wielded so effectively," Smoke reminded her.

That brought a laugh from the older woman. "Vingie heard the commotion and came outside to see what was going on. She knew I was late getting back from the store, and she was worried about me. She may be a bit flighty when it comes to young men, Mr. Jensen, but she's a good girl at heart."

"I'm sure she is. You know, you can call me Smoke if you want."

"Is that actually the name your mother gave you?"

"No, ma'am. My real name is Kirby."

"Kirby Jensen," Dorothy said. "That has a nice ring to it, as well. How in the world did you wind up being called Smoke?"

His mind went back to the day he and his father, and the scruffy old mountain man called Preacher, had been ambushed by a bunch of Pawnee warriors. Preacher had called that a "baptism of fire" for young Kirby, and he had taken the tendril of powder smoke curling from the muzzle of the .36 Colt Navy in the young man's hand as a sign. "Smoke," Preacher had dubbed him at that moment, and Smoke it had been ever since.

But instead of sharing the memory of that long-ago day with Dorothy Bacon, he said, "Oh, it's just something I picked up somewhere along the way, and I reckon it fit well enough to stick."

She seemed to accept that, because she went on. "After Vingie saw what was happening and I told her what those men had done, she ran back into the hotel and grabbed that pitcher from somewhere. I suppose she just found the first thing she could put her hands on to use as a weapon. I called out to her to stop, but—well, I doubt if this will come as a great surprise to you, Mr. Jensen, but Vingie can be a bit headstrong at times. She ignored me and went after that big ugly fellow with the braided beard."

That was a good description of Watt Calder. The end of his long, brown beard had been twisted into two braids held in place by beaded cords. Smoke had been keeping an eye out for Calder and his friends this morning. It was possible they wouldn't try to even the score for what had happened the previous evening, but they seemed like the sort that might hold a grudge.

Nothing unusual about that. Smoke was used to living with

the potential for violence. It had never been far from him in the dozen-plus years since he had left the farm in the Ozarks.

"I'll admit, I was surprised when I saw who had walloped Calder over the head like that," he said, "but now that I've gotten to know Miss Virginia a little better, it does seem like something she'd do. I know I'm going to try to stay on her good side."

"She set her sights on you immediately."

Smoke shook his head. "That didn't mean anything. She was just trying to make Captain Litchfield jealous. I understand that."

"I'm not sure that's all it was. You're a handsome man, Smoke." Dorothy laughed. "Don't get the wrong idea. *I'm* not flirting with you like Vingie was. Just stating the facts. Philip has been pursuing her for a while, and even though she's perfectly content to string him along, I don't believe she's really interested in him. Or in that young cowboy Mr. McKinley, for that matter. Driving them insane is just something to do to pass the time." A touch of melancholy came into the woman's voice as she went on, "I'm not sure Vingie is really suited for life here in the West, or army life in general. Yet it's all she's ever really known."

"Colonel Griffin is your brother, is that right?"

"That's right. Andrew is considerably older than I am. Our parents passed when I was fairly young, and he's always been, well, almost as much like a father as an older brother to me." She looked up at Smoke. "He's a good man. Very gruff, very much the commanding officer, but a good man. I hope you'll be able to work with him successfully."

"I'm sure it'll be fine," Smoke said. "He needs horses, and I've got good ones."

They walked in front of the old mission, which was a large, imposing structure with a tall bell tower and beautiful stained-glass windows, as well as ornate brickwork and elegantly carved double doors at the entrance. After admiring the mission, they turned their steps back toward the hotel.

By the end of that day, Captain Brant had given his stamp of approval to all the horses in the two corrals on the edge of the settlement. After hearing that news, Smoke found Dean McKinley and told him, "Ride out to the bed-ground and send three of the other boys to help get these horses down to where we'll be holding them until the others are inspected."

Smoke would have to split his group of cowboys again—four with the horses north of town, four with the animals being held to the south of the settlement, and four free to indulge in the pleasures Socorro had to offer, as long as they stayed out of trouble. He hoped that arrangement would work out.

"You stay with the bunch north of town," he went on to McKinley.

McKinley frowned. "You mean I can't come back into town?"

"We have work to do, Dean," Smoke said. "You had a night in town."

"Yeah, but I thought—"

"I know what you thought. You'll get to spend more time with Miss Griffin once we're all on our way to the fort."

"That trip will take just a day or two," McKinley complained. "Then we'll have to head home."

"You knew that all along," Smoke pointed out. "Don't let a pretty girl turn your head too much, Dean. There are a lot of pretty girls in the world."

The young cowboy sighed. "Yeah, I know. You're right, Smoke. I'll do what you say."

"Good man," Smoke told him. McKinley fetched his horse, mounted up, and rode out of Socorro to carry out the instructions Smoke had given him.

Smoke sympathized more than he let on. If he'd been in McKinley's place, he wouldn't have liked surrendering the field to an hombre like Philip Litchfield, either.

Dean McKinley admired Smoke Jensen more than any other man he'd ever met, and the idea of going against Smoke's orders really rubbed him the wrong way.

However, the thought of Captain Philip Litchfield squiring Virginia Griffin around town put a giant-sized burr under Dean's saddle. It was almost like having a cactus under there, it was so blasted annoying.

Carl Moore, Alvie Rogers, and Walt Pogue were going with the horses that had been inspected already to the new bed-ground south of town. One of the other men would join them there once another hundred horses had been moved to the corrals in Socorro first thing the next morning. Smoke had told Dean to remain with the part of the herd north of town, but he figured as long as he was doing necessary work, Smoke wouldn't get too upset with him if he adjusted those orders a mite. He would help drive the next batch of horses into town and then go on to join Carl, Alvie, and Walt. That would accomplish the same end, Dean told himself.

And maybe on his way through town, he could see Virginia again, even if it was only briefly. Just the thought of being with her, of gazing into her lovely green eyes and smelling the fresh scent of her thick auburn hair, made the blood race in his veins and his heart slug heavily in his chest.

Because of that, Dean didn't tell the other men everything that Smoke had told him to do. Instead, the next morning he mounted up along with Tom Parsons, Chuck Stanley, Wayman Jones, and Bob Wallace to push another hundred head into Socorro.

The corrals were empty when they got there. Carl, Alvie,

and Walt had already moved the first bunch of horses to the bed-ground south of town.

Captain Brant was waiting, along with the burly sergeant who was in charge of the detail Litchfield had brought with him and a couple of troopers from that bunch. The sergeant was white, a red-faced Irishman named O'Malley, and the troopers were Black, two of those buffalo soldiers Litchfield had mentioned.

Dean didn't see Smoke anywhere around the corrals. That was good. If he could find Virginia and visit with her for a minute, then slip on out of town without Smoke seeing him, he might get away with not exactly following orders.

The cowboys got the horses into the corrals, and the troopers closed and fastened the gates after Captain Brant and the sergeant went inside to examine the animals. Dean faced Parsons, Stanley, Jones, and Wallace and said, "All right, boys, you're free to look around Socorro and have yourselves some fun as long as you don't get carried away."

"We've been working for Smoke longer than you, McKinley," Wallace said. "What makes you think you got the right to go handin' out orders?"

"Because Smoke gave those orders to me to pass on," Dean replied. "If you don't like it, you can take it up with him." He looked around. "I don't see him right now, but I'm sure he's somewhere around town."

Chuck Stanley, who was a little older and more levelheaded than his companions, said, "No, that's all right, kid. We're not lookin' for trouble. When do you think that army horse doc will be through with this bunch?"

"Maybe by the end of the day, but more likely sometime tomorrow morning."

"So, we'll be spendin' the night in town?"

"Until you hear differently, I reckon you can figure on that.

Once Captain Brant is through examining the horses, whether it's today or tomorrow, you'll take them on and join the others south of town."

"Let's hope it's tomorrow, then," Tom Parsons said with a grin. "That way we get a night in town."

Stanley gestured to the other men. "Come on, boys." He glanced at Dean. "Where are you headed?"

"On out to join the fellas with the first bunch of horses, once I've taken care of a little business."

Dean didn't add that seeing Virginia was the business he spoke of.

While the others rode off in search of whatever pleasures and diversions Socorro might have to offer, even though it was fairly early in the day, Dean turned his mount toward the Grand Central Hotel. He dismounted a block away and led the animal so he wouldn't be so noticeable. As he approached, he looked for Smoke, Virginia, her aunt, or Litchfield, but he didn't see any of them in the street or on the boardwalks.

He knew where Dorothy Bacon's suite was located on the hotel's second floor; that had come up during the conversation the previous evening. Dean tied his horse to a hitchrack several buildings away, tugged his hat down to shield his face a little better, and walked toward the alley between the Grand Central and the two-story brick building next to it. The hotel had a rear entrance he intended to use.

He was just turning in to that alley when Virginia stepped out the Grand Central's front door, arm in arm with Captain Philip Litchfield. She saw Dean, and as their eyes met, a smile broke out on her face and she called his name.

CHAPTER 7

Once Virginia had hailed him, the only thing Dean could do was stop. He couldn't be rude and ignore her. After all, he had gone against Smoke's orders and come back into town for one reason, and that was to see her again.

Besides, Litchfield looked mighty annoyed to see him, and Dean enjoyed that, too.

So instead of going into the alley, he took off his hat and moved toward them. "Good morning, Virginia," he greeted the auburn-haired beauty, as he smiled at her. Litchfield got a curt nod and an equally brusque, "Captain."

"I thought I wouldn't see you again until we all started for the fort," Virginia said. "This is a very nice surprise."

"Well, I, uh, helped bring in the next batch of horses for the army doctor to examine," Dean explained. "And later today I have to go out and help the fellas holding the part of the herd that's been checked over already."

"But you don't have to leave right now, I hope."

"No, not right now," Dean answered without hesitation, even though the longer he remained in Socorro, the greater the chance he would run into Smoke. He'd hoped for a moment alone with Virginia, but judging by the stubborn look on Litchfield's face, he wasn't going to get it.

"Philip and I are going for a walk," she said. "Join us."

Litchfield said, "I'm sure McKinley has better things to do."

That made up Dean's mind, right there. He said, "No, I'd be happy to join the two of you."

"Let's stroll around the plaza," Virginia suggested. She offered her other arm to Dean, who took it as he fell in beside her.

That just made Litchfield's face flush a dark red with anger.

With an obvious effort, the captain kept his voice level as he asked, "How are things going with the horses?"

"Mighty fine," Dean answered. "The doctor didn't find anything wrong with the first bunch, and I don't figure he'll find anything wrong with any of the others. Smoke raises some mighty fine horses." He ventured a question. "Have you seen Smoke this morning, Miss Virginia?"

"Why, yes. He had breakfast with Aunt Dorothy and me, and when Philip and I left the hotel, they were sitting in the lobby visiting. They seem to be getting along very well."

Dean was glad to hear that. There was at least a chance Smoke would stay in the hotel talking to Mrs. Bacon long enough for Dean to have his visit with Virginia and then get out of town.

"Smoke's a mighty good man. I haven't known him all that long, but I reckon he's the best man I've ever met."

"What are your ambitions, Mr. McKinley—Dean? Would you like to have a ranch of your own someday?"

"Well, yeah, I reckon I would. Most fellas who work with cattle would like to have a spread of their own."

Litchfield said, "From what I've seen, most cowboys are too shiftless to ever accomplish anything like that. They're perfectly content to work for pitiful wages and then spend the little money they make on liquor and loose women."

"Philip!" Virginia exclaimed. "That's a very rude thing to say."

"I'm not trying to be rude, just honest." Litchfield looked over at Dean. "Do you think I'm wrong, McKinley?"

Dean kept a tight rein on his temper as he replied, "Cowboys are like hombres in any other line of work, Captain. They're all different. You're right about some of them when you sum it up that way, but not all of them are like that. Not hardly. Plenty of them are hard workers and mighty ambitious."

Litchfield snorted. "Perhaps you've met some like that. I certainly haven't."

"Philip, you're just trying to stir up trouble," Virginia scolded him.

Litchfield smiled, but it wasn't a very sincere expression. "My apologies, my dear," he murmured.

"You don't need to apologize to me," she said. "It's Mr. McKinley you should be apologizing to."

"I don't believe that's necessary," Litchfield said coldly. "He and I understand each other. Don't we, McKinley?"

"Oh, I reckon we do," Dean said, with just as hard an edge to his voice as the one in Litchfield's words.

They turned the corner of the plaza, walked in front of the picturesque old mission, and started back toward the hotel. Several familiar faces down the street, glimpsed between passing pedestrians and riders, caught Dean's attention. He looked closer and recognized his friends from the Sugarloaf crew. They were walking along the street and looking around. From the steadiness of their steps, Dean knew they hadn't been drinking much—yet.

The day was pretty young, though.

Up the street the other way, Dean saw some blue uniforms and realized they were being worn by three of the Black troopers from Fort Craig. The buffalo soldiers were sitting on a bench in front of a domino parlor. People passing by didn't appear to be paying much attention to them; this close to the fort, the citizens of Socorro had to be used to seeing Black troopers in town.

Dean's natural live-and-let-live attitude had kept him from feeling much prejudice. The army needed horses, and he didn't care what color the fellas were who were going to ride those horses.

The three of them were back to the street in front of the hotel now. Litchfield didn't look like he intended to go anywhere, so Dean was forced to ask, "Do you reckon I could have a word with you in private before I head on out of town, Miss Virginia?"

Before she could answer, Litchfield said, "I'm afraid I can't allow that, McKinley. Miss Griffin's safety is my responsibility, and I can't let her or the colonel down."

"I'm sure I'll be perfectly safe with Dean, Philip," Virginia said, with a touch of exasperation in her voice. "Clearly, he's a gentleman, and it's broad daylight, after all."

"Nonetheless, he was brawling in this very street last night. I won't risk your well-being, Virginia. If anything were to happen to you, your father would—"

She interrupted him by saying, "Have you forgotten that *I* was brawling in this street last night?"

"You were simply coming to the defense of your aunt."

"So were Mr. McKinley and Mr. Jensen."

"I don't want to cause trouble—" Dean began, although in truth, he didn't mind Litchfield being put out.

"You're not causing trouble," Virginia said quickly. With smooth skill, she disengaged her arm from Litchfield's and turned toward Dean. "Why don't we walk around the plaza again, by ourselves this time?"

"I'd sure like that," Dean said. As the two of them turned away from Litchfield, Virginia pressed closer against his side.

He felt the warmth of her body through the nice dress she wore, and it set his heart to racing again.

Behind them, Litchfield said harshly, "Virginia, I forbid this—"

She stopped, looked back at him, and said, "I'm not under your command, Philip. You can't forbid me to do anything."

Dean couldn't resist smiling at Litchfield as he and Virginia started walking again.

In hindsight, he realized that probably wasn't the smartest thing he could have done. That understanding came to him abruptly when Litchfield grabbed his shoulder, jerked him around, and punched him in the face.

Virginia cried out as the blow knocked Dean away from her and sent him stumbling backward in the street. He caught himself, and the pain of being struck on his already bruised face, as well as the sight of the sneer twisting Litchfield's lips under that narrow mustache, made fury explode inside him.

Virginia stood to one side, her startled gaze switching back and forth between the two men. As Dean started forward, she cried, "No!" but that plea wasn't enough to make him contain the rage boiling up.

With a yell, he charged Litchfield.

The arrogant confidence on the officer's face never budged. He danced aside from Dean's bull-like rush, raised his fists in a pugilistic stance, and stepped in to pepper a right-left-right combination to Dean's head.

Litchfield didn't look like a particularly impressive physical specimen, but appearances could lie. The punches landed with crisp, stunning force, driving Dean off his feet. He rolled in the dirt and came up hard against the long water trough in front of the hotel.

"Philip, stop this!" Virginia said.

"He started it," Litchfield said.

"No, you did! You struck first."

Litchfield wasn't moved by that accusation. He said, "He started it by forcing his unwanted attentions on you. I had to take action to defend your honor."

"You're not defending anything! And his attentions weren't unwanted."

That seemed to throw Litchfield for a loop, Dean noted as he struggled to his feet, but he couldn't be sure, because his head was spinning. He tried to shake that off and just made himself groggier. He was able to stay upright, though.

"Go back in the hotel, Virginia," Litchfield said. "This brute has been begging for a thrashing ever since he rode into town, and I'm just the man to give it to him."

"I told you, you can't order me around."

He glared at her. "Your father has put me in charge of you, so I daresay I can!"

"Ohhh!" Virginia's face was bright red and her eyes blazed with fury.

Her reaction was so emphatic that Litchfield's gaze was drawn to her, and in that moment, Dean summoned up the strength and speed to spring at the officer. Litchfield didn't have a chance to get out of the way this time. Dean landed a roundhouse right on him that knocked him backward.

Litchfield's knees struck the edge of the water trough, and he toppled over into it with a huge splash.

Litchfield shot back up, soaked and with water streaming off of him, but Dean had only a second to enjoy that ludicrous sight.

The next instant, strong arms clamped around him from behind and whirled him away.

"Leave the cap'n alone, cowboy!" a deep voice bellowed in his ear.

He realized that the buffalo soldiers had noticed the fight and come running to protect their officer. One of the burly troopers had hold of Dean while the other two loomed in front of him. One of them said, "Lemme have a shot at him, Obadiah!"

The blue-clad soldier slammed a fist into Dean's belly. Dean grunted in pain and would have doubled over if the first trooper hadn't had hold of him.

"I'm next," the other soldier said. "Hang on to him, Obadiah!"

Before that man could launch a punch, a shrill whoop sounded somewhere nearby. A figure flashed in front of Dean and tackled the soldier who'd been about to hit him. The men rolled in the street. Dean recognized Bob Wallace.

Chuck Stanley was there, too, throwing wild punches at the other trooper. The men from the Sugarloaf had arrived to help Dean. He knew they must have seen the battle from where they were walking along the street.

The arms wrapped around him abruptly let go. He fell to his knees. Shapes made indistinct by the rising dust swarmed around him. Fists thudded heavily on flesh and bone. It was a wild melee between the three buffalo soldiers and the four cowboys. Dean saw as he struggled to his feet, being buffeted back and forth by the brawlers around him, that despite being slightly outnumbered, the troopers seemed to be holding their own.

He spotted Virginia and Litchfield a few yards away. Litchfield had climbed out of the water trough and looked like a wet rat, but he had hold of Virginia's arm and was trying to steer her toward the hotel entrance.

"Hey!" Dean shouted. "Let her go!"

He started toward them. Litchfield saw him coming, shoved Virginia behind him, and reached for the flap of the holster on his hip that held his service revolver.

Maybe too late, Dean realized the son of a buck was fixing to shoot him!

* * *

Smoke was enjoying his conversation with Dorothy Bacon. The middle-aged widow was a handsome woman, and happily married or not, Smoke appreciated spending time with a good-looking lady.

More important, Dorothy was also smart, with a wicked sense of humor and a keen understanding of the human condition. She didn't have any blinders on when it came to her niece, either. She was perfectly aware that Virginia had quite the coquettish streak in her.

"I'm sure she'll settle down, though, once she meets the right man," Dorothy said.

"But that's not Captain Litchfield," Smoke guessed.

"Good heavens, no. He couldn't keep up with Vingie." Dorothy's lips tightened with disapproval. "Besides, he has a venal quality to him that I don't care for. He's a competent officer, though, as far as I know, and Andrew seems to like him."

"That might be enough right there to keep Miss Virginia from getting serious about him."

That brought a laugh from Dorothy. "I'd say you're right about that, Smoke. I—what in the world is that?"

The front doors of the Grand Central were closed, but that wasn't enough to keep the sound of excited shouts from reaching the hotel lobby. The sudden commotion in the street prompted Dorothy's question and made Smoke glance toward the windows flanking the doorway.

Through the glass, he saw people crowding around what appeared to be a fight. Probably none of his business, he told himself, but he thought he should go make certain of that.

His interest got more urgent when, through the press of townspeople, he caught a glimpse of a familiar face.

What was Dean McKinley doing in Socorro? He was supposed to be with the part of the horse herd that was still north of town.

"Excuse me, Mrs. Bacon," he told Dorothy, as he came lithely to his feet. "I need to see what that's about."

"You're like a firehorse when you hear the bell, aren't you, Mr. Jensen? Any sign of trouble and you're there."

Smoke paused long enough for a grin. "I actually said that same thing to a friend of mine not long ago," he told her. He'd been holding his hat on his knee as they talked. He clapped it on his head and started for the doors.

As he stepped out into the street, he spotted Captain Litchfield and Virginia Griffin only a few feet away. The captain was bareheaded and soaking wet for some reason. He had a tight grip on Virginia's arm and was forcing her toward the hotel entrance.

Dean McKinley loomed behind them and yelled at Litchfield to let Virginia go. The officer jerked around, shoved Virginia behind him, and started fumbling at the holster on his hip.

A brawl was going on in the street between some blue-uniformed cavalry troopers and several men in range clothes whom Smoke recognized as belonging to the Sugarloaf crew. He didn't know what had started the battle, but at the moment, that didn't matter.

What was important was that if Litchfield got his gun out and opened fire, innocent folks were almost sure to be hurt.

Smoke stepped past Virginia, who looked pale and frightened, and clamped his left hand around Litchfield's right wrist. The captain had gotten the holster flap unfastened, but his fingers hadn't closed around the butt of the Single Action Army revolver. And now they couldn't because of Smoke's iron grip on his wrist. Litchfield gasped in surprise and pain.

"That's a bad idea, Captain," Smoke said.

"Let go of me, blast it!" Litchfield exclaimed. He glared at McKinley. "This man—"

"This man works for me," Smoke interrupted him. "If he's done something wrong, I'll deal with him."

Virginia caught hold of Smoke's sleeve. "Dean didn't do anything wrong," she told him.

"Well, he disobeyed my orders."

McKinley had come to a stop in front of Litchfield and Smoke. He looked a little shame-faced now, almost like a little boy who'd been caught misbehaving.

"He's a disreputable scoundrel!" Litchfield said. "He forced himself on Miss Griffin—"

"He did not!" Virginia cried. "We were going for a walk around the plaza, that's all."

Before that argument could continue, a new voice bellowed, "Fall in, you scalawags, fall in!" A tall, broad-shouldered figure in a sergeant's uniform pushed through the crowd. The three cavalry troopers stopped punching and wrestling with Smoke's men and snapped to attention.

"You boys settle down!" Smoke ordered the Sugarloaf hands. "Stanley, Parsons, Wallace, Jones! That's enough!"

The four cowboys moved away from the troopers and stood scowling at the men they'd been battling. Their clothes were torn and disheveled, and their faces were bloody and bruised.

Smoke still had hold of Litchfield's wrist. In a sullen voice, the captain said, "All right, Jensen, you can let go of me. There won't be any gunplay."

"Better not be," Smoke warned. He released Litchfield's wrist and stepped to the side. Looking hard at Dean McKinley, he went on, "I don't know what's going on here, but this fight is over."

"Aye, that it is," the big redheaded sergeant said. "You men get out to the corrals now and wait for me."

One of the troopers said, "But Sarge, that fella was beatin' up on the cap'n—"

"Now, I said!" the sergeant roared.

Tight-lipped, Litchfield said, "I'm perfectly capable of fighting my own battles."

The sergeant nodded and said, "Yes, sir, 'tis sure I am that you are. The lads just wanted to pitch in and help a bit."

He turned back to the troopers and followed them, glaring, as they picked up their forage caps, which had gotten knocked off in the fight, and then filed away toward the edge of the settlement.

Dorothy Bacon had followed Smoke out of the hotel. She took hold of her niece's arm, and said, "Come along, Vingie. We'll go up to my suite."

"I'm perfectly all right, Aunt Dorothy," Virginia insisted. "I was just enjoying a pleasant walk with these gentlemen—"

"I'm sure you were," Dorothy said, "but it doesn't appear that the gentlemen wound up enjoying it as much as you did. Let's go."

Her tone didn't brook any argument, and with a weak smile in the general direction of both Litchfield and McKinley, Virginia allowed herself to be maneuvered back into the Grand Central.

Litchfield's black hat with its yellow cord and crossed sabers insignia floated on the water in the trough. He stepped over to it and picked it up with a disgusted expression on his face.

"I suggest you take better control of your men," he said stiffly to Smoke. "It's clear to see that they're lacking in discipline."

"All due respect, Captain, I'll handle my men the way I see fit," Smoke replied, his voice flat and hard with dislike.

"Don't forget, Jensen, you're dealing with the army now. Colonel Griffin is the one who'll be making the final decision about those horses."

"The colonel and I have a deal. He's taking these horses, and the army's paying the agreed-upon price, assuming they're all healthy, which they are."

"But as to whether there are any more such arrangements in the future—"

"Colonel Griffin and I will negotiate that," Smoke said.

Litchfield drew in a breath and nodded. "Very well. My apologies, sir, if I spoke out of turn."

"Everybody's blood is running a little hot right now. We can let it go at that, Captain."

"Of course." Litchfield nodded again and turned away. His high-topped black boots squelched with every wet step he took as he stalked into the hotel. Smoke managed not to smile at that.

But he had no trouble looking serious as he turned to Dean McKinley and said to the young cowboy, "Now, let's talk about what in blazes you're doing here—although I've got a pretty good idea I already know."

CHAPTER 8

Smoke made his disapproval clear, but he didn't waste a lot of time and breath raking McKinley over the coals. The crestfallen young man seemed to understand that if he disobeyed Smoke's orders again, he wouldn't be going back to the Sugarloaf with the rest of the crew.

"Go on out to the new camp and watch that part of the herd with Alvie, Walt, and Carl," Smoke told him. "There shouldn't be any need for you to come back into Socorro before we all head for Fort Craig."

"If there's any trouble out there—" McKinley began.

"One of the others can come and fetch me," Smoke said firmly.

McKinley heaved a sigh but nodded his agreement. Smoke knew he was thinking that he would be able to see Virginia again during the trip to the fort. He hoped McKinley would have enough sense not to stir up any more trouble during that time.

When McKinley had mounted up and ridden out of Socorro to the south, Smoke walked to the corrals. All six of the Black troopers were sitting nearby now, a couple of them smoking pipes while the others puffed on cigarettes they had rolled. Inside one of the enclosures, Captain Brant continued his inspection of the horses.

The burly sergeant spotted Smoke and walked over to him. "Sergeant Seamus O'Malley, sir," he introduced himself through the corral bars. "Apologies for my men gettin' out of hand."

"They believed they had a good reason, Sergeant. It didn't appear that any real harm was done to either side."

"I'd venture to say some of 'em will be a bit sore in the morning, but nothing they won't recover from."

Smoke nodded toward the horses in the corral. "Has Captain Brant come across any problems so far?"

O'Malley shook his head and said, "Nary a one, Mr. Jensen. That's as fine a bunch of horseflesh as these old eyes o' mine have ever seen."

"Thanks, Sergeant. I appreciate hearing that. When do you think the doctor will be finished?"

O'Malley thought about the question and said, "Sometime fairly early tomorrow mornin' with this batch, I'd say, and then if all goes as planned, he can finish his examinations by the middle of the day after that. We ought to be able to start for the fort around noon, day after tomorrow. That's what you were wonderin', ain't it, sir?"

Smoke nodded. "That's exactly right. I'll probably be at the hotel in case you need me."

"We shouldn't, sir. Despite the little fracas earlier, I'd say we have this assignment well in hand."

"So would I, Sergeant, so would I."

Smoke lifted a hand in farewell and headed back to the Grand Central.

He didn't see Virginia, Dorothy, or Litchfield in the lobby. He supposed the ladies were in Dorothy's suite, and he didn't care where Litchfield had gotten off to.

Someplace where he could dry his soaked clothes, Smoke

supposed with a smile. Despite his annoyance with McKinley, he had enjoyed seeing the captain get some comeuppance.

In the middle of the following day, Captain Brant came to the hotel to let Smoke know he had finished his examination of the second bunch of horses, and once again, all of the animals were healthy and approved for use by the army. Brant was about to begin checking out the third and final group of horses.

This whole thing had been a waste of time and an unnecessary delay, Smoke thought, but he kept that to himself and didn't complain to Brant. The man was just following orders and doing his job, and besides, Smoke liked the veteran officer.

Virginia and Dorothy came down to the lobby that afternoon. Virginia seemed rather subdued. Smoke wondered if her aunt had laid down the law to her about trying to stir up trouble.

Dorothy wanted to know more about Smoke's past, so he found himself spinning yarns, although he edited them so that they weren't quite as bloody and tragic as the real events had been. Virginia got interested in spite of herself and listened raptly, as did her aunt.

"The West is certainly a dangerous place," Dorothy commented.

"It can be," Smoke agreed. "The parts that are already settled, folks had to risk a lot to do that. But I reckon when you look around, you can see that it was worthwhile."

"Oh, absolutely," Dorothy said, nodding.

"I'm not sure some of it is worth settling," Virginia put in. "I can't think of anything in the Jornada del Muerto that anyone would ever want. There's hardly any water, very little grass, just rock and dirt. My father calls it badlands, and that's what it is."

Smoke nodded. "Nobody's going to argue that, but if you can carry enough water with you, it's a good route up from the border. That's why it's part of the old Spanish Camino Real—the King's Road."

"And if you didn't want to be found," Dorothy said, "that would be a good place to hide. People say that the Desert Wolf has a stronghold somewhere down there."

"I still don't believe that," Virgina scoffed. "I'm not even sure the Desert Wolf exists. I think he might be just a story that parents make up to frighten their children. 'Be good, little ones, or the Desert Wolf will get you!' It's nonsense."

Dorothy shook her head. "I wouldn't be so sure about that. I know Andrew takes the threat seriously."

"My father worries too much," Virginia said, "and he's just as susceptible to gossip and wild stories as anyone else."

"Well, I hope we never find out whether the Desert Wolf is real or not. Thankfully, Captain Litchfield and his troops, along with Mr. Jensen and his men, will be traveling with us to the fort. I can't imagine anyone bothering such a large, well-armed group."

Neither could Smoke, but he knew not to disregard the possible threat. He couldn't speak for the soldiers, but he knew he and his men would keep their eyes open during the journey to Fort Craig.

The day passed peacefully. Smoke paid a visit to the corrals in late afternoon and was assured by Captain Brant that the examinations would be finished the next morning. Brant hadn't rejected any of the animals and continued to be impressed by their quality. They would be some of the best remounts the army had gotten, he told Smoke.

The final four punchers from the Sugarloaf were in Socorro now, enjoying their visit to the settlement after driving in the last bunch of horses. Smoke had warned them to stay out of trouble, and so far, it appeared that they had. That evening, after dark, he left the hotel for a final stroll around the settlement before turning in. Music came from the saloons and cantinas, laughter could be heard on the street, and Socorro appeared to be in a good mood tonight.

He moved on, turning back toward the hotel.

He was passing the alley next to the Grand Central when light suddenly spilled from a door that opened at the building's rear corner.

The door was ajar just long enough to allow a cloaked and hooded figure to slip through it into the alley. Then it swung closed, and thick darkness plunged down again.

But that brief moment had been long enough for Smoke's keen eyes to catch a glimpse of auburn hair sticking out from under the hood. The sight stopped him in his tracks.

More than likely, Virginia Griffin wasn't the only redheaded young woman in Socorro—but she was the only one Smoke had seen, and the hair on the head of the one who'd just slipped out of the Grand Central matched exactly.

Smoke heard the woman's quick footsteps receding into the night. Whether that was Virginia he had seen or someone else, the person was hurrying off on what was apparently an urgent errand.

He was curious about that, but was he curious enough to investigate something that might not be any of his business?

On the other hand, he thought, if that *was* Virginia he had seen, she might be sneaking out to meet Dean McKinley. And it was indeed Smoke's business if McKinley had disobeyed orders by coming back into Socorro yet again.

That was a good enough reason for him to find out more, Smoke told himself as he started along the alley after the mysterious figure, moving with graceful stealth and silence.

His hearing was sharp enough for him to follow the woman's footsteps along the alley that ran behind the buildings. Smoke stuck to the shadows, figuring that the hooded figure skulking around might look back from time to time to check for followers. The steps continued until he caught another glimpse of the indistinct shape crossing a small patch of moonlight in front of a large barn.

Someone else stepped from the barn into the silvery illumination to meet the hooded figure. This person was definitely a man. He opened his arms, embraced the smaller shape, and drew it to him.

Smoke stopped short and watched the intimate scene. Doing so made him a little uncomfortable. The moonlight, with a thin screen of clouds obscuring it, was too dim for him to make out facial details, but he recognized the clothing worn by the man who came out of the barn. The tight trousers, short jacket, and flat-crowned hat with a band of silver conchas were all familiar.

This was the young Mexican Smoke had seen riding into Socorro with a trio of vaqueros a couple of days earlier.

The man reached up, took hold of the hood, and pulled it down, revealing the long, thick hair of the young woman he was kissing. Smoke had no doubt now that she was Virginia Griffin.

And she was kissing this man with a lot more passionate intensity than she had shown with either Dean McKinley or Philip Litchfield. She wrapped her arms around his neck and pressed her body against his.

The embrace and kiss went on for long moments. Smoke stayed where he was, in dense shadows at the back of a building about fifty feet away. He had a good view of Virginia and the stranger from here, but they couldn't see him.

When the kiss finally ended and their heads parted, Smoke heard the soft murmur of voices as they spoke, but he couldn't make out any of the words. From the looks of things, they had to be words of endearment.

Smoke hadn't expected this development, but now that he thought about it, he wasn't too surprised. The idea that Virginia could have a third young man wrapped around her little finger made perfect sense. It appeared that she took this relationship more seriously, but Smoke told himself not to assume that. He didn't know her well enough to say what she was capable of.

And none of it mattered one blasted bit, he reminded himself. Virginia Griffin wasn't his responsibility. He liked Virginia's aunt, though, and he thought he might say something to Dorothy about it being a good idea for her to keep a closer eye on the girl.

For now, he was just going to head back to the hotel as quietly as possible. He had spied on those two long enough. He turned away from the couple standing close to each other just outside the barn.

As he did, a patch of shadow moved in front of him, and something sharp touched his belly, penetrating his shirt to prick his skin.

"Do not move, señor," a soft voice whispered. "I would hate to have to spill your guts in this filthy alley."

Smoke's fingers were already clasped around the butt of his right-hand Colt. They had flashed to the gun as soon as he realized someone was lurking in the shadows. Equally quietly, he said, "And I'd hate to blow a big hole in *your* belly, amigo, but I reckon I'd have plenty of time to do it before I died."

By now, Smoke could make out the lean sombrero-wearing figure in front of him and knew this man was probably one of the riders who had accompanied the Mexican dandy into Socorro two days earlier.

For a moment, the man had no response. Then he said, "Perhaps I will take my knife away, señor, and you will take your hand off your gun."

"That sounds like a good idea to me, especially since I mean no harm to your *patrón*."

"How do you know he is my *patrón*?"

"Are you saying he's not?"

The man didn't answer that. Instead, he moved the knife away from Smoke's belly and took a step back. Smoke let go of the Colt and relaxed—but not much.

"Señor Vaca!" the vaquero called softly.

Virginia gasped and pulled away from the man who had been holding her. The man stiffened and turned swiftly toward the spot where Smoke and the vaquero stood in the shadows.

"I was going to suggest that we just go away and leave those two alone," Smoke said to the man who had stuck a blade against his belly.

"I cannot do that, señor. You were spying on Señor Vaca. He must decide what to do with you."

"I don't reckon it makes any difference that I don't know who your Señor Vaca is?"

"None at all," the vaquero said.

Vaca put out an arm, thrust Virginia behind him, and strode through the moonlight toward Smoke. He drew the revolver on his hip as he approached.

"Ernesto?" he said. "That is you?"

"*Sí, señor.*"

"What are you doing here?"

"Watching over you, as your grandfather ordered us to do."

"My grandfather did not order you to interfere in my personal affairs!"

"Protecting you from any danger that might befall you is our duty, señor."

Vaca gestured curtly toward Virginia, who still stood tensely near the barn's open doors.

"And you believe the *señorita* to be dangerous?" he demanded.

"You would be a better judge of that than me, señor," Ernesto replied dryly.

Even though the man had prodded his belly with the point of a knife, Smoke had to chuckle at that.

Vaca strode over and confronted Smoke. "Who are you, señor?" he asked, with the same arrogance in his voice that Smoke had seen in his face a couple of days earlier.

"Smoke Jensen," Smoke answered. "I'm friends with Miss Griffin and her aunt."

Even though Smoke had known Virgina and Dorothy for only a short time, he felt comfortable in claiming friendship with them.

Virginia spoke up, taking a step forward and saying, "Mr. Jensen, what are you doing here?"

Smoke looked past Vaca at her and said, "I saw you slipping out of the hotel and thought maybe you were sneaking out to rendezvous with young McKinley."

Vaca's head jerked toward her. "McKinley?" he repeated. "Who is this McKinley?"

"Oh, he's nobody," Virginia said. "Just a boy who follows me around making calf eyes at me."

"Another one besides your soldier?"

"Captain Litchfield is not *my* soldier. I've explained to you, José, that I have to be polite to him. He's one of my father's favorite officers."

"You should inform him that there will never be anything serious between the two of you. The same is true of this man McKinley."

"I know what I'm doing," Virginia said, with a note of defiance in her voice.

"We will speak of this another time," Vaca said. He turned back to Smoke and went on, "Señor Jensen, I am José Antonio Vaca. Perhaps you have heard of me."

Smoke knew it was liable to offend him, but he was honest as he replied, "Nope, can't say as I have."

"My grandfather is Don Alejandro Vaca."

The young man probably couldn't see it in this bad light, but that information made Smoke quirk an eyebrow. Now that he thought about it, he *had* heard of Don Alejandro Vaca. The man was a *hacendado*, the owner of one of the biggest ranches across the border in the Mexican state of Chihuahua. Smoke had never met Don Alejandro, but he'd heard that some of the finest cattle in the Southwest came from his ranch.

"I know who that is," Smoke said. "He's a very well-respected hombre."

"As well he should be," Vaca said.

"But he's in Mexico, the last I heard, and you're here."

"My affairs and where I am are none of your business, Señor Jensen."

Actually, Smoke couldn't argue with that. But he was uneasy about leaving Virginia here with José Vaca, even if that was where Virginia wanted to be. He had a hunch Mrs. Bacon wouldn't agree with that.

He ignored Vaca's statement and turned to Virginia. "Miss Virginia, I'd be happy to escort you back to the hotel. I'm sure you'd like to get back before your aunt realizes you're gone."

"You don't have to worry about me, Smoke," she said. "I'm perfectly safe here with José."

"That may be, but I don't reckon Mrs. Bacon would like for you to be out at night like this. If she realizes you're not in the hotel, she's going to think you're missing and that something might have happened to you. She's liable to raise a ruckus and have Captain Litchfield and his troopers searching all over Socorro for you."

Virginia caught her breath, turned to Vaca, and said, "Mr. Jensen is right, José. It probably wasn't wise for me to sneak out and meet you like this. It's just going to cause trouble for both of us."

"I am not afraid of any trouble it may cause," Vaca said. "Any moment I can steal with you is worth the risk it may entail."

"That's sweet of you, but I think I should go."

Smoke could tell that Vaca was angry by the stiff way the young man stood and the note of strain in his voice as he said, "The day may come when you have to choose, *querida*."

"And you promised me I wouldn't have to choose," she shot back at him. "At least not yet."

He shrugged. "That is why I said the day may come." He drew in a breath and went on, "Very well. Go back to the hotel with Señor Jensen. I will see you again."

"Not any time soon," she said. "We're leaving for the fort tomorrow."

"Then when you and your aunt return to Socorro—"

"I don't know how long we'll be gone." There was a little catch in her voice as she went on. "I'm sorry, José. This isn't how I intended for this conversation to go. I—I wanted to let you know that things can't continue the way they have been. There's too much chance of ruining everything for both of us—"

He stopped her by reaching out and taking hold of her shoulders. Smoke tensed, and so did the vaquero called Ernesto, but for different reasons. Smoke was ready to step in if Vaca treated Virginia roughly, and Ernesto was prepared to stop Smoke from interfering with his *patrón*.

But evidently, Vaca's grip was gentle. Virginia didn't try to pull away from him. In fact, she went eagerly as he pulled her to him and embraced her again.

"You cannot mean to end things this way," he murmured.

"Maybe not forever," she managed to say. "But for now . . ."

Ernesto touched Smoke's sleeve. "Amigo, we step away for a moment, no?"

Smoke hesitated to do so, but he figured Vaca wouldn't try anything now that he knew someone had discovered his romance with Virginia. Smoke was still unsure just how serious it was, but he sensed that Virginia felt differently about Vaca than she did either Dean McKinley or Captain Litchfield.

He said, "Sure," and walked a few feet into the gloom with

the vaquero. He could still see Virginia and Vaca as they embraced and kissed one more time. What might be one final time, Smoke reflected. Then Virginia stepped away from the young man and hurried to Smoke's side.

"We'll go back to the hotel now," she said quietly.

"Sure."

Virginia didn't look back as they walked away. Smoke did glance over his shoulder once, but he didn't see any sign of Vaca or Ernesto. They had disappeared into the night already.

"I feel like I owe you an apology," he said to Virginia. "When I followed you, I just wanted to make sure you were safe. I didn't mean to ruin things for you."

"They were already ruined," she said. "They started out that way. José thinks he can change the way things are in the world, but no one can do that."

"Maybe, maybe not," Smoke said, "but it's a pretty thing to think about."

CHAPTER 9

Smoke was waiting at the corrals the next morning when Captain Brant finished his examinations. The army veterinarian came over to Smoke, pulling his gloves off as he approached, and said, "Mr. Jensen, it's official. Your herd is approved for use as army remounts."

"All of them?" Smoke asked.

Brant nodded. "Every one. I've said all along that they're fine-looking horses, and my examinations bear that out. They're all healthy as, well, horses."

Smoke smiled and said, "I knew that, but it's good to hear it, doctor. Or should I call you Captain?"

"Either is fine," Brant said with a wave of his hand. "I'll find Captain Litchfield and give him my report. I probably should have spoken to him first before telling you the results, but I've never been quite as much of a by-the-book officer as he is."

"I won't mention to him that you told me, then."

"Oh, I don't care," Brant said. "I'm too old and too close to retirement to worry about what some young officer thinks." He stuck out his hand. "It's been a pleasure working with such fine animals."

"I appreciate it, doctor," Smoke said as he shook hands.

Brant headed for the hotel. Smoke knew it was likely he would find Litchfield there.

Two of the Sugarloaf cowboys were leaning on the corral fence; the other two sat on the bottom rail, leaning forward with their hands clasped between their knees. They all looked vaguely ill. They were hungover, just as Smoke expected them to be.

"Looks like that's all the rest you boys are going to get," Smoke told them. "You heard the doc. The horses are ready to go. We'll drive them out to join the others and then get started on the trip to Fort Craig this afternoon."

The two who sat on the bottom fence rail groaned. One of them said, "It's awful hot and dusty, Smoke."

"At this time of year, it won't be any less hot and dusty if we wait, will it?" Smoke asked.

The man sighed. "No, I reckon not. Come on, boys."

As Smoke anticipated, the men perked up once they were in the saddle and working. They got the horses pushed out of the corrals and into a bunch that they started south, toward the campsite where the rest of the herd was being held. Spread out around the horses, the riders called out and swung coiled ropes against rumps to keep them moving.

Smoke returned to the Grand Central Hotel to gather his gear and check out.

Captain Philip Litchfield was waiting in the lobby when Smoke walked in. He gave Smoke a curt nod and said, "Captain Brant has informed me that he's approved all of your livestock, Jensen. I'm just going to tell Sergeant O'Malley to have the troopers prepare to depart for the fort."

"Do Mrs. Bacon and Miss Griffin know that we're getting ready to leave?" Smoke asked.

"Yes, I've told them. They already knew that was the plan for today unless something unforeseen came up." Litchfield took out a pocket watch and flipped it open to check the time. "I expect to depart no later than a half hour from now."

"There's no need to rush the ladies."

"They come from a military family," Litchfield said. "They know how to respond efficiently to a situation."

"My men and I can go ahead and start the herd moving," Smoke said. "Your party will be able to travel faster, so you won't have any trouble catching up to us."

"That's agreeable." Litchfield summoned up the faintest of smiles. "We'll see you on the trail."

Smoke nodded and returned the smile. He was perfectly willing to be cordial as long as Litchfield was, but he was glad that this association would soon be over.

He made it to the campsite south of Socorro just a few minutes after the Sugarloaf hands arrived with the last bunch of horses. Anticipating that they would be leaving today, Arbogast and the young wrangler, Perry Severs, who also served as the cook's assistant, already had the team hitched to the chuck wagon.

"Move 'em out?" the cadaverous Arbogast called from the driver's seat.

Smoke grinned and said, "Move 'em out!" He took off his hat and waved it in the air above his head to confirm the order.

Several members of the crew, including Dean McKinley, whooped with excitement and waved their hats, as well. They were already in their saddles and urged their mounts into motion, spreading out around the herd. Smoke took the lead, and the three hundred horses surged forward, following him as the Sugarloaf crew pointed them south.

Smoke knew that as long as they kept the Rio Grande in sight on their left, there was no way they could miss Fort Craig. The fort was built on a shallow bluff just west of the river. Except for occasional bluffs like that, the terrain on both sides of the Rio Grande was flat and covered with clumps of hardy grass and brush. Mesquite trees grew here and there but were rare. To the east and south, a few hills and flat-topped mesas were visible in the distance. To the west loomed the Magdalena Mountains, which were fairly small compared to the towering ranges to the north but still a welcome relief to the vast plains. The landscape wasn't what anybody would call picturesque, Smoke thought as he rode along at the head of the herd, but it possessed a stark beauty that never grew old to a true Westerner.

They hadn't gone much more than a mile when Vic Russell rode up alongside Smoke and told him, "Dust cloud coming up behind us. Reckon it must be the soldiers and those ladies."

"Bound to be," Smoke agreed, "but I'll swing back there and make sure."

He remembered what Litchfield had said about Apache raiding parties. While it seemed highly unlikely—almost impossible, in fact—that such a group would attack the herd this close to Socorro, Smoke couldn't rule out the possibility entirely. For his own peace of mind, he wanted to be sure who was closing in on them.

There was nothing to worry about, he saw a few minutes later as he came in sight of the approaching party. An army ambulance wagon, a vehicle with a canvas-covered bed considerably smaller than the prairie schooners used by immigrants, was in the lead with a mounted figure riding alongside it. That rider had to be Captain Litchfield, Smoke thought.

Another wagon, this one without a cover over the bed, followed with a rider alongside it, and then four troopers on horseback. Two saddled but riderless cavalry mounts were tied to the back of the second wagon, which told Smoke that a trooper was driving each of the vehicles.

The party didn't slow as Smoke approached. As he came

closer, he confirmed that Litchfield was riding beside the ambulance, while Sergeant O'Malley accompanied the other wagon. Captain Brant was on the seat of that vehicle along with the driver.

Smoke didn't see Virginia Griffin or Dorothy Bacon, but he assumed they were in the back of the ambulance, out of the sun that was already beating down with intensity as the hour approached midday. The second wagon's bed was piled high with the ladies' bags as well as crates and barrels of supplies.

When he was close, Smoke reined in and waited, turning his horse so that he could fall in beside the others. Litchfield nodded a greeting and said, "I can see the dust from your herd up ahead. I expected to catch up to them fairly quickly. I like to set a brisk pace."

"The ladies are inside the ambulance?" Smoke asked.

Virginia must have heard his question. She leaned out the front next to the stolid-faced driver, waved, and called, "Hello, Mr. Jensen."

Smoke smiled and ticked a finger against his hat brim. "Miss Griffin. Good to see you again, even though it hasn't been very long. I'm glad to see that you're staying in the shade."

"My father sees to it that Aunt Dorothy and I travel in comfort. Well, as much comfort as you can get out here."

"This is the frontier, Virginia," Litchfield said. "Not some drawing room back East."

"Oh, goodness, I know that, Philip. I didn't mean anything. I appreciate what my father does, and what you do to make things easier for us, too."

Litchfield nodded his acknowledgment of Virginia's gratitude, and then said, "You'd better get back inside and draw the flap over the front and back openings. The dust will be worse while we're going around the herd."

"All right." Virginia withdrew into the ambulance wagon.

Smoke said, "I've been thinking about that plan of yours, Captain. Are you sure it's a good idea for your party to go around the herd and take the lead?"

"Why wouldn't it be?" Litchfield asked. The sharpness of the question showed that he didn't like having his judgment questioned.

"You said that Apache war parties sometimes roam around here. It might be better to let us scout ahead first."

"We've made the trip back and forth from Socorro to the fort with the ladies several times and never encountered any trouble." Litchfield shrugged. "It's true that the size of the escort is a bit smaller this time since Colonel Griffin knew we'd be traveling with you and he assumed that you would assist us if there was any trouble."

"Of course we would," Smoke said. "My men will always pitch in if there's a fight."

"Yes, I saw ample evidence of that in Socorro the other day," Litchfield said stiffly. He had some bruises on his face, reminders of the ruckus with Dean McKinley.

"As for which part of the group goes first," he continued, "I don't want to breathe that herd's dust the entire way, and I'm sure Miss Griffin and Mrs. Bacon don't, either. And it seems to me that the Apache could sneak up and attack us from behind just as well as they could if we're in the lead."

Smoke considered that and nodded. "I can't argue with your logic, Captain," he said. "No matter who's in front, we all need to keep our eyes open for any sign of trouble."

"Exactly."

Litchfield's voice had a smug tone to it that rubbed Smoke the wrong way, but he let it pass.

"If there's anything I can do for you, let me know," he said. "I'd suggest that once you're out in front of the herd, you can catch up with my chuck wagon and travel with it. Arbogast is pretty experienced at picking out a good place to camp. You folks are welcome to share our grub this evening, too. You might not think it to look at him, but that old pelican can put together a mighty good surrounding."

"Thank you. We'll consider it."

Litchfield's words were still a little stiff, but he seemed to be making an effort to unbend a little. After the clash with McKinley, that probably took quite an effort on the captain's part. He wasn't the sort to forgive and forget.

Smoke waved a farewell and rode ahead of the army detail toward the herd. It didn't take him long to catch up. He was heading for the point again when Dean McKinley, who was riding on the left flank, motioned him over.

"Did you see Miss Griffin while you were back there talking to Litchfield, Smoke?" the young cowboy asked.

"Yes, and Mrs. Bacon, too. They're fine. Virginia seems to be enjoying the trip so far."

"I'm glad to hear it. I hope I get a chance to visit with her when we make camp this evening."

Smoke figured it might be a good idea to take some preventive measures, even though he knew McKinley wouldn't like it.

"You're going to keep your distance from Miss Griffin, Dean," he said.

McKinley stared at him for a couple of heartbeats, then demanded, "What do you mean by that, Smoke?"

"You're a smart young fella. I think you know exactly what I mean."

McKinley's jaw tightened with anger. "I'll bet that Litchfield polecat won't be keeping his distance. He'll be falling all over her and trying to impress her with what a handsome hombre he is."

"That's between the two of them." Being only a few years older than McKinley, Smoke didn't really cotton to talking to him as if he were dispensing fatherly advice, but that might be what the circumstances called for. "Look, Dean, we'll reach the fort late tomorrow and turn these horses over to the army. We'll probably spend one night there and then start back to Colorado. There's a good chance you'll never see Virginia Griffin after that, so it doesn't make sense to keep stirring up trouble over her."

"I'm not trying to stir up trouble, Smoke. I swear I'm not. I just can't stand the sight of that soldier boy hanging around her. That arrogant, full-of-himself stuffed shirt just rubs me the wrong way, blast it!"

Smoke had to smile at the passion of McKinley's response.

"I agree with you about Litchfield," he admitted, "even though my reason for feeling that way is different than yours. But what he does is none of our business—and neither is what Miss Griffin does."

McKinley shook his head as his horse jogged easily alongside Smoke's mount. After a moment, he said, "You claim I'll never see her again after we leave the fort, but that's not necessarily true. Don't you plan on striking a deal with the colonel for more remounts?"

"I do," Smoke said.

"So, you'll have to be bringing more horses down here in the future."

"That doesn't mean I'll bring you along with me."

McKinley frowned. "You'd do that? Order me to stay at the Sugarloaf?"

"I'm a businessman, Dean. I'd be foolish to bring somebody along knowing that it was liable to cause a problem."

"Maybe I wouldn't ride for the Sugarloaf anymore. Maybe I won't even go back to Colorado with you the day after tomorrow."

Smoke's voice hardened. "If you want to draw your time once we've delivered those horses, I won't have any way to stop you. I doubt that Colonel Griffin is going to let you just hang around the fort, though, unless you decide to up and enlist."

McKinley didn't respond to that for a few moments. Finally, he said, "I never intended to be a soldier. I'm not sure I'd fit in too well." He brightened a little. "But I could stay in Socorro, maybe get a riding job at some spread around here. Or work in town at something. That way I could see Virginia every now and then, anyway."

Smoke's voice softened as he said, "You'll have to make up your own mind how you want to live your life, Dean. I can't stop you, and you're old enough to know what you want and what you're prepared to do to get it. Just help us get these horses to the fort, and then you can go your own way if that's what you decide."

"Why, sure, Smoke," the young cowboy replied instantly. "I signed on to do a job, and I'd never turn my back on that, no matter what. I'm just going to have to do a whole heap of thinking between here and Fort Craig."

Smoke smiled. "Nothing wrong with that. I always like to see a fella using his noggin for something more than a place to hang his hat." He grew more serious as he added, "But I meant what I said about keeping your distance from that girl in camp tonight. I don't want any more trouble."

"I understand," McKinley said, "and I'll go along with what you say."

He didn't look like he was happy about it, though.

Smoke nodded and nudged his horse to a faster pace, waving at the other hands as he passed them and resumed his place at the front of the herd.

Not long after that, the two wagons rolled around the horses and pushed ahead, followed by the cavalry escort. The troopers at the reins had the teams moving along briskly. Wagons and riders dwindled quickly and by early afternoon were out of sight, although Smoke could still see their dust rising in a thin column a mile or so ahead.

The semi-arid miles rolled on behind them. Sometimes the

easiest path ran along the riverbank, while in other places their course veered away from the Rio Grande. When they weren't close to the river, Smoke could still keep track of where it was from the strip of greener vegetation along it. The more colorful growth really stood out from the vast sweep of brown and tan and gray on both sides of the stream.

The horses had had it fairly easy for the past few days, all of them having had a chance to rest and recover somewhat from the long trip down here into New Mexico Territory. Because of that, Smoke didn't hesitate to move the herd along at a fairly fast pace. The horses seemed glad to be on the move again and didn't give any trouble.

Maybe they sensed they would soon be at their new home, Smoke thought.

Even though the horses were rested, he didn't want to push them too hard. They needed to be at their peak when they arrived at Fort Craig and Colonel Griffin inspected them. Even though Captain Brant had signed off on their good health, the final word on whether or not the army would accept the animals rested with the colonel.

Knowing that, Smoke called short halts every now and then to let the horses blow. The cowboys took advantage of those opportunities to dismount and stretch their legs, too, although a couple remained in the saddle at all times just in case any of the horses decided to head for the hills. Smoke didn't expect that to happen, but no matter how well trained they were, in most cases, every day was a new day for a horse.

During one such halt, Smoke and Dean McKinley were still mounted while the other members of the crew swung down and walked around a little. Smoke rested his crossed hands on the horn and leaned forward as he scanned the herd for any signs of restlessness. The horses all seemed calm and were content to crop halfheartedly at clumps of bunch grass.

Smoke's mind drifted a little as thoughts of Sally stole into his brain and reminded him of what he was missing. It would be good to get home . . .

That was when a familiar sound, faint with distance, came to his ears and caused his head to jerk up. The pop and crackle of gunfire came from somewhere ahead of them.

And there was nothing up there except the army detail and the two women—and whoever was doing all that shooting.

Chapter 10

Dean McKinley heard the ominous rattle in the distance as well, and he jumped to the same conclusion as Smoke. He didn't wait for any orders, either.

"Virginia!" he cried, as he rammed his bootheels into his horse's flanks. The horse leaped forward and landed in a dead run that carried the young cowboy southward.

Smoke wheeled his horse. Pogue, Rogers, and Moore were the men closest to him. He shouted, "Walt, Alvie, Carl, come with me! Vic, you and the rest of the boys stay here with the herd!"

Vic Russell looked like he wanted to argue, but he wasn't going to disobey Smoke's orders. Pogue, Rogers, and Moore leaped into their saddles as Smoke sent his mount pounding after Dean McKinley.

All the saddle horses were good ones, including McKinley's. The animal flashed across the landscape. The sandy soil was fairly well packed and easy to run on. There were few obstacles to avoid, just the occasional runty mesquite tree or creosote bush.

With the swift rataplan of hoofbeats filling his ears, Smoke couldn't hear the gunfire anymore, but he suspected it was still going on. From what he had heard in that brief volley, it had sounded as if the entire escort detail was involved.

That had been an actual battle, not somebody taking potshots at a rattlesnake or anything like that. The soldiers were in trouble, and that likely meant the two women were, as well.

Smoke drew even with McKinley, who glanced over at him with a very worried expression but didn't try to say anything over the pounding hoofbeats and the wind. Smoke looked back and saw the other three Sugarloaf men not far behind them. Whatever they found waiting for them, Smoke knew they would probably need to strike hard and fast.

One of the bluffs that overlooked the river in places along this stretch loomed up on the right. It was fifteen to twenty feet tall, with a very ragged edge formed by numerous short canyons and crevices. It ran like that, sometimes closer to the river, sometimes farther away, as far south as Smoke could see.

The dust column from the wagons and riders was no longer visible, but he spotted a thinner, more widely dispersed cloud to the right, lingering in the air in front of the bluff. Dust like that was usually caused by a lot of riders milling around or charging back and forth.

Knowing that, Smoke wasn't surprised when he caught sight of at least two dozen men on horseback. Some of them rode hard toward the mouth of one of those little canyons. Rifles cracked and powder smoke roiled and blended with the dust. Other attackers fired at the canyon mouth from the sides.

Shots came from the canyon and forced the straight-ahead assault to turn back. None of the riders toppled from their ponies, so the volley from the canyon likely hadn't wounded any of the enemy, at least not seriously.

Smoke was close enough now to see the brightly colored headbands holding the attackers' long, dark hair back, as well as the loose light-colored shirts and trousers they wore, the high-topped soft boots on their feet, and the equally bright cloth sashes around their waists.

They were Apaches, Smoke knew. Chiricahuas or Mescaleros, he wasn't sure which. But they had to be one of those raiding parties Litchfield had told him about, probably dissatisfied young men who had run away from the Fort Stanton reservation. Warriors desperate to reclaim even a part of their former glory, and made dangerous by that desperation.

From the looks of this scene, the war party had jumped the military escort, and the soldiers had made a dash for that canyon and taken cover there. The wagons must have made it to safety because Smoke didn't see them anywhere.

Nor were there any dead troopers or horses sprawled on the dusty ground. They had been lucky so far.

It appeared to be a standoff, but only for the moment. It wouldn't be long before some of the Apaches circled around, climbed the bluff somewhere else, and attacked the canyon's defenders from above.

If Smoke and his men were going to help, it needed to be now.

He reined in a little and motioned for McKinley to do likewise. McKinley didn't want to, Smoke could tell; he wanted to keep charging right into the middle of this fracas. But he did as Smoke ordered and pulled back on his reins, slowing his horse.

Smoke twisted in the saddle and motioned for the other three men to spread out and move up alongside him and McKinley. They obeyed instantly, Pogue and Moore going to the right, Rogers to the left. The five riders formed a line. Smoke leaned forward and pulled his Winchester from its saddle sheath. The other men did the same.

Then Smoke put the reins in his teeth, worked the rifle's lever to throw a cartridge into the chamber, and sent his mount charging toward the Apaches at full speed.

He didn't have to tell the others what to do. They followed

his example, riding side by side as they charged toward the Apaches. They were already in rifle range, but it wouldn't hurt their chances to get closer.

The warriors had all their attention turned on the quarry they had trapped in the canyon. They were probably enjoying this fight, filled with eager anticipation at the thought of all the blue-belly soldiers they were going to kill. They might or might not be aware of the women's presence, but first things first—slaughtering those troopers.

They probably never saw Smoke and his men coming.

They knew it, though, when rifle bullets began to rip through them and several warriors spilled from their ponies. They whooped in outrage and whirled to meet this new threat. Smoke and his companions continued spraying lead through the war party as fast as they could work the levers on their rifles.

Not all the Apaches turned away from the canyon. About half of the force charged again. They weren't shooting this time; instead, they bent low over their ponies' necks to make themselves smaller targets.

Smoke caught a glimpse of what they were doing and realized instantly what it meant. The Apaches might lose a few men on the way, but they were determined that some of the warriors would reach the canyon, leap off their mounts, and wreak bloody havoc on the defenders in hand-to-hand battle.

It was a daring move, but it might well succeed in killing most or all of the trapped party, even though there was a good chance it would cost the lives of all the warriors, too.

Such a fanatical effort was unusual for any Indian war party. No matter what the tribe, they liked to fight when they had the advantage and retreat when they didn't.

Apparently, this bunch was really eager to kill those they considered enemies.

Those thoughts flashed through Smoke's mind in the second it took him to jack the Winchester's loading lever down and back up as they smashed full blast into the war party. He fired again and blew one of the Apaches backward off a paint pony, then shouted, "Dean, come with me! The rest of you boys cover our backs!"

More than half of the warriors who had tried to stop them were down, sprawled motionless on the ground, and others sagged on their ponies, badly wounded. Smoke and his men had dealt a mortal blow to the war party—but the ones attacking the canyon still posed a terrible threat. Smoke and McKinley pounded after them while the other three cowboys wheeled their horses and continued firing at the remnants of the war party to keep them at bay.

One of the Indian ponies racing toward the canyon mouth fell suddenly, its forelegs buckling as it was brought down by a shot from one of the defenders. It was a spectacular collapse that raised a cloud of dust as the dying animal rolled over and flailed its legs. The rider was thrown screeching over the pony's head, landed hard, and rolled several times before coming to a stop. He didn't get up.

Another warrior threw his arms out to the sides and somersaulted backward off his mount. When Smoke saw that, he knew a bullet must have smashed into the man's chest.

That left at least ten men charging toward the canyon, however. It was difficult to be sure because of all the dust billowing in the air. Smoke and McKinley were closing in on the attackers from behind, but the Apaches who survived the charge were going to reach the canyon before Smoke and McKinley could get there.

They were close enough to hear the attackers' shrill war cries, punctuated by the crack of rifle fire. Smoke's Winchester was empty by now, so he rammed it back in the saddle boot and drew both Colts. The rest of this fight was liable to be close work, anyway.

The two riders burst out of the dust and saw the knots of

struggling men just inside the canyon mouth. The Apaches had reached the defenders and were battling them at close quarters now. The wagons were parked about fifty yards inside the canyon, and individual fights were going on all over the area in front of them.

The troopers from Fort Craig were outnumbered, but they were giving a good account of themselves, fighting with rifle butts and bayonets. The Apaches had knives and lances.

One of the soldiers had tripped and fallen backward, Smoke saw. A warrior loomed over him, lance raised as the Apache prepared to ram it through the trooper's body.

Smoke drilled the warrior through the head, a snap shot with the left-hand Colt directed with deadly accuracy. The Apache dropped the lance and crumpled lifelessly to the ground.

Dean McKinley flashed by on Smoke's right. Smoke turned in that direction and saw that McKinley was heading toward the ambulance wagon where Virginia and her aunt had to be hiding. Captain Philip Litchfield stood beside the wagon, pistol in his hand, ready to fire.

A knife-wielding Apache lunged at him. Litchfield jerked the pistol toward the attacker and fired, but he hurried the shot and it went wild. The Apache knocked the captain's gun hand up with his free arm and rammed his shoulder into Litchfield's chest. Litchfield went down and the warrior landed on top of him, poised to plunge the knife down into his chest.

Smoke would have risked a shot at that moment, but he held his fire because McKinley veered his horse into the line of fire. A split second later, the young cowboy left his saddle in a diving tackle. He wrapped his arms around the Apache and drove the warrior off of Litchfield before the knife could fall in its killing stroke. McKinley and the Apache rolled across the ground beside the ambulance wagon.

The Apache made a desperate swipe at McKinley's throat with the blade. McKinley caught the man's wrist and turned the knife aside at the last second. At the same time, he clawed his revolver from its holster, jammed the barrel under the warrior's chin, and pulled the trigger.

The Apache's head exploded in a shower of gore. McKinley rolled away from him, came up on one knee, and fired again, knocking another warrior off his feet.

Smoke's Colts blasted, left, right, left, right, and every time flame leaped from a gun muzzle, another attacker fell.

Suddenly the canyon was quiet except for fading echoes and harsh breathing.

A ragged cry came from above, followed by a rifle shot. Smoke saw Sergeant Seamus O'Malley stagger and fall. He jerked his head up and spotted one of the Apaches on the rim of the canyon. The warrior had gotten up there somehow during the battle.

Smoke's right-hand Colt roared again. The shot was a tricky one, angled up like that, but the Apache dropped his rifle and bent forward, clutching at his middle where Smoke's slug had ripped through his guts. He toppled off the canyon rim and rolled limply down the steep slope.

This time when a hush descended on the canyon, it remained.

McKinley scrambled up and ran to the ambulance, dodging past Litchfield to do so. The captain still lay on the ground looking dazed.

"Virginia!" McKinley called urgently, as he thrust aside the canvas cover at the back of the wagon. "Virginia, are you all right?"

Smoke saw the auburn-haired young woman lean over the ambulance's tailgate and throw her arms around McKinley, embracing him tightly. Her face was pale and strained, but she appeared to be unharmed.

He rode to the front of the wagon and leaned over in the

saddle to peer into the back through the gap between the canvas covers behind the driver's seat.

"Mrs. Bacon? Are you in there?"

Dorothy Bacon appeared, looking just as shaken as her niece.

"Mr. Jensen!" she said. "Thank God you got here when you did."

"Are you wounded?"

Dorothy shook her head. "No, and neither is Vingie. We both stayed as low as we could while the fighting was going on."

"I'm glad to hear it," Smoke said.

"What about Seamus? And . . . and the other troopers?"

"Sergeant O'Malley is wounded. I was about to check on him."

Dorothy climbed hurriedly over the seat. She held out a hand, and Smoke grasped it to steady her as she got down from the ambulance. As soon as her feet were on the ground, she looked around, found O'Malley, and ran to his side.

Obviously, she had a soft spot for the sergeant, Smoke thought. Even under these grim circumstances, the shadow of a smile flickered over his face.

He swung down from the saddle and looped his reins around the wagon's brake lever, then joined Dorothy to see how O'Malley was doing. She had helped the sergeant sit up and had her arm around his shoulders, supporting him and keeping him from standing up at the same time.

"You're wounded, Sergeant," she told him. "Just sit there until someone can look at your leg."

Blood stained the right leg of O'Malley's uniform trousers between the knee and the hip. It looked to Smoke like the bullet fired by the Apache on the rim had passed through the sergeant's thigh muscle. The bone must not have been broken, though, or he wouldn't have been trying to stand up.

"Blast it, ma'am, I'm all right," he protested. "I've hurt meself worse than this trippin' on a rock."

"Do what the lady says, Sergeant," Captain Samuel Brant ordered as he bustled up. He knelt beside O'Malley. "I'll see how bad you're hurt."

"Beggin' your pardon, Cap'n, but you're a horse doc!"

Brant grinned. "I know, and you're a big ox, but I think I can manage."

The sound of hoofbeats made Smoke turn away from the wagons. He saw Carl Moore riding toward the canyon. Walt Pogue and Alvie Rogers were still out where a number of Apache bodies littered the ground.

"The fight's over out there, Smoke," Moore reported as he reined in. "Two or three of those varmints were still alive, but they realized they didn't have a chance and took off for the tall and uncut." He looked around. "Any of them left in here?"

"Only dead ones, I think," Smoke replied. "I was just about to check on that."

"I'll give you a hand," Moore said as he dismounted.

It didn't take them long to determine that none of the Apaches had survived the battle. Some had been bayoneted, others had had their heads busted open by rifle butts.

One trooper was dead, having been run through with a lance, and a couple of others had bloody but not fatal knife wounds. Overall, these buffalo soldiers had acquitted themselves very well in battle, which confirmed what Smoke had heard about them. They were supposed to be excellent fighting men.

When Smoke turned toward the wagons again, he saw that McKinley had helped Virginia out of the ambulance and was standing talking to her as he held one of her hands in both of his.

Not far away, Captain Litchfield had made it back to his feet and stood there shaking his head groggily. As Smoke watched, the captain seemed to get his wits back about him.

And the first thing he noticed was the way McKinley and Virginia were standing so close together. Litchfield's jaw tightened, his lips pulled back from his teeth in a grimace, and for a second, the look Smoke saw on the officer's face was one of naked hatred and rage directed at Dean McKinley.

Then Litchfield seemed to remember he was in command of a detail that had just been attacked and had fought a desperate battle for survival. He stalked over to where Captain Brant was wrapping a dressing around O'Malley's leg and snapped, "Sergeant, report!"

O'Malley looked like he wanted to bolt upright, but Brant's firm grip on one shoulder and Dorothy's hand on the other shoulder kept him on the ground. O'Malley looked up at Litchfield, and said, "The, uh, hostiles have been defeated, sir."

"What are our losses?"

O'Malley wouldn't know that yet, so Smoke said, "You have one man killed, Captain, and a couple wounded."

"And the Apache?"

"All dead," Smoke said.

"Good. I don't know where they came from. We were just moving along fine, and then suddenly they were all around us . . ."

Litchfield's voice trailed off. Smoke nodded and said, "That's the way it usually is with Indians, Captain. Even when it doesn't seem like there's any place for them to hide, most of the time you don't know they're anywhere around until they want you to see them."

"I've fought Indians before, you know," Litchfield said. "You don't need to lecture me, Jensen."

Smoke shrugged. "I wasn't trying to lecture you, just letting you know where things stand." Although he wasn't sure why he did it, he extended an olive branch by adding, "After being jumped like that, by a war party that size, you did mighty good just getting in here where you could fort up without suffering a lot worse losses than you did."

He didn't get a chance to see if his words mollified the officer—and honestly, he didn't care whether they did or not—because at that moment rapid hoofbeats sounded and Smoke looked around to see Alvie Rogers riding fast toward the canyon. Rogers waved an arm toward the north and shouted something.

"What's he yellin' about?" Carl Moore asked.

Smoke stiffened and replied, "He's saying there's more gunfire coming from north of here. From the direction of the horse herd!"

Chapter 11

As Smoke and Moore ran to their horses, Smoke called to McKinley, "Dean! Let's go!"

McKinley looked around, confused. "What—"

"Trouble at the herd!"

Smoke jerked his horse's reins loose and swung into the saddle. As he pulled the animal around and headed out of the canyon, he saw McKinley mounting up. The three men galloped out of the canyon mouth and joined Rogers. Walt Pogue was already riding north.

The five men formed into a loose bunch. Pogue was still in the lead. He glanced back over his shoulder at the others, then yelled, "Smoke!" and waved his hand at something behind them.

Smoke looked back, too, and saw a blue-clad figure riding hard after them. He realized a moment later that it was Captain Philip Litchfield on their trail.

Those horses were Litchfield's responsibility, too. Smoke could understand why the captain would want to find out what was happening. But at the same time, Smoke wished Litchfield had stayed where he was to make sure the women remained safe.

The threat from the Apache war party might be over, but other dangers could lurk on this mostly untamed frontier.

It didn't take long for them to come in sight of the herd. When Smoke saw the dark mass of horses with riders circling around them to keep them under control, he felt a surge of relief, but that reaction didn't last long. He realized a moment later that the herd looked smaller than it ought to.

Some of the horses were gone.

One of the cowboys turned his mount and loped out to meet them. As Smoke reined in, he called to the man, "Where's Russell?"

The cowboy pointed. Smoke saw two riderless horses off to the side of the herd. One man was on the ground, and the other knelt beside him.

The herd was under control but the horses still looked spooked from whatever had happened. Smoke turned to McKinley, Pogue, Rogers, and Moore and told them, "Help the other boys keep those horses calm."

Then he nudged his mount into a fast trot toward the spot where one man was tending to an injured companion. The sound of hoofbeats made Smoke glance over his shoulder. Litchfield was following him. The captain was bareheaded. Evidently, he hadn't taken the time to find his hat after the battle in the canyon.

As Smoke came closer, he saw that the man on the ground was Vic Russell. He was sitting up as the cowboy with him knotted a strip of cloth around his upper left arm, securing a makeshift bandage with a small bloodstain showing through it.

Smoke reined in and swung down. "Vic, how bad are you hurt?" he asked.

Russell shook his head. "The varmints just winged me, Smoke," he said. His voice caught a little as he went on, "But they got away with half the herd, blast their ugly hides."

"What happened?" Smoke asked, as Russell got to his feet with the assistance of the other Sugarloaf hand.

"We had slowed down a little after you rode off because we didn't want the whole herd blundering into the middle of a battle. I was about to call a halt just to be sure of that when a bunch of riders came up on us from behind. I don't know where they came from. We hadn't seen any dust on our back trail. They must have been off to the west somewhere, keeping an eye on us, and swung out behind us when we drove the horses past."

Smoke nodded. "That makes sense," he told Russell. "I reckon they must have been Apaches."

He could see now how the plan had worked out. A war party had attacked the wagons and the escort detail, both from the desire to kill soldiers and as a distraction so another bunch of warriors could jump the herd.

But to his surprise, Russell shook his head. "No, they weren't Apaches or any other sort of Indian," he said. "All the ones I saw looked like Mexicans."

Litchfield had been listening to the exchange. When Russell said that, the captain exclaimed, "The Desert Wolf! It had to be that blasted bandit and his men. I told you they might be somewhere around here, Jensen."

Smoke frowned in thought and scraped a thumbnail along his jawline. "Moving parallel to us, maybe," he speculated, "and waiting for an opportunity to hit the herd?"

"That's the only explanation," Litchfield said with an emphatic nod. "That devil was looking for a lucky break, and those Indians gave it to him!"

The theory seemed reasonable to Smoke. He said to Russell, "I guess you boys fought back."

"Sure, we did, but the varmints had us outnumbered more than two to one. There must have been at least twenty of them.

When the shooting started, we were too busy to keep the herd bunched up. The horses scattered, and then some of those no-good thieves kept us busy while the others gathered up half the stock and drove it off to the west."

"Did you bring down any of them?" Smoke asked.

Russell shook his head. "Not that I saw. They were good at what they did, Smoke." He craned his neck to look over what remained of the herd and the men riding around it. "Do you know if any of the other boys were hurt?"

"You were the only one I noticed when we rode up."

"Well, there's that to be thankful for, anyway."

"I'm not thankful for any of this," Litchfield said, with a note of bitterness in his voice. "I'll be thankful when the Desert Wolf is strung up like the thief he is." The captain sighed. "But chasing him down will have to wait. My orders are to deliver the herd—and the ladies—to the fort as soon as possible, so that's what I have to do."

"Half the herd is gone," Smoke pointed out.

"And half of it is still here. Those animals have to go on to Fort Craig."

"I can split up my men. Half of them can take the herd to the fort while the rest of us go after those thieves."

"And you'll be six men against twenty or more," Litchfield argued.

"I've faced high odds before," Smoke said.

Litchfield looked like he was reluctant to say what he said next, but he continued anyway.

"Jensen, without your help it's possible, even likely, that those Apache would have wiped us out today and taken Miss Griffin and Mrs. Bacon prisoner. You know what sort of horrible fate that would have been for them."

"It would have been pretty bad," Smoke agreed. A war party raiding off the reservation wouldn't have taken the women back to a village and made slaves of them, as had happened with other female prisoners in the past. Instead, the warriors would have taken their pleasure with the women and then cut their throats to be rid of them.

"I'm asking you to accompany us the rest of the way to the fort," Litchfield said, "just as was planned. Once the ladies are safe there and the remaining horses have been delivered, then you can discuss your next move with Colonel Griffin."

Vic Russell said angrily, "What's to discuss? We're going after those blasted bandits and getting those horses back!"

"That'll be up to the colonel. He's in charge of this region."

"He's not in charge of me," Smoke snapped.

"That's where you're wrong, Jensen. Everything south of Fort Craig through the badlands of the Jornada del Muerto is under the jurisdiction of the United States Army."

That didn't seem right to Smoke, but he knew he'd be wasting his time arguing with Litchfield. Instead, he said, "According to Vic, the thieves took the stolen horses west, not south into the badlands."

"Yes, but that's where they'll wind up. The Desert Wolf's stronghold is somewhere down in the Jornada. The bandits may have gone west, but I'm confident they'll swing south somewhere this side of the Magdalenas and then bypass the fort on the way to their hideout."

It was possible the captain was right, Smoke realized, and he could understand Litchfield's concern over the safety of the two women.

"That war party isn't going to give us any more trouble," he said.

"But several of the savages got away. There may be more of them lurking in the area. If there are, those survivors will head straight for them and bring them back to make another try for us. They'll be even more vicious now, motivated by the desire for revenge."

That was a distinct possibility, and Smoke couldn't dispute

Litchfield's assessment of the danger. Virginia and Dorothy *would* be safer if the men from the Sugarloaf accompanied them the rest of the way to the fort. The escort detail had lost a man, and three more were wounded, including Sergeant O'Malley.

Even so, it sure rubbed Smoke the wrong way to let those thieves get away with the horses without even going after them. In this case, though, it might be the right thing to do.

"All right, Captain, we'll stay together," he said. "And I do mean together. No pulling out so far ahead of the herd like you did earlier."

Litchfield nodded. "That's a reasonable precaution." He made a face. "I was perhaps a bit too hasty in my eagerness to get back to the fort."

Smoke was surprised to hear the captain take even a smidgen of blame like that. It didn't raise his opinion of Litchfield, but it made the officer seem a bit more human.

Smoke turned to Russell and asked, "Vic, are you able to ride?"

"Sure, Smoke. It's my arm that got winged. I can still sit a saddle just fine."

"All right. Let's get these horses moving south again. We'll join up with the cavalry escort and then push on south as far as we can today. We should still make it to Fort Craig sometime tomorrow."

"Assuming we don't run into any more trouble," Litchfield said.

Smoke shrugged and said, "Out here, that can be a mighty risky assumption to make."

When the herd reached the canyon where the escort detail was waiting for them, the troopers dug a grave for their comrade who had been killed in the fighting and laid the man to rest. It was a lonely place for a man to spend eternity, but Smoke had seen worse.

The bodies of the slain Apaches were left where they had fallen. The members of the war party who had escaped might come back for them, or they might be disposed of by scavengers. Either way, those bodies would be dealt with.

Captain Brant had tended to all the wounded as best he could. Once they reached the fort, the regular army surgeon there would take over caring for them. Smoke was no sawbones, but he had plenty of experience with such things and didn't believe that any of the injuries were life-threatening.

Once the grim burial chore was over, everyone mounted up and the party pushed southward again, still following the Rio Grande.

Late in the afternoon, they came upon the chuck wagon where Arbogast had stopped to make camp for the night. Smoke had been worried about the scrawny old-timer; the war party might have found him first and killed him.

But as the wagons, the riders, and the horse herd approached, Arbogast stepped out of the shade under the canvas cover he had rigged over his Dutch oven and waved a greeting.

"I thought I heard shootin' earlier in the day," he said as Smoke dismounted. "It looks like you lost some hosses. Rustlers?"

"Yeah, and that's not all." Quickly, Smoke filled him in on the two attacks.

"But the two bunches who jumped you weren't connected?" Arbogast asked with a puzzled frown.

"Evidently not. Apaches don't get along with Mexicans any better than they do with gringos. I can't imagine that war party working with a bandit gang to hit the cavalry escort and the herd at roughly the same time."

Arbogast shook his head. "Sounds like you just had some plumb bad luck, then."

"That's what it looks like," Smoke agreed.

He wasn't entirely convinced, however. Even though he

couldn't put his finger on it, he sensed that something else might be going on, some possibility that nagged at the back of his brain without revealing itself. But if that truly was the case, he might have to wait for time to uncover more information.

Arbogast fed the entire group, and it was a subdued supper after the losses they had suffered today.

Smoke posted extra guards and so did Captain Litchfield, so the camp had half a dozen sentries standing watch during the night. That precaution proved unnecessary, as the hours of darkness passed quietly and peacefully.

Early the next morning, the party prepared to get on the move again as the sun came up.

Sergeant O'Malley insisted he was able to ride with his wounded leg, but Dorothy Bacon overruled that idea.

"Don't be foolish, Sergeant," she told him. "This is an ambulance wagon. It was built for carrying wounded soldiers, not just so pampered ladies could ride inside it and not have the sun burn their fair skin."

"The men need me out there riding with 'em, ma'am—" O'Malley began.

Dorothy wasn't hearing any of it. "I'm sure Captain Litchfield is perfectly capable of issuing any commands that need to be issued," she said.

Smoke overheard the conversation as he was saddling his horse. He didn't necessarily share Dorothy's confidence in Litchfield, but he kept that thought to himself.

The woman's confidence might not be completely genuine, either; if she had feelings for the sergeant, as Smoke suspected was true, she probably just wanted to fuss over him and spend time with him.

That didn't really matter, because with O'Malley wounded, he actually didn't need to be riding horseback all day. With obvious reluctance—and with Dorothy Bacon's assistance—he climbed into the ambulance wagon.

Smoke and Litchfield took the point. Arbogast wouldn't go on ahead as he had earlier in the journey. The chuck wagon would stay with the two army vehicles and the group wouldn't split up again until they reached Fort Craig.

Without further incident, they arrived around four o'clock that afternoon. The wagons, the accompanying riders, and the horse herd had moved up onto the shallow bench west of the river. Still riding out in front, Smoke spotted a flagpole with the Stars and Stripes fluttering slightly in the hot wind above the parade ground. A low, dark line on the ground marked the location of the earthworks surrounding the fort's outer perimeter.

As they drew closer, Litchfield said, "The only access is through a narrow gate on the north side of the earthworks. After we have the wagons inside, your men can drive the horses to the stables and corral in the northwest corner of the compound. Our hostlers will take care of them from there."

"Colonel Griffin is expecting us, I reckon?"

"He will be. The lookouts in the tower on the guardhouse at the gate will have spotted us by now and sent word to him that we're here."

Litchfield turned in the saddle and waved for the two army wagons and the troopers to follow him. Smoke dropped back with the herd.

"Looks like we've made it," Dean McKinley commented, as Smoke joined him on the herd's left flank. "I know I ought to be happy about that . . ."

"But you've still got that girl weighing on your mind, don't you?"

"I have to be honest, Smoke. As soon as I laid eyes on her, I felt like there was something special about her. That there could be something special between her and me. Did you feel like that when you first met Miss Sally?"

"I reckon I did," Smoke admitted. "It took her a little while to come around to seeing things the same way." He paused, then added, "Like I said, I'm not going to tell you what to do, Dean. But it might be a good idea for you to have a good talk with Miss Griffin before you make any decisions that you can't take back."

McKinley nodded slowly. "I reckon that's the smartest thing to do. But sometimes it's hard to be smart when your heart is telling you one thing and your brain is saying you probably ought to rein it in a mite."

Smoke chuckled and said, "That's true enough. For right now, let's just concentrate on getting those horses the last little bit they've got to go."

"And then figure out what to do about the ones that were stolen?"

"That's right," Smoke said with a nod. He was eager to talk to Colonel Andrew Griffin and see what Fort Craig's commanding officer would have to say about the situation.

CHAPTER 12

Smoke estimated that the earthen wall surrounding the fort was about a dozen feet tall, as they rode closer. Next to the narrow gate was a square, sturdy-looking guardhouse made of adobe, with a covered wooden platform on its roof where sentries could use field glasses to scan the approaches to the fort.

The gate was made of thick iron-banded beams that must have been freighted in. There were no trees around here big enough to have provided them.

The gate swung inward as the group approached. Through the opening, Smoke could see some of the adobe buildings at the southern end of the compound, on the other side of the open parade ground. Even though they weren't visible from this angle, he knew similar structures would be arranged around the outer edges of the fort: officers' quarters, barracks, the sutler's store, a blacksmith shop, storage buildings, a powder magazine. The largest building he could see at the other end was probably the post headquarters. Another flagpole rose in front of it with a regimental guidon hanging from it.

Although the details differed from fort to fort, all the frontier outposts Smoke had visited had the same feeling to them—brisk efficiency coupled with crushing monotony and a nagging sense of possible danger. In a place like this, surrounded by desolation, where the weather was hot and arid most of the year, monotony tended to have the upper hand.

That was probably why a number of heads sporting forage caps of the 9th Cavalry popped up at the top of the earthworks to watch as the escort detail and the horse herd approached the fort. This was the most excitement Fort Craig had seen in a while.

More than likely, the excitement level would rise even higher once word got around about the battle with the Apaches and the daring raid on the herd by the Desert Wolf and his bandits.

Captain Litchfield was the first one through the gate, followed by the ambulance wagon and the supply wagon with Captain Brant riding on the seat next to the driver. The five surviving troopers from the escort detail came next. The supply wagon swung off to the left, but the ambulance headed straight across the parade ground toward the headquarters building.

As Smoke rode through the gate, he saw a tall, stiffly held figure in a blue uniform and black hat step out onto the building's low gallery and stand there waiting.

That would be Colonel Andrew Griffin, Smoke thought. He couldn't make out many details at this distance, but the man certainly carried himself as if he were in command.

Litchfield reined in, dismounted, and handed his reins to an orderly who hurried out to meet him. A single step up took him onto the gallery, where he came to attention and saluted the officer waiting for him. The colonel returned the salute, the two men spoke for a moment, and then they emerged from the shade of the thatch awning over the gallery and walked out to the ambulance wagon.

Virginia Griffin climbed over the seat onto the driver's box. It wasn't a very ladylike move because she had to pull up her skirts in order to do so, revealing a fetching bit of ankle and stocking. But obviously, she was eager to greet her father. The colonel stopped beside the wheel and reached up to help his daughter off the wagon.

As soon as her feet were on the ground, Virginia threw her arms around the tall officer. She might not be that fond of the fort, but clearly, she had missed her father. As Smoke rode up, Virginia stepped back a little and smiled up at the man who rested his hands on her shoulders.

"It's good to see you again, Colonel," she said, with a mischievous sparkle in her eyes.

"At ease, Private Griffin," the colonel responded in a dryly affectionate tone.

"Are you ever going to promote me to corporal?" she asked.

"When you earn it," he said. Then he hugged her again, and went on, "Ah, Vingie, girl, you're a sight for sore eyes, indeed you are."

Litchfield stepped up to them and said, "I felt the same way when I first saw Miss Griffin in Socorro, sir. She's always welcome here at the fort. She brings a refreshing bit of loveliness to these somewhat stark surroundings."

"Yes, yes," Colonel Griffin responded, with a slight note of impatience in his voice. He seemed to realize that Litchfield was currying favor and wasn't overly impressed by the effort.

Dorothy Bacon climbed down from the wagon as well and hugged her brother.

A worried frown appeared on Griffin's face as he said, "I was sorry to hear from Captain Litchfield that you and the others ran into trouble on the way down here from town. Are you all right, Dorothy?"

"I'm fine," she assured him. "But Sergeant O'Malley was wounded, along with several other troopers, and one man was killed."

"Yes, the captain told me about that."

"I'm confident that O'Malley will recover completely, sir," Litchfield put in.

"I hope so. He's one of the finest noncommissioned officers we have." Griffin turned back to his daughter and sister and went on. "You two go into my office and get out of this heat. I'll be in shortly, as soon as I've dealt with business."

"All right, Father," Virginia said. She linked arms with her aunt and they went across the gallery into the headquarters building. The adobe walls were quite thick and would help keep some of the heat at bay.

Griffin and Litchfield turned to Smoke. Litchfield said, "Colonel, this is Smoke Jensen."

Griffin extended his hand. "Colonel Andrew Griffin," he introduced himself, which wasn't really necessary. "I'm the commanding officer of this post. It's good to finally meet you, Jensen, after the letters we've exchanged."

Smoke clasped the man's hand firmly and said, "I'm happy to meet you, too, Colonel."

Griffin cut an impressive figure in his crisp, blue uniform. In his mid to late forties, he was an inch or two taller than Smoke and probably twenty pounds heavier. He had a rather long face with a deep permanent tan that spoke of many years spent outdoors in the wind and sun. His pale blue eyes were deep-set and surrounded by tiny wrinkles formed by all the time he had spent peering into the distance, searching for foes. The reddish-brown hair under his hat was touched liberally with gray.

Smoke didn't feel any instinctive liking for the colonel, but he didn't dislike Griffin, either. He sensed that the man was accustomed to getting his own way, which was to be expected in a high-ranking military officer. Griffin would have to accept, though, that Smoke wasn't under his command.

"I just wish the circumstances weren't quite so unfavorable," Griffin continued. "But I appreciate that you and your men rendered some assistance to Captain Litchfield when his detail came under attack by hostiles."

Smoke glanced at Litchfield, who returned the look expressionlessly. If not for the timely arrival of Smoke and the other men from the Sugarloaf, the Apache war party probably would have overrun the escort detail. Smoke knew that, and doubtless Litchfield did, too.

But Smoke didn't see any point in dwelling on that. Litchfield could self-aggrandize all he wanted to; it was none of Smoke's business.

So, he said simply, "I'm glad we were able to lend a hand, Colonel. Right now, though, I'm more concerned with going after those stolen horses and getting them back."

Griffin shook his head. "I'm afraid you won't be doing that."

Smoke leaned back a little in surprise and frowned. "What do you mean, Colonel?" he asked. "I'm not in the habit of letting bandits steal from me and get away with it."

"Those horses are United States cavalry remounts. Therefore, it's the responsibility of the U.S. army to recover them, if possible."

Smoke shook his head. "Begging the colonel's pardon, those horses haven't been turned over officially to the army yet. I tried to do that in Socorro and was told it would have to be done here at the fort." He glanced at Litchfield and then turned his attention back to Griffin. "Not only that, but I haven't been paid for them, either. I expect the army *won't* pay for them unless they're recovered."

"That is correct," Griffin admitted. "You make good points, but I still have to overrule any plans you have to pursue those horse thieves. According to the best information we have, the stronghold of Lobo del Desierto is located somewhere in the badlands south of here, and that area is under military jurisdiction."

Anger welled up inside Smoke, but he kept a tight rein on his temper. Yelling at a man like Griffin would just make him dig in his heels even more, and if the colonel got mad enough, he might throw Smoke in the guardhouse. He wouldn't have any legal authority to do so, but Smoke would still be behind bars.

"With all due respect, Colonel, I'm not sure you have the right to put the area off-limits. The old Camino Real runs through there. It's a public road and has been for a couple of hundred years. Freighters run their wagon trains up and down through the Jornada del Muerto all the time."

Litchfield said, "They used to—until they began suffering too many losses of cargo and men to the Desert Wolf. For the past few months, the trail through the badlands has been all but shut down."

Smoke hadn't been aware of that. When Litchfield had told him about the Desert Wolf, it was the first time Smoke had heard of the bandit.

"All that may well be true," he said, "but I still believe I have a right to go after the varmints who stole my horses. And for now, they *are* my horses." Smoke gestured toward the corrals. "I won't argue about the ones that are already in your custody, Colonel. But until I've officially delivered those others—"

Griffin held up a hand to stop him. Smoke figured the colonel was fixing to tell him to go pound sand, but Griffin surprised him by saying, "As I told you, your points are well-taken. And I'm aware that you have some friends in high places, Jensen. If I refuse your request, you'll return to Socorro and send telegrams to those friends complaining about me, won't you?"

"I stomp my own snakes," Smoke said, with a chilly note in his voice. "I don't ask friends to do it for me."

"Nevertheless . . ." Griffin drew in a breath. "I'll be sending out a detail first thing in the morning to locate the trail of those stolen horses, follow it, and recover them. Upon further consideration, if you want to accompany that detail, I'll allow it."

"Who's going to be in command of the detail?"

The colonel answered without hesitation. "Captain Litchfield is my finest and most dependable officer." He turned to Litchfield. "Captain, you'll be in charge of finding those horses and bringing them back."

Litchfield stiffened and gave Griffin a curt nod. "It'll be my honor, sir," he told the colonel. With a glance toward Smoke, he added, "But I'm not certain about sending a civilian along—"

"I've made my decision, Captain. You'll leave first thing in the morning. Pick twenty men for the detail, but none of the troopers who were part of the escort detail. Since Sergeant O'Malley is wounded, you'll take Sergeant Dunn with you, as well."

"Very good, sir."

Griffin turned back to Smoke and said, "If you'd like to have a couple of your men accompany you, that's agreeable, as well."

"Thanks, Colonel. I'll do that."

Smoke thought of Dean McKinley right away. Not only was the young cowboy a steady, dependable man, he was a good shot and cool under fire. And getting him away from Fort Craig would also mean getting him away from Virginia Griffin.

McKinley wouldn't like that, of course, but Smoke would feel better about things if McKinley came along, especially since Smoke wasn't going to be here at the fort while they were chasing those horse thieves. He wouldn't be able to keep an eye on McKinley and see to it that the young man didn't stir up any more trouble where Virginia was concerned.

He wasn't sure which of the other men he would ask to ride with him, but they were all good hands and he would be happy to have any of them along.

"It's settled, then," Colonel Griffin said. "Your men are welcome to spread their bedrolls in our barracks, or they can camp outdoors if they prefer. There's an empty cottage in our officers' quarters you can use. And of course, you'll have supper with me and my family this evening."

"It would be my pleasure, Colonel," Smoke said. He would have preferred taking all of his men with him to chase down those horse thieves, but he could tell that Griffin had already unbent as far as he was going to.

"Now, if you'll excuse me, I'm going to go catch up with my daughter and sister. I'm sure they have a great deal to tell me about everything that's been going on in Socorro." Griffin smiled slightly and then went into the headquarters building, leaving Smoke and Litchfield standing in front of it.

"I think the colonel is making a mistake," Litchfield said bluntly, in a voice that wouldn't carry to anyone except Smoke.

"By letting me and another man go along to help you chase down the Desert Wolf?"

"I don't need your help, and civilians are more trouble than they're worth."

"They're still my horses and my responsibility," Smoke said.

"I suppose you're going to bring McKinley with you," Litchfield snapped.

"As a matter of fact, I am. I know the two of you don't get along, but I figured you'd rather have him out in the badlands chasing bandits, rather than here where Miss Griffin is."

Litchfield frowned as if that angle hadn't occurred to him. He said, "As long as he follows orders, that's all I care about."

"He'll follow my orders."

"That's not what I meant. I'm in command—" Litchfield broke off what he was about to say and went on, "No, never mind. We're all going to have to work together if we're going to find those horses and recover them."

"And what about the Desert Wolf? I noticed that Colonel Griffin didn't give you any orders about what to do with him."

"I'm sure that's because the colonel anticipates the same

thing I do. The Wolf will never surrender those horses peacefully. We'll have to take them from him, and he'll put up a fight."

"The odds should be fairly close to even, from what we've heard about his gang."

Litchfield shook his head. "Numbers aren't the most important thing. A band of undisciplined Mexican rabble won't be any match for the troopers of the Ninth Cavalry."

"You'd better hope you're right, Captain, or . . ."

"Or what?"

"Or it could be that none of us will come back from the Jornada del Muerto," Smoke said.

Chapter 13

Dean McKinley stepped back from the corral gate, took off his hat, and dragged the sleeve on his other arm across his face to wipe off some of the sweat. A few drops had gotten in his eyes, and the salt tang was making them sting. He blinked rapidly as he crammed his hat back on his head.

He glanced toward the far end of the parade ground. A short time earlier, Virginia and her aunt had gone into the building there, which Dean assumed was the headquarters for this frontier outpost. Smoke still stood in front of the building with that no-good varmint Litchfield. Another officer—Colonel Griffin, Virginia's father, Dean assumed—had just gone inside, as well.

Smoke and Litchfield exchanged a few more words before Smoke turned away and led his horse toward the corral.

A couple of troopers had just swung the gate closed and fastened it. Vic Russell slapped the hand on his unwounded arm against one of the rails and said, "Well, that's those nags accounted for, anyway."

"I reckon Smoke told the colonel we're going after the ones that got stolen," Dean said.

He wasn't sure how he felt about that. On the one hand, the herd being raided like that and half of the stock driven off by thieves put a mighty big burr under Dean's saddle. He was offended, insulted, and downright mad. Getting those horses back and dealing with the bandits who'd stolen them loomed large in his mind.

At the same time, that would mean leaving the fort and not being able to see Virginia again until they got back. He had been counting on spending a little more time with her before he and the rest of the Sugarloaf crew headed back to Socorro and then home. He hoped to have a good talk with her, and that was going to help him make up his mind what to do next.

He wasn't going to join the army, that was for sure. But he might draw his time from Smoke and stay around these parts. That would be hard—he had never met a man he admired more than Smoke Jensen—but sometimes a fella's heart just didn't allow him much leeway.

"The army's liable to go after those horse thieves, too, you know," Russell said, breaking into Dean's thoughts.

"You think so?"

"It wouldn't surprise me."

"The missing horses don't belong to them yet. They're still Smoke's."

"You heard the way Captain Litchfield talked about that colonel. He thinks he's the big skookum he-wolf around here and runs everything. Civilians, too."

"Well, I don't know about that. I'm not sure Smoke would stand for it."

"You can ask him about it," Russell said, with a nod toward Smoke, who was still approaching. "Here he comes now."

Smoke walked up leading his horse and nodded at the animals milling around inside the corral. "It's good to see those critters where they belong," he said. "We got that much done, anyway."

"And we'll get the others back," Dean said confidently. "You're going after them, aren't you, Smoke?"

"I am. And so are you, Dean."

Russell said, "What about the rest of us?" Before Smoke could reply, he added, "Don't worry about this arm of mine that got winged. It doesn't amount to anything. I can still ride and shoot just fine."

Smoke shook his head. "Colonel Griffin is sending a cavalry detail to track down those stolen horses. He agreed I could go along and said I could bring another man with me. I figure on Dean for the job." His voice softened a little. "I know you're not hurt bad, Vic, but it'll do you some good to rest up a mite. And I need you to keep an eye on things here at the fort, too, while I'm gone with the cavalry."

Russell frowned but nodded. "I'll do like you say, Smoke. But I wish I was going out there to track down those bandits, too."

Dean felt both excitement and dismay going through him. He wanted to help Smoke bring those thieves to bay, but at the same time he was going to have to leave Virginia, just as he'd feared.

Something else occurred to him. He said, "Who's going to be in charge of that cavalry detail, Smoke?"

Smoke smiled, but the expression was wryer than anything else.

"Captain Litchfield," he said.

"Blast it!" Dean burst out. "Don't they have any other captains here at this dang fort?"

"Colonel Griffin trusts him. He must, or he wouldn't have sent Litchfield to fetch his daughter and sister."

Dean nodded and said, "Well, I'm not surprised. That seems to be the way my luck's going these days."

"Shoot, kid, it could be worse," Russell said. "If Litchfield's out chasing the Desert Wolf, he won't be here courting Miss Griffin, will he?"

"No, I reckon not. I just hope he doesn't get us all killed."

That wasn't likely, though, Dean told himself. Not with Smoke Jensen along.

* * *

Arbogast parked his chuck wagon not far from the stables and set up to cook the evening meal for the Sugarloaf crew. After they had eaten, they pitched their bedrolls nearby. Accustomed to sleeping under the stars while they were on the trail, none of the men found the idea of spending the night in a stuffy barracks appealing, at least as long as the skies were clear and there was no rain.

Smoke had been invited to have supper with the colonel and his family and to use one of the empty cabins in the officers' quarters. Dean figured Smoke would have rather been with the crew, but it was probably a good idea not to antagonize the commanding officer.

After supper, the men sat around the chuck wagon, smoking and talking, while Arbogast and Perry Severs cleaned up after the meal. Dean didn't pay much attention to the conversation. His gaze kept straying across the parade ground to the largest of the buildings in the row of officer's quarters. That was the colonel's residence. Yellow lamplight glowed warmly and appealingly in its windows.

Virginia was in there, he thought. He would have given a lot to be able to walk over there, knock on the door, and ask her to come out for a walk with him. The sun was down, the sky was shading to a deep blue, and pinpricks of stars were beginning to shimmer into existence here and there. The heat from the day had already begun to fade as the dry air cooled rapidly, as it always did. This part of New Mexico Territory might not be the prettiest country in the world, but an evening such as this was truly beautiful.

Sharing it with Virginia Griffin would just make it more beautiful, Dean knew.

But if he marched over there like he wanted to, more than likely the colonel would come to the door and threaten to have him locked up.

Not only that, but Smoke would be angry with him, too, and Dean didn't want that. He liked even less the idea of letting Smoke down.

So, with a sigh, he leaned back against the wagon wheel where he was sitting, stretched his legs out in front of him, and told himself to take it easy, rest after an eventful and dangerous day, and not brood so blasted much.

That wouldn't be easy, but he would give it a try.

He tried to distract himself with the raucous talk and horseplay of the cowboys around him, but his thoughts kept straying back to Virginia, and he couldn't keep his eyes off the house where he knew she was.

After a while, as his frustration grew greater, he wondered if he might be able to take his mind off it by walking around the fort. He got to his feet.

"Where are you goin'?" Alvie Rogers asked.

"I'm just going to take a walk," Dean replied. "It'll be time to turn in soon, and I wanted to get a little night air first."

"Well, watch where you're steppin'," another cowboy warned. "This is the time of the evenin' when rattlesnakes start to move around."

That was true. Once the air began to cool off, the snakes that had been lying torpid in the heat all day began stirring. Dean hated snakes with a passion, but he was too wound up inside to stay still. Besides, one reason cowboys wore high boots like they did was to turn aside serpents' fangs.

"I'll keep my eyes open," he said.

He strolled around the parade ground, not getting in any hurry. His steps took him away from the colonel's house at first, but once he reached a corner and turned, he was going toward those quarters again.

Dean could still see where he was going, even though the shadows of dusk had begun to gather fairly thickly. Lamps burned in most of the cabins along this side of the post, but the ones in Colonel Griffin's house seemed brighter and more compelling to him. He ought to turn back and return to the chuck wagon, he told himself.

But he didn't.

Instead, he continued toward the sturdy adobe house at the end of the row of officers' quarters. He was only halfway along that row, however, when he stopped short and peered through the gloom.

He would have sworn he had just seen someone slip around the corner of the colonel's house. It might have been some trooper carrying out an errand, Dean told himself, but that argument didn't convince him. There had been something furtive about the shadowy figure's movements.

And that set off alarm bells in Dean's mind and caused his heart to start slugging harder in his chest.

A few members of the Apache war party had gotten away earlier in the day. They might still be in the area, and so might others who hadn't attacked the cavalry detail. Dean was no expert on the Apache or any other tribe, but slipping into the fort to attack the commanding officer and his family seemed like something the hostiles might do.

Without thinking too much about what he was doing, he curled his hand around the walnut grips of the Colt on his hip and stole forward carefully, sneaking through the shadows as he approached Colonel Griffin's house.

The cottage next to the colonel's quarters appeared to be vacant. The windows were dark, anyway. Dean pressed his back against its wall and listened intently. He didn't hear anything except the normal night noises of the fort.

The space between this cottage and Colonel Griffin's house was already so thick with shadows that Dean couldn't make out anything moving along it, nor did he hear any telltale sounds. But that didn't mean the mysterious figure wasn't still lurking back there.

He eased around the corner and slid along the adobe wall toward the rear of the cottage. He kept his hand on his gun in case he bumped into trouble.

He didn't encounter anything. When he reached the corner, he stopped again to listen. It was even quieter back here. Maybe he'd just imagined seeing something, he thought. Maybe there really wasn't anything to worry about.

A few cottonwood trees grew between the quarters and the earthworks. Their large leaves rustled as they stirred in the gentle evening breeze. Dean studied the thick shadows under those trees, searching for any signs of movement. He didn't see any, and the gathering night remained quiet other than the whispering of the leaves.

Patiently, he waited while more time went by and the darkness deepened. The heavens above were black now and dotted with millions of stars. Dean was about to decide he was being foolish and ought to just go back to the chuck wagon when he heard soft footsteps from the front of the colonel's quarters. Those footsteps came along the narrow passage toward him.

Dean pressed his back against the wall and held his breath. He was absolutely silent and motionless as someone slipped past him, close enough to reach out and touch if he'd wanted to.

And he did want to, because the fragrance that drifted to his nose was familiar. It was the scent that Virginia Griffin wore, mixed with the clean smell of her hair.

What in the world was she doing out here, sneaking around after dark with no lantern?

Dean wanted to stop her, but he restrained that impulse. If someone reached out of the dark and touched her, it would frighten her, probably make her cry out. He didn't want to scare her, and he didn't want to draw attention.

Maybe if he waited to see what she was doing, then he could approach her and steal a few minutes of time with her. He needed to talk with her and find out if he even had a chance of any sort of friendship—or more—with her. That would help him make up his mind what to do.

But if she yelped or even screamed, more than likely somebody would come running to see what was wrong, and any chance to talk to her—maybe even kiss her—would be gone.

As Dean watched, Virginia walked toward the trees. She stopped just short of them, and in the starlight that flooded down on the scene, Dean saw that she had a shawl wrapped around her shoulders. The nights could get cool out here, even though the air was still a little warm right now. Was the shawl a sign that she intended to stay out here for a while?

He was about to step out of the shadows and call softly to her when more footsteps pattered quickly behind him. It had seemed like Virginia was trying to be quiet, but this newcomer wasn't being so careful. Another figure hurried past the spot where Dean stood motionless.

He didn't have to wonder for long who it was. A female voice that he recognized demanded, "Vingie, what are you doing out here?"

That was the same thing Dean wanted to know.

Virginia turned sharply where she was standing and said, "Aunt Dorothy! Please go back inside—"

"Your father thinks you've gone to bed," Dorothy Bacon said, "but I saw you slip out of the house. What in the world do you think you're doing?"

"Nothing you need to be concerned about. I'll be back inside in just a few minutes, if you'll give me a chance—"

Whatever it was Virginia planned to do, she wasn't going to get that chance, because at that moment another figure appeared, emerging swiftly and smoothly from the shadows under the cottonwood trees. The unknown man darted behind Virginia, wrapped his left arm around her waist, and clapped his right hand over her mouth to silence her as he began dragging her toward the darkness.

CHAPTER 14

Dean was so shocked by what he had just seen that it took a moment for him to shake off the temporary paralysis of surprise gripping him.

During that moment, two more men rushed from the shadows under the trees. One of them grabbed Dorothy Bacon and silenced her roughly with a hand over her mouth, just as Virginia had been silenced.

As Dorothy began to struggle, the other man took hold of her, as well, and between them, they forced her toward the cottonwoods. They were too strong for her; she couldn't throw off their grips.

Dean broke free of the invisible hands that held him. He charged out of the gap between Colonel Griffin's house and the empty cabin and yelled, "Leave those women alone!"

More figures flitted from the shadows and raced to intercept him. This was a raiding party, all right, no doubt about that. Dean figured they were Apaches even though it was too dark to get a good look at them.

He yanked his gun from its holster. He couldn't shoot toward the ones who had grabbed Virginia and her aunt for fear of hitting the women, but he could give a hot-lead welcome to those varmints looming up right in front of him.

Before he could pull the trigger, one of the attackers left his feet in a diving tackle that crashed into Dean. The man's arms wrapped around his waist, and his shoulder rammed into the young cowboy's belly. That impact knocked the air out of Dean so that he couldn't even yell as he went over backward and slammed onto the ground.

Even worse, the hard landing jolted the Colt out of his hand. He couldn't maintain his grip on the gun and felt it slip from his fingers.

The man who had tackled Dean dug a knee in his belly and heaved up to give himself room to throw a punch. The hard fist slashed down, caught Dean in the jaw, and bounced his head off the ground, making the world spin crazily around him.

He knew if he didn't fight back soon, his opponent would beat him senseless.

Dean bucked hard and twisted his body. At the same time, he shot his hands up, grabbed the front of the man's shirt, and heaved. The weight pinning him to the ground went away. Dean rolled the opposite direction and scrambled in the dirt to get his hands and knees under him.

He managed to do that, but before he could make it all the way to his feet, another of the attackers sunk a foot in his ribs in a vicious kick. That sent Dean rolling over a couple more times.

When he came to a stop on his back, one of the figures was looming above him, blotting out some of the stars. Dean sensed as much as saw the foot coming down at his face, intended to stomp him into unconsciousness or even death. He flung his hands up just in time to grab the foot and twist it as hard as he could.

That move sent the attacker down with a startled but muffled exclamation. Dean realized they were trying to be quiet so as not to draw any attention from the troopers. He opened his mouth to shout for help, but before he could get any sound out, another man leaped on him. The fellow's chest covered Dean's face, making it impossible for him to yell and difficult to even breathe.

The attacker twisted enough to give him room to hook several fast punches into Dean's midsection. Dean grabbed hold of the man's shoulders and tried to push him off, but the man seemed to weigh a ton. Once again, Dean realized he was on the verge of passing out.

That desperation saved him a second time. He brought his knee up and drove it into the man's groin. That brought a groan from the man's lips and ended the attack. Dean shoved him aside as the pain made the man curl up into a ball. Rolling onto his belly, Dean again made it to his hands and knees.

But again, one of the enemy was waiting for him. From the corner of his eye, Dean saw something coming at his head. He tried to jerk aside from it, but the object clipped him hard enough to knock him down. The thing that struck him felt like a gun barrel, which was a little surprising because Dean still figured the attackers for Apaches. But they could have handguns, too, he supposed.

Whatever it was, it hit him yet again as he tried to get up, and this time the blow was enough to tip him over the edge of a black, bottomless hole. Somewhere along the way as he plummeted into that darkness, oblivion claimed him.

Dean had been knocked out a couple of times before in his life, so he knew that when he came to, he probably wouldn't have any idea how much time had passed while he was unconscious. It might not seem like much at all, but he couldn't count on that.

As awareness flooded in on him and brought a wave of pain with it, he bit back a groan and forced his eyes open. At first, he saw nothing but black and wondered if maybe he hadn't come to, after all.

His head wouldn't be pounding like a giant drum if that were the case, though. After a moment, he realized he was lying on his belly with his face pressed to the dirt, and that was why he couldn't see anything.

He lifted his head. That made the booming inside his skull even worse, but he clenched his teeth and ignored it.

Now he could see the trees and the earthworks beyond them. The air had a glittery quality to it. He didn't know if that was from the starlight—or from being walloped on the head with a gun a couple of times.

Dean looked around and saw no sign of Virginia, Dorothy, or the men who had attacked him. If the raiders had killed the ladies, the bodies would still be there. It made more sense that Virginia and her aunt had been taken prisoner and carried away from the fort.

That thought made a terrible chill go through Dean. What kind of fate could they expect as captives of the Apaches? Nothing good, he knew.

But at the same time, something stirred in his brain. The cobwebs were dispersing, and he began to think faster and straighter.

This whole thing was wrong somehow. When he'd grabbed the shirt of one of the men he'd been fighting with, it wasn't a loose, blousy garment such as the Apache warriors wore. It had been tighter, with a slick, silk-like quality about it. It might have even been silk.

Not only that, he'd been close enough to smell the breath of another attacker, and it was laden with fumes of wine and pepper, reminiscent of a cantina. Then there was the matter of him being pistol-whipped, not a common Apache tactic.

None of that was solid evidence of anything, but he suddenly wondered if he'd been fighting Apaches at all.

No sooner had that doubt begun to form in his head than a new sound distracted him. He heard hoofbeats—not close, but not terribly far away, either—and they were moving fast, dwindling with distance.

Dean pushed himself to his feet and broke into a stumbling run through the trees. The explosions inside his head had subsided to a dull throb that sped up as he came to the earthworks and began clawing his way up the slanting, hard-packed surface.

It wasn't an easy climb, but a man could make it. The outer face of the fortification was much more sheer and had a deep ditch on the other side of it to make an ascent even more difficult. No parapet had been constructed along the top of the rampart. If the troopers had to defend Fort Craig, they would simply lie on the ground and fire their rifles over the crest.

When Dean reached the top, he peered out into the night, trying to locate the fading hoofbeats. His sharp eyes found a dark, moving mass heading southwest, away from the fort.

When he saw that, he knew he hadn't been unconscious for very long—probably just mere minutes. Those were the men who had slipped into Fort Craig, and unless he was very wrong about what he supposed, they had Virginia Griffin and Dorothy Bacon with them!

Dean didn't stop to think about what he was doing. He pulled himself onto the top of the rampart, scrambled across it, and lowered himself on the other side. It was a fairly easy drop into the ditch on the outside. He needed only a few moments to climb out of it. As soon as he was back on level ground, he started running after the departing riders.

He hadn't gone very far before he realized how futile this was. He couldn't catch men on horseback when he was on foot. He couldn't even keep up with them well enough to follow them. And he was wasting what could be valuable time when he should have been raising the alarm and getting a bunch of cavalrymen chasing after those skulking varmints, whoever they were.

He slowed to a stop, heaved a sigh, and started to turn back. Disappointment with himself was like a knife in his guts. He had had a chance to save Virginia from whatever was happening to her at this moment, and he had failed. Whatever her fate might be, it was on his head . . .

That bitter self-recrimination was torturing him as he swung around and a shadowy form leaped at him, seemingly from nowhere, starlight reflecting from the blade of a knife held high, ready to plunge down in a death stroke.

Dean yelped in surprise. He couldn't hold back the exclamation. But at the same time, he was twisting aside in a desperate attempt to avoid the knife.

The shadowy figure's momentum was committed to the attack. He couldn't alter the blade's path in time to bury it in Dean's breast. Instead, the tip caught the left sleeve of Dean's shirt and ripped along the forearm, but the cold steel missed the flesh itself.

Dean whipped his right arm around and hammered the side of his clenched fist against the man's head. That knocked off the broad-brimmed sombrero the attacker wore.

The distinctive headgear confirmed that it wasn't the Apaches who had raided Fort Craig tonight, after all. The most likely suspects were the bandits led by Lobo del Desierto—the Desert Wolf. Why they would sneak into the fort and kidnap Virginia Griffin and Dorothy Bacon, Dean didn't know—and he had his hands full right now just staying alive, so he didn't have time to ponder the question.

The blow to the head staggered the knife-wielder, but as he caught his balance, he swung a backhanded swipe with the blade that forced Dean to suck in his belly and leap back to avoid having his guts spilled.

While the attacker was turned half away from him as a result of the missed stroke, Dean kicked the man in the hip. This time he couldn't stay upright but went down in a floundering fall.

Dean leaped after him, pouncing on this opportunity. He brought his bootheel down sharply on the wrist of the man's knife hand. The man let out a thin little scream as he let go of the knife.

Dean tried to drop on top of him, but the man rolled aside to avoid being pinned. He jerked a leg up and straightened it in a kick that crashed into Dean's side, which already ached from being kicked earlier. Dean wound up on his belly with his face in the dirt again.

He pushed himself up and saw the man going after the knife on hands and knees. Dean dived after him, landed on top, and got his right arm around the man's throat from behind. He tightened his grip and locked it in place with his left hand, clenching his teeth from the effort, as he tried to choke the attacker into unconsciousness.

The man bucked and heaved himself over. Dean was suddenly on the bottom with his opponent's considerable weight on top of him. He didn't let up on his hold, though, as the man struggled fiercely.

Then the man rammed an elbow in Dean's stomach and the grip weakened. A second blow racked Dean, and the man broke free. He writhed over and got his hands around Dean's neck. The fingers clamped down like iron bands, and now it was Dean who was being choked until he passed out—or died.

Dean pounded at the man's head with both fists, but the man raised his shoulders to protect himself and hunkered down to the task of killing the young cowboy. Dean slapped the ground around him, searching for anything he could use as a weapon, when fate guided his hand to an actual weapon.

His fingers brushed the handle of the attacker's knife, which was wound with strips of leather and had a brass ball at the end of it. It tried to slide away from him on the sand, but he grabbed the handle and brought it up in a roundhouse blow. The brass ball crashed into the attacker's head with stunning force. It was enough to knock loose the man's grip on Dean's throat.

The attacker slumped over and rolled onto his back.

Gasping for breath, Dean rolled onto his side and lifted the knife, reversing it so that he gripped it to use the blade now. He could have driven it deep into the man's chest and pierced his heart. The hombre had it coming after the way he had tried to kill Dean.

But for some reason, the young cowboy hesitated. From the looks of it, the man who had jumped him was out cold, knocked senseless by that blow to the head, and Dean couldn't bring himself to kill a defenseless man.

At that moment, a horse whickered somewhere nearby.

Dean jerked his head up and spotted the horse standing about fifty feet away. His attacker must have had the animal hidden, maybe in a clump of mesquite, several of which dotted the area.

Dean's brain leaped to the most logical conclusion: the Desert Wolf had left this man behind to dispose of any pursuers.

Dean reached to the man's waist, found the gun holstered there. He pulled it from the sheath and saw in the moonlight that it was a .45 like his own that he had lost during the fight inside the fort. He pouched the iron in his own holster and stuck the knife behind his belt.

Then he came to his feet and bent to snag the sombrero he had knocked from the man's head. He placed the wide-brimmed hat on his own head and carefully approached the horse, which danced around a little skittishly.

Dean didn't know much Spanish, but he used what he could, speaking in a low, soothing voice. He might not smell like this horse's usual master, but at least he could approximate the man's shape and sound.

The horse settled down as he reached it and caught hold of

the dangling reins. It had accepted him, and he meant to put the mount to good use.

He left the sombrero on as he swung up into the saddle. He was going to try to stay out of sight, but if any of the Desert Wolf's men happened to spot him following them, maybe with the big hat on they would mistake him for the man they had left behind to guard their back trail.

All he wanted to do was to get close enough to find out where they were going. The Wolf was supposed to have a hide-out somewhere in the badlands to the south of here. If Dean could locate it, he could return to the fort and then lead the cavalry right where they needed to go.

The idea that he ought to head back to Fort Craig immediately and raise the alarm crossed his mind, but the Wolf's stronghold had to be well hidden; otherwise, the army would have found it by now. If he went back to fetch a troop of cavalry, the bandits might well have enough of a lead to slip away with their captives and never be found.

No, his best chance of saving Virginia and her aunt lay in following the gang and finding the hideout. Dean had reached that decision in a matter of seconds as soon as he laid eyes on the unconscious man's horse.

Anyway, he told himself, as soon as Colonel Griffin realized that his daughter and sister were gone, he would send out a search party. Smoke Jensen was at the fort, too, and Smoke was a great tracker. Chances were, once Dean located the bandit stronghold and headed back, he would run into the rescue party pretty quickly.

Virginia Griffin and Dorothy Bacon would be free in no time, Dean vowed to himself—as long as he didn't allow those varmints to give him the slip.

He pushed the sombrero down tighter on his head, leaned forward in the saddle, and rode quickly into the night after his quarry.

Chapter 15

Smoke found the dinner he shared with Colonel Griffin, Virginia, Dorothy, and Captain Litchfield somewhat uncomfortable, even though the colonel seemed to be making an effort to be a good host.

However, none of them could forget everything that had happened earlier in the day. All of them except Griffin had been in deadly danger, and that strain took a toll on people. The smell of gun smoke and the sight of blood always lingered.

Also, a trooper had been killed and several more wounded, including Sergeant O'Malley. Smoke had a hunch that Dorothy was worried about the sergeant, although she didn't bring up the subject.

Then there was the matter of the stolen horses and the cavalry detail that would leave first thing in the morning to search for them. Smoke wished that Colonel Griffin had picked someone other than Captain Litchfield to be in command of that detail, but at the same time, he wasn't acquainted with the other junior officers at the fort. It was possible that Litchfield actually was the best qualified to be in charge of the pursuit.

The whole situation put a bit of a pall over the gathering. The conversation was pleasant enough but restrained. The food prepared by the mess sergeant was good—simple but well cooked and appetizing.

When the meal was over, the ladies withdrew, leaving the men to smoke and sip brandy. Smoke didn't use tobacco and wasn't much of a drinker, so he sipped from a cup of coffee while Colonel Griffin packed and lit a pipe and Captain Litchfield fired up a cigar.

"I'm curious about this Desert Wolf," Smoke said. "What do you know about him?"

"He's a bloody-handed thief," Litchfield snapped. "What more do you need to know about him?"

Griffin ignored the captain's response and said, "We first began hearing rumors about him a year or so ago. Not many freight wagons use the old Camino Real anymore. It's simply too dry and difficult to make it through that stretch. But the freighters who made the attempt were stopped and held up. Ranches to the east, over in the Sacramento Mountains, and to the west, beyond the San Mateos and the Magdalenas, began losing stock to rustlers. As the crimes continued, it began to appear that a single organized gang was behind them."

"And the Desert Wolf is the leader of that gang?" Smoke asked.

"So the authorities along the river say." Griffin puffed on his pipe for a moment as he frowned in thought. Then he continued, "The farmers tell a different story about the Wolf, though."

"They're liars," Litchfield said. "Fanciful, romantic liars. Or else they're too frightened of the Wolf's vengeance to tell the truth."

That piqued Smoke's interest. "What do they say about him?"

"That he helps them," Griffin replied. "He claims that his goal is to protect them from Apaches and bandits."

"*Other* bandits, you mean," Litchfield said. "He won't allow any other gangs in the area so that he can prey on the peasants himself."

Griffin shook his head. "There haven't been any reports of farmers being attacked or robbed, not that they have much to steal." The colonel gestured with his pipe. "But just because the Wolf leaves them alone doesn't mean he's innocent of the other depredations up and down the Rio Grande. The Mexicans may believe him to be some sort of heroic outlaw, like that Joaquin Murrieta fellow, but that's ridiculous."

Smoke nodded slowly as he mused over what he'd been told. He thought about his own history, as well, and after a moment, he said, "Just because an hombre is accused of being an outlaw, that doesn't mean he really is. But chances are, you're right about the Desert Wolf. We ought to be able to tell once we find out where he's holed up."

"I'm still not fond of the idea of taking civilians along on a military mission," Litchfield said.

"The army sometimes uses civilian scouts, isn't that right?" Smoke countered.

Griffin nodded. "That's true."

"Just think of me and McKinley as scouts, Captain. I've had some experience at tracking, and I had just about the best teacher any man could have when it comes to that. A man known as Preacher."

Griffin's eyebrows rose. "The mountain man called Preacher? I've heard stories about him. General Carson spoke highly of him, back during the war."

Smoke knew Griffin was talking about the famous frontiersman Kit Carson, who had crossed trails with Preacher on several occasions.

"Preacher and I are friends," Smoke said, which greatly simplified the relationship between them. Preacher had been

Smoke's mentor and almost a second father to him for many years.

"You mean he's still alive?" Griffin asked. He sounded amazed. "The stories about him go back a long time. Decades, in fact."

That drew a chuckle from Smoke. "The last I heard, he was alive and kicking. I'm not sure Preacher will ever die. He's sort of as unchanging as the mountains."

Litchfield said, "We have good trackers, too, so I'm not sure your services will be needed in that area, Jensen." He shrugged. "Of course, I'll comply with the colonel's orders. You and your man will accompany us when we leave at first light tomorrow morning. But you'd better keep up, and you'll be responsible for taking care of yourselves. I'll not put troops at risk for you."

Griffin pursed his lips as if he didn't care for Litchfield's bluntness, but he didn't contradict the captain. He had placed Litchfield in command and wasn't going to undermine him. Smoke could respect that, even though he didn't like Litchfield.

He changed the subject by asking, "What makes you think the Wolf's hideout is in the Jornada?"

"The freighters who have been held up reported that the thieves fled in the direction of the hills along the western edge of the badlands," Griffin said. "The farmers have also spoken of the Wolf's stronghold as being in that area, although I'm not sure how much faith we should put in their word. They're sympathetic to him, after all."

"They're too . . . *uncomplicated* to lie," Litchfield said. He managed to make it sound like an insult. "Fortunately, those stolen horses should have left enough of a trail that we can tell which direction they started. Once we're into the Jornada, though, in most places the ground is too hard and rocky to take any tracks. Finding the Wolf's hideout won't be easy, but I can assure you, I'll give it my utmost effort, Colonel."

"I know you will, Philip," Griffin said. "And you and Mr. Jensen had better turn in. First light comes early."

Litchfield puffed on his cigar for a moment and then took it out of his mouth to say, "I can't wait to get on the trail. It's time someone brought the Desert Wolf to heel." He looked at Smoke. "Don't be late, Jensen. We won't wait for you."

"McKinley and I will be there," Smoke said, keeping a tight rein on his temper. He drank the coffee that was left in his cup and stood up from the table. "Good night, Colonel. Thank you for supper, and please pass along my compliments to the ladies."

"Of course."

Smoke got his hat and left the colonel's house. He thought he might see Virginia or Dorothy on his way out, but he didn't encounter either of them. The fort was quiet as he walked along the row of officers' quarters to the one he'd been given the use of for the night. He'd already checked out the cottage and knew it would be comfortable, although sparingly furnished.

Honestly, he would have been just as happy to pitch his bedroll around the chuck wagon with the other members of the Sugarloaf crew, but he hadn't wanted to appear ungrateful for the colonel's offer of hospitality.

In one way, though, Smoke felt the same as Captain Litchfield.

He was ready to get on the trail of the Desert Wolf.

Living with danger had become second nature to Smoke, so naturally, he was a light sleeper and had the ability to come awake instantly and completely when he needed to.

That was what happened when someone hammered on the cottage door early the next morning. The urgent summons brought Smoke out of the bunk in a flash. With bare feet and wearing the bottom half of a pair of long underwear, he crossed the room to the door and pulled it open.

He had a Colt in his hand, too, ready to fire if he needed to.

He held off on that when he saw Arbogast standing there. The sky had lightened slightly in the east with the approach of dawn, but the sun was still a long way from rising. Smoke was able to recognize the chuck wagon cook's tall, gaunt figure, though.

"That McKinley kid is gone," Arbogast reported.

"For how long?" Smoke asked.

"Nobody's seen him since last night, but we didn't realize that until just now when the boys started rolling out of their sugans to get breakfast."

Smoke nodded. His face was expressionless, but inside, he was worried. Dean McKinley was an impulsive youngster; there was no telling what he might have done or where he might be, but chances were that some trouble was involved.

"I'll get dressed and be over there in a minute," he told Arbogast. The cook nodded and headed back to the chuck wagon.

Smoke had already buckled on his gun belts and was pulling on his boots when more hammering sounded on the door. He stomped his feet into the boots and opened the door again.

This time it was Colonel Andrew Griffin standing there. Griffin wore boots and uniform trousers, but his suspenders hung loose and he had only the woolen, army-issue long underwear above the waist. His hair was tousled from sleep and he had stubble on his lean cheeks.

"Vingie is gone," he said. "So is Dorothy. You haven't seen either of them, have you, Mr. Jensen?"

Smoke bit back a groan. Knowing that Dean McKinley had disappeared, he wasn't surprised that Virginia Griffin was missing, too. Those two things had to be connected. He couldn't quite see how Dorothy Bacon vanishing tied in with that, but he was sure it all centered around the reckless young cowboy and his infatuation with Virginia.

If McKinley had been here right now, Smoke would have been tempted to kick his rear end.

That would have to wait until McKinley and the two women were located, though.

Those thoughts flashed through Smoke's mind as Colonel Griffin waited anxiously for his response. "I haven't seen them," Smoke said. "Do you know how long they've been missing?"

"Neither of their beds has been slept in. I haven't seen either of them since right after supper last night."

Again, that jibed with McKinley's disappearance.

"I've sent men to search the fort," Griffin went on. He noticed that Smoke was fully dressed except for his hat. "You're ready to leave with Captain Litchfield?"

"Yes, but we may have somebody to look for besides the Desert Wolf. One of my men is missing, too."

Griffin's eyes widened. "You think he's been captured by whoever took Vingie and Dorothy?"

"I think there's a chance your daughter and my cowboy ran off together," Smoke said bluntly. "Maybe your sister went after them to try to stop them."

"What in blazes are you talking about?"

"Captain Litchfield didn't tell you about the trouble he had with Dean McKinley over Miss Virginia?"

Griffin stared at Smoke for a moment and then sighed. "Good grief," he muttered. "Not an affair of the heart, surely."

"I reckon you could call it that," Smoke said. "I'm headed over to the chuck wagon to talk to my men and see what I can find out about it."

"I'll come with you," Griffin declared.

As they walked along the edge of the parade ground in the

predawn gloom, Smoke asked, "Have you told Captain Litchfield about the ladies yet?"

"Yes, he's in charge of the search being carried out."

It was easy to see that something was going on inside the fort. Troopers scurried here and there, carrying lanterns. Men called to each other. Smoke hoped they would turn up some sign of the missing women, but he had a hunch that they wouldn't.

A lantern burned at the chuck wagon, too, its bail hanging over one of the supports for the canvas cover extending from the vehicle's side. Arbogast, Perry Severs, Vic Russell, and the other Sugarloaf hands were gathered nearby.

They turned toward Smoke and Griffin as the two men strode up. Russell said, "We've looked all over, Smoke, but we can't find Dean. I don't know where in blazes he's gone off to."

Colonel Griffin pulled his suspenders up over his shoulders, glared, and said, "It appears that he's run off with my daughter and possibly my sister."

"The ladies are missing, too," Smoke added, addressing Russell and the other hands. "You fellas haven't seen either of them, have you?"

Russell and the others looked shocked. "We sure haven't," Russell said. "Smoke, you don't think—blast it, Dean wouldn't have—"

"He might have," Smoke broke in. "He can be pretty hotheaded at times."

"When we find him, I'm gonna kick that boy all the way back to Colorado," Russell fumed. "It's a good thing I got shot in the arm, because my kickin' leg is just fine!"

"You may have to wait until I've had my turn with him," Smoke said. "For now, let's see if we can turn up any trace of him."

The Desert Wolf and the stolen horses were forgotten for

the moment. The safety of Virginia and her aunt took precedence over everything else, and Smoke was also concerned about McKinley. He was angry with the young cowboy, but at the same time, he didn't want anything bad to happen to him.

And it was possible, Smoke reminded himself, that they might all be wrong about what had taken place at Fort Craig during the night. Maybe McKinley hadn't run off with Virginia. Dangers lurked in the badlands, and some of them might have ventured out of the darkness and made a daring foray into the fort.

As the search continued, Smoke suggested to Colonel Griffin, "It would be a good idea to take a look around outside, too. We might be able to tell if somebody was in the area who shouldn't have been."

"Such as more Apaches?" Griffin's face twisted with emotion. "Good Lord! Do you think the savages would have been bold enough to sneak into the fort and kidnap my daughter and sister?"

"I don't think we can rule it out. There's still the Desert Wolf to consider, too."

Griffin jerked his head in a nod and turned to bellow, "Sergeant Dunn!"

A lean, middle-aged man in uniform trotted up. "Yes, sir?"

"Get a couple of troopers and come with me, Sergeant."

Griffin stalked toward the gate.

Smoke didn't ask for permission to come along; he just went outside the fort with Griffin, Sergeant Dunn, and two of the buffalo soldiers. The sergeant carried a lantern, and so did one of the troopers. Even though a reddish-gold arch was forming in the eastern sky, it was still too dark to see the ground very well without the light from the lanterns.

The group walked about fifty yards away from the fort and then began making a slow circuit around it. They were almost at the halfway point when Smoke noticed some odd markings on the ground. He dropped to a knee and said, "Could you bring that lantern over here, Sergeant?"

Dunn did so, holding the lantern closer to the ground so that Smoke could study the scuff marks in the dirt.

"There's been a fight here," he said to Colonel Griffin, who leaned forward to peer over his shoulder. He pointed to several dark splotches on the ground. "Unless I miss my guess, that's blood."

"Blood!" Griffin sounded shaken.

"There's not a lot," Smoke went on. "Whoever was hurt, it was just a minor wound, nothing serious."

"That doesn't make me feel a great deal better. The struggle that took place here happened last night?"

"That's the way it looks to me," Smoke said.

"Sergeant!" the trooper with the lantern called. "Look over here."

Smoke, Griffin, and Dunn hurried over to look where the soldier was pointing on the ground.

"Those are hoofprints, all right," Smoke agreed. He nodded toward the southwest. "A single rider headed off in that direction."

"We'll follow these tracks," Griffin said.

The five men did so, moving fast but not hurrying so much that they risked losing the trail. After another hundred yards, Dunn paused and said, "Quite a few horses waited right here, Colonel. You can see the way they milled about."

Smoke said, "And there are enough droppings to indicate that they were here for a while."

"How many horses?" Griffin asked.

"Eight or ten, I'd say," Smoke replied.

"Then it could have been more Apaches, brought here by the survivors from that war party."

Smoke shook his head. “Not likely, Colonel. These horses were shod. Some Indians ride shod horses, but most don’t. Apaches don’t, as a rule.”

“Then who—?” Griffin stopped short for a moment, then said, in a voice fraught with both anger and fear, “The Desert Wolf.”

“That’s more likely.”

“The effrontery of the man! To come right into my fort and steal away my daughter and sister! I wasn’t inclined to give him the benefit of the doubt, no matter what the Mexican farmers say, but I wasn’t going to convict him without proof, either. But this—this is too much!” The colonel turned to Smoke. “I’m aware of your reputation, Mr. Jensen. I’m asking you, as a personal favor, to find those ladies and bring them back safely to me.”

Smoke nodded and said, “I’d already decided that’s what I’ll do, Colonel.”

“And when you do, it’s likely you’ll find those stolen horses, as well. Evidently, the Wolf’s villainy knows no bounds!”

“Are you still sending Captain Litchfield and a patrol?”

“Certainly. If you’re going up against that bandit and his gang, you’ll need a formidable force. The captain will remain in command.” Griffin paused and then said, “He’s a good officer, Mr. Jensen, no matter what your personal feelings toward him may be.”

“Of course, Colonel,” Smoke said. He honestly didn’t mind the troopers coming along; from everything he had seen of the 9th Cavalry so far, they were a good outfit. Sergeant Dunn had impressed him, too, in the brief time he had known the man.

“This man of yours that’s missing . . .”

“Dean McKinley.”

“Is there any chance he was working with the bandits?”

“No chance at all,” Smoke said, and he meant it completely.

"It's more likely that he found out somehow what was happening and tried to stop it." He glanced at the marks that a struggle had left on the ground, along with a few drops of blood. "And he's still alive, or we would have found his body. Seems likely to me that he's out there somewhere"—Smoke nodded toward the badlands to the south—"on the trail of the Desert Wolf."

CHAPTER 16

Dean McKinley took off the sombrero, set it aside, and eased his head up until he could see over the crest of the saw-toothed ridge. A short time earlier, he had spotted a thin thread of smoke rising into the dawn sky and had followed it here.

Behind him lay the flat, arid, almost completely barren Jornada del Muerto, stretching eastward for several miles before ending in rugged hills covered with scrubby vegetation. A similar range of hills ran along this western edge of the badlands. Dean had been riding carefully along the base of them most of the night as he followed the riders who had taken Virginia Griffin and Dorothy Bacon.

Dean had hung back far enough that he caught only occasional glimpses of his quarry in the starlight. That was fine as long as he didn't lose them. Anytime he couldn't see them, they couldn't see him, he told himself. Thankfully, they hadn't given him the slip.

He had planned to drop back even farther once the sun came up, but then he'd spotted the smoke and changed his mind. He pressed closer instead, while still being cautious. Maybe they had made camp, he told himself, or even reached their hideout.

When he'd realized that the smoke was coming from somewhere on the other side of this ridge, he had dismounted, tied the horse to a gnarled mesquite that came up only as high as his knees, and climbed the slope on foot. His eyes narrowed as he intently studied the scene before him.

On the other side, the ridge sloped down to a little valley perhaps half a mile wide. On the far side was a forty-foot-tall bluff running as far north and south as Dean could see. The bluff's face wasn't solid, though; canyons cut into it here and there, giving the bluff a ragged appearance. Most of them looked narrow and probably petered out quickly.

However, roughly opposite the point where Dean lay was the mouth of a much larger canyon a couple of hundred yards wide. He couldn't tell how deep it was because shadows still hung over its far end.

Somewhere in there was a camp or a dwelling, though. That was where the smoke came from. That had to be the Desert Wolf's stronghold.

Dean was surprised to see that a narrow stream ran out of the canyon. From what he knew of the Jornada del Muerto, there was no water to be found out here in this wasteland except for a few *tinajas* that occasionally held rainwater. There certainly shouldn't have been any running streams forming a pool such as the one that lay in the valley with a fringe of vegetation around it—but he could see it with his own eyes right there in front of him.

Grass grew along the stream's banks, too. Not much, but enough for horses to graze on the hardy clumps. Several were doing that as Dean watched. He wondered if they were wild mustangs. It seemed likely that if the Desert Wolf had his hideout in the canyon, the gang's mounts would be corralled up there somewhere rather than allowed to roam loose.

He had to get in there, Dean decided. That was the only way to know for sure. He couldn't cross the ridge and approach the canyon head-on; the terrain was much too open for that. If this was the Wolf's stronghold, he was bound to have guards watching the entrance.

But there might be a back door, and if there was, Dean would find it.

He grabbed the sombrero and hurried back down the slope, sliding a little as rocks and dirt moved under his feet. He mounted up and rode north, the way he had come from.

If he kept going, there was a chance he would run into a search party from Fort Craig within a few hours. Then he could bring them right back here.

But if the smoke wasn't coming from the Desert Wolf's hideout—if there was just some old prospector holed up in the canyon, or something like that—then Dean would have wasted a lot of valuable time. The Wolf and his prisoners would have such a big lead that nobody would ever catch them.

No, the thing to do was to make sure, he told himself, even though that would be a risky proposition.

The ridge played out after about a mile. That was far enough for Dean to be unobserved as he cut west into the hills and then turned south. There was no trail and the way was hard going, with ravines and bluffs that had to be skirted, so he wasn't able to move very fast. The sun was up now, an orange orb poking above the distant mountains to the east.

Every minute he spent working southward toward that isolated canyon seemed much longer to Dean. The delay gnawed at his guts. Virginia and her aunt were in the hands of those ruthless bandits, and there was no telling what might be happening to them. Dean tortured himself with thoughts of the possibilities.

But eventually, he was able to see the smoke again and knew he was getting close. He even caught a faint whiff of burning wood and cooking meat. Whoever was in the canyon, they were preparing a meal.

That was just more evidence he had found the Wolf's hideout, he told himself.

Even though he had an idea of what he was looking for, he was surprised when he found it. The ground dropped away in a sheer cliff. Dean reined in, stopping short, and dismounted, taking the sombrero off again as he stole forward for a better look. He went to one knee and leaned forward to peer over the brink.

Fifty or sixty feet below him, a large adobe house, built in the Spanish style with an interior courtyard, sat at the end of the canyon. The red slate roof and the thick adobe walls showed signs of age and neglect, as did the six-foot adobe wall that surrounded the house at a distance of twenty or so feet, but overall, the place didn't appear to be in bad shape.

Several other adobe buildings were nearby. A couple had thatched roofs that had fallen in, and some of the walls had collapsed in places, more signs of how old they were. Several of the buildings were still intact, though, and probably in use.

Several dozen horses were penned up in two corrals. Dean studied the animals but didn't recognize any of them. They hadn't come from the raid on the Sugarloaf herd. These horses were the bandits' saddle mounts, he decided. They had to be holding the stolen horses somewhere else.

The rising sun sparkled on another pool of water that lay against the canyon's far wall. There had to be a spring over there feeding it. The stream that trickled out into the valley originated here, completely unknown to the outside world.

Unknown, except to Lobo del Desierto and his men, of course.

This was an old *rancho*, Dean realized. Somebody had gotten the idea, a hundred years or so ago, of starting a spread here. That seemed like an awfully foolish idea considering the inhospitable terrain in these parts, but maybe things had been different in those days.

Or maybe whoever built that hacienda and the other buildings was just loco. Dean didn't know, and it didn't matter. The Desert Wolf had found the place and moved in with his gang, and that was where the bandit boss had brought his prisoners. That was all Dean cared about.

Nobody was moving around down there. The bandits had had a busy night, sneaking into Fort Craig and kidnapping the commanding officer's daughter and sister. They were probably tired this morning.

Dean had hoped to find a back entrance to the hideout. In what was probably just a wild flight of fancy, he had even thought about sneaking into the stronghold, rescuing Virginia and Dorothy, and galloping away from here in triumph. Surely that would make Virginia see that he was a lot better than that blasted Captain Litchfield.

Such a rescue attempt wasn't really feasible, though, so he was about to stand up and go back to the horse when movement below caught his eye.

From where he was, he could see into the open courtyard in the middle of the house. A figure strolled into Dean's field of vision, and even a glimpse of the auburn hair, bright in the morning sun, was enough to tell him who it was.

Virginia.

He caught his breath and leaned forward, then put a hand on the ground to keep himself from toppling over the edge in his eagerness to watch Virginia as she walked across the courtyard. She sat down on a wrought iron bench. As far as Dean could tell, she was unharmed.

She wore different clothing than the last garments he'd seen her in, though. Instead of a simple but stylish dress, she wore a short-sleeved white blouse that left quite a bit of her shoulders bare, as well as a long, dark skirt. The outfit looked like something a Mexican girl might wear.

Carefully, Dean leaned forward to study the cliff face below him. It wasn't as sheer as he had thought at first. There were enough ledges and protrusions that he believed he might be able to climb down. It would be dangerous, and he couldn't rush the descent. Anyone below who happened to look up would be able to see him.

And yet, now that he had laid eyes on Virginia, he couldn't just ride away and leave her here.

Smoke would find them, he thought. As soon as the folks back at the fort realized that he, Virginia, and Dorothy were gone, they would come looking for them, and if there was anybody in the world who could find this hideout, deal with those bandits, and set things right, it was Smoke Jensen.

Dean knew that even if he was able to climb down into the canyon, Virginia would never be able to climb back up that cliff and escape with him. Her aunt Dorothy surely couldn't manage that, either.

But he had a Colt with a full wheel, and every loop on his shell belt held a fresh cartridge, too. If he could round up Virginia and Dorothy, find some secure place inside the old hacienda, and hole up there with them, he might be able to keep them safe until Smoke arrived with a bunch of troopers from the fort. It was a long shot, no doubt about that, but if it worked, that would be the least dangerous situation for the women.

He had to give it a try, Dean decided.

He stood up and moved away from the brink. The horse had drifted away a short distance but didn't spook as Dean approached it and took hold of the reins again. There was no brush up here to tie them to, but he weighed them down with a good-sized rock. That would hold the horse for a while.

And if he never came back—which was all too possible—the animal would be able to get free eventually and go in search of food and water.

Not needing the sombrero, he left it where he had dropped

it on the ground. He went to the edge and studied the cliff again. He tried to trace a path in his mind that would lead all the way to the ground, but there were a few places where he couldn't see any footholds or handholds from up here.

He would just have to find good places to hang on to when he got there, Dean decided. He eased his legs over the edge and hung on firmly as he reached down with a foot until it was resting on a small outcropping that seemed solid. Carefully, he put more weight on the foothold until he was satisfied it would support him.

With his back to the canyon, Dean couldn't see what was going on below him, if anything. He listened intently, his ears primed for any outcry or alarm. If he was spotted, he might get a little warning—but probably not enough to make any difference. He would be an easy target for any decent marksman who tried to line sights on him.

He didn't hear anything except his own pulse pounding inside his head. The morning was quiet and peaceful, and already getting hot. The air cooled slightly as Dean descended the cliff, but not enough to keep sweat from popping out on his face.

This was the craziest thing he had ever done, he told himself. Risking his neck climbing down a cliff into a stronghold full of killers, and for what? A pretty girl with hair the color of flame when the sun hit it just right? What hombre in his right mind would do a thing like that?

Well, maybe he wasn't in his right mind, he thought. All he knew was that he couldn't ride away and leave Virginia Griffin here, defenseless in the hands of bandits. Not if there was the slightest chance he could save her.

His foot slipped off the rock where it had found purchase. The little knob just wasn't big enough. He started to fall, but his hands clamped down hard on a tiny ledge.

He grimaced and bit back a groan as his weight hit his fingers. Somehow, he managed to hang on. His other foot, flailing desperately, found a tiny crack. He wedged the toe of his boot into it and almost groaned again as that eased the incredible strain on his hands, arms, and shoulders.

He hung there for a long moment, trembling as he tried to regain his strength and nerve. Tipping his head back, he looked up the cliff and was surprised to find that he was more than halfway to the ground. Once his heart wasn't racing quite as fast as it had been, he took a deep breath and resumed the descent.

He came to a place where he couldn't find any more holds, but he was less than a dozen feet off the ground by then, so he pushed away from the cliff and dropped the rest of the way. That was a risk, too—you never knew for sure how you were going to land—but he figured it was one he had to take.

He landed easily, his weight tipping him over and causing him to fall, but he rolled and came up on his feet with no trouble. Immediately, he dropped into a crouch and scurried behind a small clump of brush. From there, he surveyed the hacienda and looked for signs of trouble.

Everything was still quiet. He was behind the house, and as he studied its rear wall, he saw the single door back here, a sturdy-looking portal with iron bands reinforcing it. There were no windows, but he saw a few rifle slits. That old *hacendado* had built the place to be defended, Dean thought. But unless someone just happened to be peering through one of those slits, he figured he could approach without being seen.

No time like the present for that. He pushed himself up and broke into a run that carried him across the hundred feet or so separating him from the house.

When he reached the wall, he pressed his back against it next to the door. Where he was, nobody could see him from any of the rifle slits. He stood there for a moment, catching his breath, and then leaned over and stretched out his right arm, reaching for the door latch.

It tripped easily enough, but the door wouldn't budge. Barred on the inside, he told himself. That came as no surprise. He twisted his head around to study the wall above him.

When it had been built, it would have been smooth enough and tall enough that it couldn't be climbed. But the passing decades had crumbled the adobe in places, leaving cracks and hollows.

If he could climb down that cliff, he could climb *up* this blasted wall! It wasn't nearly as tall.

He turned, reached up to search for a good grip, and pulled himself up. It required quite a bit of effort—and teeth-clenching—but he slowly neared the top. Finally, he was close enough to throw an arm over and lever himself high enough to get a leg on top of the wall, too.

The wall was a foot and a half thick, wide enough for him to lie on it on his belly as he caught his breath. He thought that Virginia might spot him up there, but a couple of cottonwood trees and some shrubs grew just inside the wall and obscured the view for anyone in the courtyard.

After a moment, Dean twisted around, let his legs dangle off the side of the wall, and dropped to the ground. He landed behind one of the trees and crouched there, hiding as best he could until he had time to take a good look around.

The bench where Virginia sat was placed at an angle to Dean's location, so she wasn't looking directly toward him. She peered straight ahead as if she were deep in thought.

A small fountain with a low rock wall around it stood in the center of the courtyard. It was dry now and looked like it had been for many years. There were some flower beds scattered around, too, but they had only cactus growing in them. Whoever had built this hacienda had tried to make it a nice place, but that would have been difficult, if not impossible, in an arid wasteland like the edge of the Jornada del Muerto.

Yet there was a good water supply here now. It should be possible to make a decent ranch out of this spread. Dean wondered how that had happened. Had the spring that fed those pools dried up for a long time and then started flowing again for some reason?

A covered walkway bordered the front part of the courtyard next to the house. Dean watched it for several minutes but didn't see anyone moving around there in the shade. Virginia seemed to be alone. He was about to step out from behind the tree and call to her. He wanted to warn her of his presence so that she wouldn't cry out in surprise when she saw him.

Then a door opened, and a man walked across the shaded gallery. He came into the courtyard and strode purposefully toward the beautiful, auburn-haired young woman.

Dean stood stock-still right where he was and continued watching as the man approached Virginia. He was tall, dark-haired, and handsome, dressed in boots, tight black trousers, and an open-throated white shirt. A sash of scarlet silk was tied around his waist.

Dean had no way of knowing if he was right, but his gut told him he was looking at Lobo del Desierto—the Desert Wolf.

His hand wrapped around the butt of the Colt at his hip. If the man made any move to threaten Virginia, he would step out of hiding and put a stop to it. The hombre appeared to be unarmed, so Dean hoped he wouldn't have to fire a shot and draw any attention, but he would if he had to. He wasn't going to let anything bad happen to Virginia.

Instead, when the man called softly to her, she turned her head to look at him—and smiled. Dean's eyes widened with shock as Virginia stood up and hurried to meet the newcomer. She turned her face up to him as he took her in his arms.

Then he kissed her with an unmistakable passion and ardor that she returned just as unmistakably.

Dean stood there as stunned as if someone had just walloped him in the head with a two-by-four.

He was so dazed he almost didn't hear a footstep scuff behind him until it was too late. At the last second, he whipped around and saw a burly bearded figure lunging at him, hands outstretched with the fingers hooked like talons.

Chapter 17

Dean reacted instinctively, jerking the Colt from leather and whipping his arm up to try to block the attack.

The man was too close. Dean knocked his left arm aside, but the man's right hand found Dean's neck and closed around it. His charge carried him into Dean and drove the young cowboy backward.

Dean grimaced in pain as the collision rammed his back against the cottonwood's trunk. The man's weight kept him pinned there as the long sausagelike fingers tried to crush his windpipe.

He knew he couldn't withstand that overpowering assault for long. He could have rammed the revolver's muzzle into the man's body and pulled the trigger, but he didn't know if Virginia and the handsome stranger had heard the scuffle. Wanting to keep from raising too much of a ruckus, Dean lifted the Colt again and chopped at the attacker's head with it.

The blow landed solidly, but it was kind of like hitting a boulder. The man didn't even grunt in pain. He just kept trying to squeeze the life out of Dean.

As a red gauzy curtain seemed to drop over Dean's vision, he clawed at the man's face with his other hand. He felt the bushy beard and tried to dig his fingers into the attacker's eyes.

That, at least, brought a response. The man bellowed in anger and jerked his head away.

No need to keep quiet now. Dean started to shove the gun into the man's side, but as he did, a booted foot struck his wrist in a vicious kick and knocked the Colt out of his grip.

Dean cried out in pain and cut his eyes over to see that a second attacker had joined the first one. This man was tall and slender, clean-shaven except for a thin mustache that drooped over both corners of his mouth.

"Don't say I never did nothin' for you, Lupe," he told the bearded attacker. "This foolish gringo was about to blow a hole in you."

The man called Lupe growled and locked his other hand around Dean's throat. With both hands choking him, it would be only a matter of moments before Dean passed out and then died, more than likely.

As the second man watched the struggle with a smug smile on his face, Dean struck back the only way he could. Dean kicked the hombre in the groin.

The man screeched in agony, doubled over to clutch at himself, and toppled forward. He fell against Lupe with enough force to knock the big man to the side. Their legs tangled together.

Dean writhed desperately and tore free from Lupe's grasp. He clubbed his hands together and swung them as hard as he could against Lupe's bearded jaw. With Lupe already off balance, the blow knocked him off his feet. The second man, still snarled up with him, went down, too.

Then Dean spotted the Colt on the ground where the man he'd kicked had dropped it. He made a dive for it, snatched up the weapon, and thrust it out in front of him as he came up on one knee.

The distinctive metallic ratcheting of a gun being cocked sounded like a death knell in the courtyard and made Dean freeze as he knelt there, trying to drag air into his lungs through his tortured throat.

He looked up and saw the handsome young man with the scarlet sash around his waist pointing a revolver at him in a rock-steady grip. The gun was a smaller caliber, a Smith & Wesson, probably, but its wielder was only ten feet away and at this range, it would be plenty deadly.

"Put your gun back on the ground, amigo," the man said in a level voice. "I really would prefer not to shoot you."

Standing a short distance behind him, Virginia Griffin stared at Dean with surprised, horrified eyes, as she raised both hands to her cheeks.

"Dean!" she cried. "What are you doing here?"

Dean struggled to find words as well as breath. "Saving you from this . . . this . . ." he managed to say.

The man held up his free hand and warned, "Have care not to insult me in my own home. My hospitality extends only so far."

"José, please," Virginia said. "This boy is my friend."

Boy, Dean thought bitterly. She had called him a boy—and declared that he was a friend. The words were like a double punch in his gut, and they put it pretty plain. She didn't think of him as a suitor, probably didn't think of him in any sort of romantic fashion at all.

What a fool he had been.

And that starry-eyed foolishness stood a good chance of getting him killed.

He dragged in a deep breath. No matter what Virginia thought of him, he had done the right thing by coming after her. He had believed her to be in great danger, and there was nothing else he could have done.

Based on what he had seen a few minutes earlier, though, she hadn't been in any real danger at all. She hadn't been kidnapped by a stranger. She knew this man. She even acted like she loved him, kissing him that way.

Maybe this slick hombre wasn't the Desert Wolf, after all.

Or maybe he was, and she just didn't care.

All those thoughts flashed through Dean's mind in a matter of heartbeats. He and the man called José were still pointing guns at each other. A feeling of tense anticipation hung in the air, a sense that gunplay could erupt at any second.

If it did, that would endanger Virginia, too.

Dean lowered the Colt in his hand. He leaned forward, placed the revolver on the ground, and came to his feet.

A few steps away, the burly bearded hombre knelt next to his lean friend, who was still curled up on the ground in pain. When he saw Dean stand up, he straightened as well, and turned toward the young cowboy. A growl sounded deep in his throat, and his powerful hands clenched into fists as he took a step toward Dean.

José stopped him with a slight gesture. "No, Lupe," he said. "I know you're angry because this man hurt Hector, but I wish to speak with him." José shrugged. "Perhaps you can kill him later."

"No!" Virginia exclaimed.

José smiled at her. "A jest, my dear. Admittedly, a poor one. Your amigo will come to no harm unless he forces it upon himself." He turned his attention back to Lupe. "Help Hector to his quarters. Send for Miranda to care for him."

Lupe lifted the other man to his feet. Hector leaned heavily on the big man.

José added, "And while I appreciate the two of you trying to deal with this interloper, I'm disappointed that he managed to invade our sanctuary in the first place. You were supposed to be on guard against such a thing."

"My apologies, Don José," Lupe rumbled. "But where did

he come from? He did not enter the canyon from the valley, this I know."

"Perhaps he flew down?" José suggested.

Lupe rolled his eyes in disbelief.

"Or climbed down the cliff?"

"Impossible! Only a madman would attempt such a thing."

José eyed Dean and said, "Or a man with a great enough reason to do so, eh?"

Dean didn't say anything. After a moment, Lupe led Hector toward the hacienda, scowling at Dean as they departed.

José motioned for Dean to step back, away from the Colt. When Dean had done so, José strode forward, picked up the gun, and backed away again, keeping Dean covered as he did so. He stuck the Colt behind the scarlet sash and in the waistband of his tight trousers, which, Dean saw now, had silver embroidery down the sides of the legs.

"Virginia, introduce me to your *friend*," he said.

"This is Dean McKinley. He works for Smoke Jensen. You know about Mr. Jensen."

"Most people in this part of the world have at least heard of the illustrious Smoke Jensen. Is he nearby, Señor McKinley?"

"You're blamed right he is," Dean answered. "And any minute now, he's going to come crashing down on this place like an avalanche with a troop of cavalry and a bunch of salty hombres from the Sugarloaf—"

Dean stopped talking as José shook his head.

"I think not. One man could approach our sanctuary without being observed, perhaps. One man *did* approach and even managed to invade our tranquility. You're here, living proof of that. But such a large group as you describe could not do so." José studied Dean intently for a moment and then nodded. "No, I believe you are here alone, Señor McKinley. You came because you believe yourself to be like a knight of olden times, come to rescue the fair maiden from the clutches of an evil brute." He smiled and lightly touched his chest with his free hand. "Myself."

"Do you always talk like a blasted dime-novel villain?" Dean snapped. "I've read plenty of 'em, and they always go on and on with a bunch of highfalutin speechifying like that."

"Forgive me. One of the ways I learned English as a child was by reading those popular novels you speak of. Perhaps I picked up some bad habits from them." The man drew himself up straighter and grew serious, his mocking half smile disappearing as he went on. "Allow me to introduce myself, señor. My name is José Antonio Vaca." An eloquent gesture took in their surroundings. "This is my *rancho*."

"You're no rancher," Dean said. "You're the Desert Wolf."

"Yes," Vaca admitted without hesitation, "I am. And you are my prisoner."

Instead of locking him up, Vaca surprised Dean by telling him to sit down on the shaded veranda at a round table with a slate top. Comfortable wicker chairs surrounded it.

Vaca and Virginia took seats as well, next to each other on the opposite side of the table from Dean. The young cowboy didn't like the idea of socializing with this varmint, but he figured that might be the quickest way to find out what was actually going on here.

A middle-aged Mexican woman emerged from the house. If Vaca had summoned her somehow, Dean hadn't seen him do it. Maybe she had been watching from in there.

Vaca told the woman to bring them coffee, then motioned for her to wait and said to Dean, "I assume it is early enough that you haven't had breakfast, especially as busy as you've been intruding in my home?"

"I'm not hungry," Dean said, knowing that he sounded surly but not caring.

Vaca smiled and said to the woman, "We'll have breakfast out here, as well, Estella."

"Sí, Señor Vaca," she said, then bustled off into the hacienda.

Dean took advantage of the opportunity to ask Virginia, "Where's your aunt? Is she all right?"

"Aunt Dorothy is fine, of course. She's simply resting in her room." Virginia smiled. "It was a bit of a tiring night."

"I imagine so, what with you being kidnapped and all."

Vaca said, "The *señorita* and her aunt were not kidnapped. But I had to speak with her, to plead my case and come to an understanding between us, and in order to do so, I had to get her away from the fort. Her father would not have allowed me to call on her as I wish I could have, in the proper fashion of a suitor calling upon a beautiful *señorita.*"

Dean snorted. "Yeah, I can see why the colonel wouldn't want a notorious bandit courting his daughter. That's why you dragged Virginia and her aunt back to this place, whatever it is."

Vaca's lips tightened with renewed anger. "I dragged no one," he said. "I would not have brought along Señora Bacon if I had not been forced to do so. Unfortunately, circumstances dictated otherwise. As for this place . . ."

He made a sweeping gesture that took in their surroundings.

"I told you this is my *rancho,*" Vaca said, with a note of pride in his voice, "but the real credit goes to my great-grandfather, Don Alfonso Eduardo Vaca, who established it more than a hundred years ago. Men told him he was mad to believe he could start a ranch in this wasteland, but he was determined to prove them wrong."

Despite the anger and confusion that gripped him, Dean found himself getting interested in what Vaca was saying. "Was there a spring in this canyon back then?" he asked.

Vaca shook his head and said, "No, but Don Alfonso believed there was water to be found underneath this seemingly arid and barren land."

Dean grunted. "Looks pretty darned arid and barren to me—except right here in this canyon."

The woman called Estella came back from the house then, carrying a silver tray that bore a coffee pot, cups, and saucers. She set it on the table and poured coffee for the three people sitting there. Dean tried it and found it to be dark and strong, and seasoned with unfamiliar spices as well as a rich sweetness. It was very good and braced him after the long, sleepless night and the strain of the early morning.

Vaca resumed the story. "My great-grandfather and his men dug a well. In rocky ground such as this, you can imagine what a back-breaking task that was. They spent long days wielding picks and shovels."

"Yeah," Dean said, nodding. "But I reckon they must have found water, or he wouldn't have gone to the trouble of building this house and all the other buildings. From the looks of it, this was a working spread for a while."

"For a while," Vaca agreed, nodding. "But then the well went dry."

Dean had seen failed ranches before, and had seen how those failures affected the men who poured their hearts and souls into the spreads.

"That's a tough break," he acknowledged. "It's a risk you run when you decide to go into the cattle business, though."

"Or any kind of endeavor where success depends as much on nature and good fortune as it does on hard work," Vaca said. "Those are things a man cannot control, no matter how much he tells himself he can."

Vaca sipped his coffee and shrugged.

"Don Alfonso was a resolute man," he continued. "He returned to Mexico City and made a successful life there for himself, marrying my great-grandmother and becoming a wealthy merchant. But his thoughts returned often to the dream he had had of running a fine ranch, and he spoke of that dream to my grandfather, Don Alejandro Vaca. My grandfather told the stories to my father, Don Pedro."

"And they passed them on down to you," Dean said. "A family legend, I reckon you could call it."

Eagerness gripped Vaca and caused him to lean forward over his cup. "*Sí.* I came to share my great-grandfather's dream. But unlike him, I had the knowledge required to make it come true."

Estella returned at that point with platters of eggs, tortillas, tamales, and sweet rolls that were good enough to rival Sally Jensen's bear sign back on the Sugarloaf. Dean hadn't realized just how hungry he actually was until he began eating.

A part of his brain reminded him that he was sitting here with an outlaw who had carried off two women from Fort Craig, along with who knew what other depredations, and scolded him for acting like he was enjoying the hombre's hospitality.

But Dean had a wide streak of practicality running through him, too. The food was here, it was good, and later he might need the strength it would give him. So, he ate heartily and did justice to the meal.

After a while, Vaca patted his lips with a napkin and went on. "As I was saying, I had knowledge that my great-grandfather wasn't fortunate enough to possess. My father has mining interests in the mountains, and he believed I would profit from an education in mining and engineering. So he sent me to the College of Mines at your Columbia University."

"My pa sure didn't," Dean said, with a shake of his head. "I never heard of the place."

"It is located in New York City."

"Reckon I've heard of that. Never been there and wouldn't go if you paid me."

Vaca ignored that comment and continued. "I learned a great deal, not the least of which was the method of excavating with dynamite."

Understanding dawned in Dean's mind. "You blew a hole in the rock where the old don's well was and started the spring flowing again!"

Vaca inclined his head in agreement.

Dean saw the way Virginia gazed admiringly at the young Mexican and felt jealousy stirring inside him again. She had made it pretty plain earlier that she wasn't interested in him that way, and he knew he ought to just accept that, but it was still hard for him to do so.

"There's no way of knowing how long the spring will flow as it is now," Vaca said, "but my hope is that the water supply will turn out to be long-lasting, perhaps even permanent. You've probably seen that it's already made a difference in the valley. Soon, there will be enough grazing land to support a herd."

Reality came flooding back in on Dean. "A herd of stolen horses, you mean?" he said in a sharp, accusatory tone.

Vaca frowned across the table at him. "I've stolen no horses," he said.

"Well, I know good and well that Smoke didn't give 'em to you."

"I don't have Señor Jensen's horses." Vaca nodded toward Virginia. "Señorita Griffin told me of the raid on the herd and that many of the horses were driven off by bandits. But my men and I did not do this thing."

"There's only one bunch of bandits around here as far as I know, and their boss is a no-good varmint called the Desert Wolf!"

Dean's anger brought him to his feet as he spoke, and Vaca stood up to meet the challenge. The two young men glared at each other across the table, and once again the potential for violence was thick in the air.

"Stop it, both of you," Virginia said. "I'm not going to have you fighting."

"Take it up with this horse thief," Dean said, practically snarling at Vaca.

"You are extremely rude, Señor McKinley," Vaca said. "Perhaps I should stop regarding you as a guest and treat you as the prisoner you actually are! I can have Hector and Guadalupe lock you in the smokehouse. I'm sure Hector would enjoy being given that task."

Virginia said, "Nobody's being locked up."

Vaca shot a quick, angry glance toward her. "Do not presume to issue orders, *mi amor*. This is my hacienda." He shifted his attention back to Dean. "And I am not a horse thief, I tell you!"

"Then who raided Smoke's herd?"

Vaca got control of himself with a visible effort and motioned toward the chair where Dean had been sitting.

"Take your seat again, señor, *por favor*. This is a misunderstanding. I am not a bandit."

With obvious reluctance, Dean sank into the wicker chair again and glared across the table at Vaca as the young grandee sat down, too.

"Everything I've heard about you tells me that the Desert Wolf sure enough is a bandit," Dean insisted. "You've been robbing wagon trains and rustling cattle for months now."

Stubbornly, Vaca shook his head. "Lies, all lies. Why would I do these things? My family is wealthy."

"Maybe they disowned you because you're no good. *Somebody's* been raising hell and shoving a chunk under the corner up and down the Jornada del Muerto. If it's not you, who is it? Are you trying to tell me there's a second gang of owlhoots holed up in this wasteland?"

"Not a second gang, because my men and I are not thieves. In fact, we have stopped the thieves from preying on the poor farmers who try to scratch out a living on the banks of the river."

Virginia said, "It's true, Dean. The farmers and the small ranchers are all grateful to José and his men. Without them, those poor people would have been wiped out or forced to flee from their homes and abandon all they've worked for. The Desert Wolf is a hero to them!"

Dean could tell that she believed every word coming out of her mouth, but to him it still sounded loco. He shook his head and said, "More dime-novel foolishness."

"Believe what you will, señor," Vaca said coldly. "I cannot change a mind set in stone. But I cannot allow you to interfere with my work, either. I will summon Hector and Lupe—"

Virginia looked like she was going to argue against the order he was about to give, but she didn't have to because at that moment, the swift rataplan of hoofbeats sounded from somewhere nearby in the canyon.

Vaca stood up, turning toward the house with a lithe move. The hoofbeats stopped, and a moment later they were replaced by quick footsteps coming from the arched passage that led into the house.

A man dressed in a sombrero and the rough, functional clothing of a vaquero emerged from the house. An ivory-butted revolver jutted from the holster on his hip. The gun, along with the spurs strapped to his boots, were the only things about him that were flashy.

He came to a stop in front of Vaca and dragged off the gray felt sombrero, then followed that gesture with a respectful nod.

"What is it, Tomás?" Vaca asked. "Have you found what I sent you to look for?"

"I have, Don José," the man replied. "I have found the lair of that treacherous serpent, Juan Covarrubias!"

Chapter 18

Vaca punched his right fist into his left palm in excitement.

"Good work, Tomás! I knew if anyone could find that snake, it was you."

"Now we go and wipe out him and his men, eh, Don José?" the vaquero asked, as he wrapped his hand around the ivory grips of his gun.

"Wait," Vaca said. He glanced around at Dean and Virginia, then turned back to Tomás. "Where is Covarrubias hiding?"

"In the hills several miles south of here. There is a trail through a ravine that looks as if it goes nowhere, but it leads to a pocket valley with a small *tinaja* that still holds a little water from the rains earlier this year. The stolen horses are there, but they cannot hold them long because the water will run out."

"You're talking about Smoke's horses?" Dean asked.

Tomás looked at him, and said, "The ones stolen from Señor Jensen, *sí*."

"I told you my men and I had nothing to do with the raid on Señor Jensen's herd," Vaca said to Dean. "Now do you believe me?"

Dean frowned. "Well, this fella showing up right when he did with some story that's supposed to clear your name, that's a mite suspicious, isn't it?"

Vaca made an exasperated sound and threw his hands in the air. "What will it take to convince you?" he asked. "Must you see the evidence with your own eyes?"

"That might go a ways toward doing it. But first, who's this Covarrubias hombre you're talking about?"

Instead of answering right away, Vaca turned back to the vaquero and said, "*Gracias*, Tomás. Go into the house and tell Estella to give you some breakfast. Wait for me, and I will figure out what to do next."

Tomás nodded. "*Sí, señor.*"

When Tomás was gone, Vaca sat down at the table again with Dean and Virginia. He said, "Juan Covarrubias is the worst bandit in the territory, just as he was the worst bandit in Chihuahua before he crossed the border. He goes back and forth, you see, sometimes tormenting the people of Mexico, sometimes stealing from, harassing, and killing the Americans. He claims he is for the people and that someday he will lead a revolution that will throw off the shackles of the oppressors, but it is all lies!" Vaca's fist thumped down on the table. "He seeks only to line his own pockets, and those of the craven dogs who follow him!"

"Sounds like a pretty bad hombre," Dean observed.

"He is. And it shames me to admit that he was once my friend, back in the days when he rode for my grandfather as a vaquero on Don Alejandro's ranch."

Again, although it went against the grain for Dean, he found himself interested in what Vaca was saying. He wanted to just stay angry and not listen, but instead he asked, "What happened?"

Vaca shrugged and spread his hands. "Juan was a top hand, as you Americans say, but he decided he would rather be rich and powerful instead of working hard and remaining poor." The young grandee chuckled, but the sound held no genuine amusement. "When he explained it like that, it made sense to many who heard him. Say what you will about him, Juan Covarrubias is the sort of man other men will follow. He can weave a web with words that will entangle many, especially those who are filled with resentment over the way their lives have unfolded. By promising riches—and the chance to strike back at those his men believe have wronged them—he has been able to recruit many to follow him."

"And he's the one who's been causing trouble in these parts, you say?"

"That's right. He might have stayed on the other side of the border and not ventured into New Mexico Territory, if not for his partner."

"What partner?" Dean asked.

Vaca shook his head. "That, I do not know. But I'm convinced he's working with some American who has been funneling money and guns to him in return for promises of power and even greater wealth when Covarrubias is successful with his so-called revolution." Again, the young man blew out a disgusted breath. "I do not believe that will ever happen, but along the way, many innocent people will suffer and die because of Juan's ambition."

Dean leaned back in the wicker chair and thought about what Vaca had said. Although he was reluctant to give up his resentment and dislike of Vaca, Dean had to admit that the man's story made sense. Of course, at this point it was just a story. The whole thing might be a pack of lies.

"If there really is some gringo working with this Covarrubias hombre, who do you think it is?"

"I have no idea," Vaca replied, shaking his head again. "It seems most likely, though, that it is someone from Fort Craig. One of the officers there would be in a good position to work with Covarrubias and get him what he needs to build his army."

"No!" Virginia said. "Absolutely not. No one under my father's command would ever do such a terrible thing."

Vaca cocked his head and said, "I believe you underestimate what some men will do for money and power, *mi amor*."

"But that would be the same as turning traitor. I just can't imagine it."

Vaca spread his hands. "Perhaps I am wrong, but the arrangement seems logical to me. Tell me, when the subject comes up at the fort, who is blamed for all the wrongdoing in this part of the territory?"

"Well . . . you are," Virginia admitted. "The Desert Wolf."

Vaca leaned forward and nodded. "Exactly. The army chases the Desert Wolf but leaves Juan Covarrubias alone. It may well be that no one at Fort Craig has even heard of Juan Covarrubias." Vaca glanced at Dean and smiled. "Because he does not have a dime-novel name, eh, *mi amigo*?"

"I don't know where you got the notion that you and me are friends," Dean said, "but I suppose you're right about that. Chasing you and your bunch would be a good distraction from what's really going on."

Virginia looked at him and demanded, "Do you believe it, too? You think someone from the fort is working with this awful bandit José is talking about?"

"I don't reckon we can rule it out. I'd need some real proof, though, before I'd say I believe it."

Vaca slapped a hand down on the table. "And proof you shall have," he said. "So will Colonel Griffin and Señor Jensen." He leaned back. "I am going to let you go."

That took Dean by surprise. "Is this some sort of trick?" he asked.

"No trick," Vaca said. "I know there must be a search party from the fort looking for Virginia and her aunt. Do you think you could find them?"

"I don't know for sure, but I reckon there's a good chance I could," Dean answered warily. He didn't trust José Antonio

Vaca as far as he could throw the varmint, so he didn't mention that he had been thinking the same thing earlier.

"And what are the chances of Señor Jensen accompanying that search party?"

"Mighty good, I reckon." Dean paused and then added, "Smoke's not the sort of fella to stand by and do nothing when a couple of ladies are kidnapped."

A look of irritation passed over Vaca's face again. "I told you, I did not kidnap—" He stopped short and raised a hand. "Never mind. We can discuss that at another time. Right now, it's more important to thwart Covarrubias's plans. I'm going to find out from Tomás exactly how to get to that hideout where Covarrubias is keeping the stolen horses, and I'm going to recover them."

"You're going to steal 'em back?"

"Exactly. With the help of the army and Señor Jensen, if you can find them in time. If not, my men and I will deal with the thieves and turn the horses over to the army later."

Virginia reached over and put her hand on Vaca's arm. "José, you can't do that," she said. "It would be the same thing as turning yourself in. I mean, Dean didn't believe your story, at least not at first—"

Dean's skeptical grunt eloquently conveyed that he still wasn't completely convinced.

"And I don't think my father would believe it, either," Virginia pressed on. "Even if you give him the horses, he might lock you up."

"That is a risk I'm willing to run if it means putting things right." Vaca clenched a fist again. "Covarrubias won't keep those horses penned up for long. You heard what Tomás said. There's only a limited amount of water where they are. He'll drive them west into the mountains, possibly all the way to Arizona, and sell them. There are buyers who are none too discriminating about such things. The cash will go to build up his army even more."

"First you claimed he's just a bandit out for loot," Dean said, "and now you're talking like he might actually stage a revolution. Which is it?"

"I truly don't know," Vaca said, shaking his head. "But either way, people suffer and die."

Dean thought about it and nodded. "Yeah, I reckon I can see that."

"Then you'll do what I ask? You'll locate the search party and bring them to Covarrubias's stronghold?"

Dean hesitated a moment longer. "What about Virginia and Mrs. Bacon?"

"They will remain here, where they're safe," Vaca answered, without hesitation.

Dean's first impulse was to argue—he wanted to take the women with him when he went to find the search party—but as he thought about it, he realized that might not be a good idea.

For one thing, he would be alone with them and would be responsible for their safety, and the Jornada del Muerto wasn't a very safe place.

For another, Smoke and whoever was in charge of the search party would want to help Vaca deal with that Covarrubias hombre, and that wouldn't be safe for Virginia and Dorothy to be around, either.

Even though he couldn't bring himself to trust Vaca or accept the man's story at face value, it did seem that the women were being treated well here and probably would remain safe until someone could come for them. Like it or not, that appeared to be the best option.

"All right," he said, "but if anything happens to them, I'm holding you responsible."

"Nothing will happen. Some of my men will stay here while the rest of us go to recover those horses. If I tell them to keep the ladies safe, they will lay down their lives to do so, if necessary."

"Let's hope it doesn't come to that," Dean said.

"Of course. Now, if you'd like to stay here for a few minutes, I'll go talk to Tomás and find out exactly where Covarrubias is hiding. We'll prepare a map for you to take with you when you leave to find the search party."

Dean nodded. "Sounds like a good idea."

Vaca looked at Virginia. "You can return to your quarters if you'd like, or . . ."

"I'll stay here and keep Mr. McKinley company," she said.

Dean could tell that Vaca wasn't particularly happy about that decision, but he didn't argue with the young woman. He just nodded and strode across the veranda to disappear into the house.

Virginia pushed empty plates aside, reached across the table, and clasped one of Dean's hands in both of hers.

"Oh, Dean," she said, "I never dreamed that you'd follow us like that. If I had known it was going to put you in danger, I—I might not have agreed to come here with José."

"Then he was telling the truth? He didn't actually force you to come?"

"He just wanted to be sure that I'd actually listen to him and give him a fair hearing. You see, a couple of nights ago, I saw him in Socorro—"

"The Desert Wolf was right there in Socorro?"

She smiled. "No one in town knows who he is. I thought it was dangerous for him to be there, too, but he assured me it would be all right. We talked there, and I told him that I—that we couldn't see each other anymore."

"But he didn't want to accept that, did he?"

Virginia shook her head. "No. José is a very strong-willed young man."

"Stubborn as a mule, you mean," Dean muttered.

"Well, that's a pretty accurate description, too, I suppose," Virginia agreed with a smile. "Anyway, he got a message to me to meet him last night behind my father's house at the fort. I did, but I didn't know Aunt Dorothy was going to follow me. And I certainly didn't know that you were anywhere around, either. I think perhaps José isn't the only one who's as stubborn as a mule."

"That's true enough, and I don't mind admitting it. I can be pretty mule-headed when I've made up my mind about something."

She squeezed his hand. "You need to make up your mind about this, Dean. I like you, I truly do. You're a good friend."

"But that's all I'll ever be. That's what you're saying."

"I'm afraid so."

Dean drew in a breath, blew it out. "All right," he said. "I learned early on it's a waste of time and breath to argue with a woman."

"I hope that maybe someday you and José can be friends."

"I wouldn't set your sights too high," he advised her. "I'll go along with him for now, but mainly because I want to know if he's really telling the truth." Dean smiled. "I reckon you could say I'm giving him enough rope to see if he's going to hang himself."

"That's not going to happen. I trust him and believe in him. He's just trying to do the right thing."

Dean didn't say anything. Time would tell whether he was right to be wary—or she was right to believe.

Vaca returned to the veranda a short time later, carrying a piece of paper. Without sitting down, he set it on the table in front of Dean, who leaned forward to study the lines drawn on it.

"Here is the map I drew from Tomás's directions," Vaca said. He rested a fingertip on the paper. "This is the *rancho*, where we are now. Juan Covarrubias's sanctuary is here—" He moved his finger to another spot. "And here is the trail leading to it through a deep ravine." His fingertip traced the route.

"What about landmarks?" Dean asked.

"These two hills together." Vaca indicated them. "They look like a camel's back. You've seen pictures of camels?"

"I sure haven't seen any of the blasted critters in the flesh. They don't live in this part of the world."

"You might be surprised. I've heard that the army brought some of the creatures over here from Arabia and tried using them instead of horses in Texas and Arizona."

Dean stared at him. "You've got to be making that up!"

"No, it's the truth. Ask Colonel Griffin when you see him again. I'm sure he's heard about it."

"Yeah, if I go asking the colonel about camels, he'll think I've been out in the sun too long, or else I got into the locoweed. I'll just keep that to myself, if you don't mind."

"As you wish, Señor McKinley. Another landmark is here, this hogback ridge, and here, some cliffs that are a bright red when the sun hits them correctly. If you follow this map, you should be able to find the hideout—but only after you've contacted the search party from the fort."

"In other words, bring reinforcements or don't come at all."

"That is about the size of it, as you gringos say. Where is your horse?"

Dean pointed up with a thumb. "I left him on the rimrock when I climbed down."

Vaca looked at him for a moment and then shook his head in amazement.

"You actually did climb down that cliff. I would have guessed that it couldn't be done, and that anyone foolish enough to try would fall and break his neck."

"Like you said," Dean told him, with a glance at Virginia, who blushed and looked down at the table, "I had a good reason to risk it."

Chapter 19

Smoke didn't take any of his men with him when he accompanied the cavalry detail, although they would have been happy to go along and, in fact, several of them practically begged for the opportunity to do so.

Captain Litchfield was adamant about not taking any more civilians, however. He was only allowing Smoke to come along because Colonel Griffin had ordered it.

"I won't risk burdening my troops with men I can't trust to follow military discipline," Litchfield told Smoke, as the detail assembled on the parade ground. "If you endanger this mission and make it more difficult to find and recover the ladies, I'll leave you out there, Jensen. You'd be well advised not to doubt that for a moment."

"I don't," Smoke replied curtly. "Don't forget I've got something at stake. One of my men is missing, too."

"McKinley?" Litchfield jerked a hand in a brusque gesture. "I still suspect he's working with the Desert Wolf. I've clashed with him enough to know he's a born troublemaker."

Somebody was a born troublemaker, all right, Smoke mused, but he wasn't sure it was Dean McKinley.

He kept that thought to himself as they all mounted up to ride out of the fort. Sergeant Dunn nodded to him, and Smoke returned it. He liked what he had seen of the lean sergeant so far. He struck Smoke as an experienced, competent noncommissioned officer, just like Sergeant O'Malley. He'd heard it said that the army truly ran on its sergeants, and he could believe it.

With Litchfield in the lead, Smoke and Dunn riding side by side behind him, and the rest of the troopers following, the detail filed out through the gate and departed from Fort Craig, heading south.

The Jornada del Muerto stretched before them, bleak and lifeless.

After a short time, the riders turned west toward the low hills bordering the desert. Those hills were almost as arid as the Jornada itself. Smoke's keen eyes searched in vain for any sign of green that would mark vegetation. He didn't find any, only an endless vista of gray, brown, and tan. Rocks and dirt—that was what those hills offered.

Yet tiny pockets of life might lurk in them, Smoke thought. Nature sometimes hid its secrets jealously.

The detail had the choice of following the trail left by the stolen horses or the tracks of the group they suspected had taken Virginia Griffin and Dorothy Bacon. The two missing women were a higher priority, according to Colonel Griffin, and Smoke agreed completely with that assessment. Recovering the horses was important to him, but rescuing the women came first.

Besides, in all likelihood, both trails would lead to the same place—the stronghold of the Desert Wolf.

The detail proceeded to the spot where Smoke had found signs of a struggle the night before. From there, the marks of the waiting horses moved off to the south and were easy enough to follow for the time being.

The harder the ground, the more of a challenge that would be later. Smoke knew that, but all they could do was push on.

The temperature rose as the sun climbed higher. The sky turned brassy and seemed to radiate even more heat down onto the parched earth. Smoke felt rivulets of sweat trickle down his back under his shirt and felt sorry for the troopers in their thick woolen uniforms. Before the day was over, they would be miserably hot.

On a day like this, Smoke missed the cool, clean air of the Colorado high country.

As he expected, they lost the trail after a while. Any experienced tracker could tell you that it was very difficult to follow a trail from start to finish without losing it at least once, unless it was a very short one. The key to successful tracking was being patient and observant enough to find it again.

That happened more than once as the morning wore on. Sometimes Smoke located the tracks again, and sometimes it was Sergeant Dunn. During one of the times the detail halted in order to rest their horses, Smoke commented to Dunn, "Sometimes I think I hear a little accent in your voice, Sergeant. It's none of my business, but I'm curious. Were you born somewhere besides the United States?"

Dunn smiled. "I don't mind answering that question at all. You have a good ear, Mr. Jensen. I was born in England, but my parents immigrated to the United States when I was just a lad of ten. I've considered myself an American ever since. But every now and then, a bit of my old speech comes out." He extended his hand. "We weren't formally introduced. James Elphinstone Dunn, at your service, sir."

Smoke clasped the man's hand and said, "Mighty pleased to meet you, Sergeant Dunn." A thought struck him, and he added, "Sergeant O'Malley is an Irishman, isn't he?"

Dunn rolled his eyes. "That he is, sir. Very much of an Irishman."

"But the two of you get along all right?"

"Of course. We're sergeants. That takes precedence over

everything else. And I suppose you could say that we're both strangers in a strange land, although we've both been here since we were tykes, so that gives us some kinship. Seamus is a good man."

"Seems like it to me, too," Smoke agreed.

He didn't express any such assessment about Captain Litchfield. He wouldn't expect Dunn to make disparaging comments about a superior officer. At the same time, he was glad to have an experienced sergeant along on this mission.

They pushed on a short time later but hadn't been on the move very long when Litchfield held up his gauntleted left hand in the signal to halt. Dunn reined in and turned in the saddle to call out the order to the rest of the troop.

Smoke brought his horse to a stop as well. He had already spotted the same thing that had prompted Litchfield to call the halt.

"Rider coming," Smoke said, as he nudged his horse up alongside the captain.

Litchfield shot an annoyed glance at him. "I can see that," he said. "It's just one man."

"Yep. And I'd bet a hat it's Dean McKinley."

They sat there watching and waiting as the man on horseback came closer. Smoke could tell he wasn't wearing a hat, but the man didn't look like an Apache. Litchfield reached in his saddlebags, brought out a pair of field glasses, and lifted them to his eyes.

"It's McKinley, all right," he announced, with a note of displeasure in his voice. "And he's alone. He's moving fairly quickly, but he doesn't appear to be fleeing any pursuers. That's good, I suppose."

"Better than being chased by Apaches or bandits," Smoke said dryly. "I'll bet his head's getting a mite hot, though. Wonder what happened to his hat."

Smoke's eyesight was keen enough that within minutes he

could tell the horse McKinley was riding wasn't one from the Sugarloaf's remuda. That was also an intriguing mystery, but he would have the answer soon enough.

When McKinley was a couple of hundred yards away, Litchfield heeled his horse into motion and rode forward to meet the young cowboy.

He didn't tell Smoke to stay put, so Smoke rode with him. He probably would have done so whether the captain had said anything or not. Dean McKinley rode for the Sugarloaf, after all.

When they were close to meeting, a hundred yards ahead of the cavalry detail, Litchfield reined in and called, "That's far enough, McKinley!"

He reached down and unsnapped the flap on his holster where his service revolver rested, as if to reinforce the order with that gesture.

McKinley looked surprised as he hauled back on the reins. He glanced at Smoke, who had come to a stop beside Litchfield, and began, "Smoke, I—"

"I'm in charge here," Litchfield interrupted, "not Jensen. Speak to me."

McKinley's face, which was already red from being out in the sun, flushed even more with anger, but with a visible effort, he kept a tight rein on his temper and said, "I have news, Captain. I've found Miss Griffin and Mrs. Bacon. They're all right."

"You left them in the hands of their captors instead of trying to rescue them?"

Litchfield's words lashed at McKinley like a whip. Smoke could tell that McKinley was having trouble controlling his reaction.

"Where are the ladies, Dean?" Smoke asked in a steady, level voice.

"At an old hacienda back yonder in the hills. I can take you there, but there's somewhere else we need to go first."

"Nonsense," Litchfield said. "Nothing is more important than their safety."

"They're safe. Vaca swore that his men would look after them and protect them."

"Vaca?" Smoke repeated as he recalled the brief encounter he'd had with Virginia Griffin and a young Mexican man in Socorro a few nights earlier. The hombre's full name came back to him. "José Antonio Vaca?"

"That's right." McKinley paused and looked unsure whether he should go on, but after a moment, he continued, "He's the Desert Wolf."

"I knew it!" Litchfield jerked his gun from its holster. "I knew you were working with that bandit!"

Smoke leaned over and closed his hand around Litchfield's wrist before the captain could raise the gun.

"Wait just a minute," Smoke said. "Let's hear him out."

Litchfield was in no mood to wait. He snarled a curse and jerked his horse to the side, away from Smoke, as if he thought that would break him loose from Smoke's grip.

Smoke didn't let go, and Litchfield suddenly found himself slipping out of the saddle. He cried out in alarm and tried to grab hold with his other hand, but the cavalry saddle didn't have a horn. Litchfield's fingers slipped off the leather, causing him to overbalance. Smoke released his grip then, and Litchfield toppled to the ground.

McKinley moved forward quickly and leaned over from his saddle to catch hold of the reins Litchfield had dropped. His firm grasp of them prevented the captain's mount from bolting. Litchfield's right boot had caught in the stirrup, and the animal might have dragged him if not for McKinley's fast action.

Litchfield had dropped the gun when he hit the ground. He kicked loose from the stirrup, rolled over, and came up sputtering and red-faced with fury.

"I'll see you behind bars for this, Jensen!" he screeched. "Assaulting a superior officer—"

"I'm not in the army, Litchfield," Smoke cut in. "And a man's got to earn it before I consider him superior to me or anybody else."

"This area is under military jurisdiction," Litchfield raged. "You have to follow my orders! I warned you that if you interfered with me—"

McKinley was the one who interrupted Litchfield's tirade this time. "I know where those stolen horses are, Smoke," he said. "Vaca didn't take them. He admits to being the one they call the Desert Wolf, but he says he's not a bandit." McKinley shrugged. "I didn't want to at first, but I kind of believe him."

Sergeant Dunn arrived then, having ridden ahead of the rest of the halted detail when he saw the altercation between Smoke and Litchfield.

"Do you need assistance, Captain?" he asked.

Litchfield leveled a trembling finger at Smoke and yelled, "Arrest him! Arrest Jensen!"

Dunn looked extremely uncomfortable as he said, "I'm not certain I have the authority to do that, Captain. Colonel Griffin issued no orders concerning a declaration of martial law, and Mr. Jensen is a civilian."

"He attacked me!"

"Nothing stopping you from taking it up on your own, mister," Smoke said. "But if you're not going to, you might want to settle down. Getting so upset in this heat is liable to give a fella apoplexy."

Litchfield glared at him with pure hatred for a few seconds, then turned away to look around for his hat. He picked it up, knocked the dust off it, and put it on.

Then he reached down to pick up the gun he had dropped. Smoke watched him closely, ready to make a move of his own if Litchfield forced the issue.

Instead, the captain shoved the gun back in its holster and closed the flap.

Smoke turned back to McKinley and asked, "Where are those horses, Dean?"

"The fellas who stole them are holed up in a little pocket in the hills a few miles south of here." McKinley reached into his shirt pocket and took out a folded piece of paper. As he extended it to Smoke, he went on, "That's a map Vaca drew of how to get to the place."

Litchfield said, "It's probably a trap. You can't trust the Desert Wolf. He's trying to lure us into an ambush."

Smoke unfolded the sweat-damp paper and studied the markings on it for a moment. That was all he needed to commit the map to memory. Even if something happened to the paper, he could find the place indicated on it, as long as it had been drawn accurately.

He looked up at McKinley. "If the Desert Wolf didn't steal the horses, who did?"

"A fella named Juan Covarrubias, according to Vaca. He's a bandit from below the border who's trying to raise an army and overthrow the government down there. Or else he's just a no-good thief pretending to be a revolutionary. Vaca wasn't sure about that."

"And you believe him?"

McKinley drew in a deep breath. "It's kind of hard not to," he said. "I've been thinking about it while I was looking for you fellas. The yarn that Vaca spins about why he's up here in New Mexico Territory and all the mischief that fella Covarrubias has been up to . . . Well, it all rings true, Smoke. And I don't mind admitting, I didn't want to believe him. Not even a little bit." The young cowboy hesitated. "You see, I reckon Virginia's in love with him."

"No!" Fury and anguish mixed equally in Litchfield's exclamation. "That's impossible! She wouldn't . . . she would never . . . He's a bandit!"

"He claims he's not," McKinley said. "And she obviously believes him, whether anybody else does or not."

"But he kidnapped her!"

McKinley shook his head. "She insists she went with him willingly. Mind you, I'm not sure Mrs. Bacon was quite as agreeable, but I didn't get the chance to talk to her about it."

Smoke asked, "What's Vaca doing up here in the territory? His grandfather has a big *rancho* below the border, I believe."

"He claims he's starting a ranch up here. It's kind of a long story, Smoke. I can tell you about it while we're on our way to where Covarrubias is holed up with your horses. Vaca's gone after him to try to get them back."

"You mean steal them for himself," Litchfield said.

McKinley shook his head. "Nope. He plans to recover them and turn them over to the army. He wants to make Colonel Griffin see that he's not as bad as he's been painted."

"Lies, all lies."

"Maybe, maybe not," Smoke said. He handed the map back to McKinley. "There's one way to find out."

A reckless grin split the young man's sunburned face. "You mean . . . ?"

"I mean let's go get those horses back," Smoke said.

Chapter 20

José Antonio Vaca tried not to wince as he rested a hand on the rock slab to brace himself. The sun was high enough in the sky that the stone had grown quite hot.

Vaca glanced over at his man Tomás, who knelt beside him. The rock face dropped off sharply in front of them to a narrow ledge where two men sat among some rocks with Winchesters across their knees.

Those two were sentries posted by Juan Covarrubias to watch the narrow ravine sixty feet below the ledge. They were typical border scum and not overly diligent about their assignment. They were smoking cigarettes that made Vaca wrinkle his nose when the smell drifted to him. He recognized the tang of hashish mixed with the tobacco. The men laughed and told bawdy stories, as well.

Just looking at them, it seemed that a herd of buffalo could have stampeded past beneath them without them ever noticing. However, Vaca knew that wasn't true. At the first sign of an intruder, the guards would be instantly alert and could hold off an army from that ledge as long as their ammunition held out.

Because of that, after talking to Tomás and finding out more about the hideout, Vaca had decided that the sentries would have to be eliminated without raising any alarm. He and Tomás had spent more than an hour working their way through the rugged terrain to reach this spot above the guard post. Tomás led the way since he had been here before to spy on the sentries.

Tomás had tried to talk Vaca out of coming along, insisting that it would be better for him to remain with the other men while he and someone else tended to the guards.

"You are too important to risk your life in such a manner, Don José," Tomás had argued. "We need you to lead us."

"A leader goes in front," Vaca had responded. "He doesn't wait for his men to run all the risks."

Tomás had given up the effort fairly quickly. He knew that arguing with the Desert Wolf was a waste of time. Once Vaca made up his mind, he forged ahead with no hesitation. Blasting that spring into existence and trying to carve a ranch out of the wasteland proved his stubbornness.

And so far, he had been right far more often than he had been wrong.

Now, as they crouched above the ledge where the sentries were posted, Vaca silently drew his knife from its sheath. Tomás did likewise. This wouldn't be an easy fight; the ledge was narrow, and they might overshoot it when they dropped down on their enemies. If they did, there was nothing to catch them and the fall would likely be fatal.

As Vaca had said, though, some risks had to be run.

As they poised there on the edge, the two men looked at each other, nodded, and then leaped forward into empty space.

Vaca tried not to put too much into the jump, but for a terrifying heartbeat he was afraid he had gone too far out. He kept his legs straight and arrowed down the dozen feet to the ledge. From the corner of his eye, he saw Tomás doing the same.

The scrape of boot leather on rock must have alerted the

guards. With their hashish-laced quirlies dropping from their lips, they bolted to their feet and tried to turn and look up.

Vaca was aimed at the man on the left. His bootheels hit the man's right shoulder and drove him down against the rock behind which he'd been sitting. The man cried out in surprise and pain as his sombrero flew off from the impact.

Vaca landed on top of him and almost overbalanced, which would have toppled him over the rock and into open air. Vaca slapped his left hand against the little boulder to brace himself and hooked his right fist into the guard's midsection.

That fist was wrapped around the handle of Vaca's knife. The cold steel went easily into the man's body, penetrating deep into his guts. The man's eyes bugged out and his mouth opened wide, but Vaca was stable enough now to take his left hand off the rock and clap it over the guard's mouth before an agonized scream could emerge.

Vaca pulled the knife out and slammed it home again, this time higher in the man's chest. The blade must have found his heart. He jerked once in a violent spasm, then sagged down. His eyes, still open wide, began to glaze over.

Vaca looked to the right and saw Tomás locked in a life-and-death struggle with the other guard. The man had reached for the Colt holstered on his hip but had gotten the gun only halfway out before Tomás's left hand closed around his wrist. Tomás hung on to keep the guard from completing his draw.

At the same time, Tomás had tried to strike with his knife, but the guard had thrown his left hand up in time to grab the wrist of Tomás's knife hand. They were locked together like that, in an apparent stalemate, faces drawn taut with effort, breath hissing between clenched teeth.

But Tomás was a little too far forward. His opponent drew up his right leg. Vaca realized the guard was about to ram his foot into Tomás's stomach in an attempt to lever him up and over the edge.

Vaca ripped the knife from the chest of the dead man lying underneath him and lunged across the space between himself and the other two men. He reached out and shoved the blade into the side of the second sentry's neck. The steel grated on the man's spine as Vaca drove in the knife as hard as he could.

The guard died with a grotesque gurgle. As he went limp, the sudden change in balance caused by Tomás straining against a grip that was no longer there tipped Vaca's man even farther toward the brink. Vaca's other hand shot out and grabbed Tomás's arm to haul him back from danger.

Both of them slid off the corpses and landed on the ground behind the rocks that lined the ledge's rim. They were breathing heavily, and their faces revealed the strain of the brief but harrowing battle.

After a few minutes, Vaca pushed himself up enough to remove his knife from the second guard's neck. He tried not to look at the horrified expression death had etched on the man's face, forever frozen there. He had seen his share of violence since coming to New Mexico Territory, had dealt death to several of Covarrubias's men in earlier battles with the bandits, but he didn't want it to ever become commonplace to take another man's life.

As Vaca wiped blood from the blade on the dead man's shirt, Tomás said, "*Gracias*, Don José. Not for the first time, you have saved my life."

"You would have handled him," Vaca said, although both of them knew that was uncertain.

They took the Colts and Winchesters from the dead sentries and carefully made their way down the narrow, nerve-racking trail to the bottom of the ravine. They had left their horses with the rest of Vaca's men and made their approach on foot, so they would have to reclaim their mounts when they rejoined the others.

"Go and tell the men the way is open," Vaca said. "I'll stay here and deal with anyone who comes this way from the hideout."

"If there are too many, you should hide and let them go on, Don José. We will take care of them when the time comes."

The Desert Wolf wasn't just about to let his men ride right into a shoot-out, especially in the narrow confines of this gorge, and they both knew it.

"If I have to, I'll go back up to the ledge and hold them off from there." Vaca shrugged. "Gunfire will alert any of Covarrubias's men left with the horse herd, but as you say, *mi amigo*, we will deal with that problem when the time comes."

Tomás nodded and trotted back along the ravine. They had left the others at the mouth of this long, narrow passage. It would take Tomás about twenty minutes to get there, and another twenty minutes for him to return with the whole group.

If fortune smiled on them, Vaca wouldn't be discovered in that time, and he and the others would be able to steal up on the little pocket where the stolen horses were being held. Then they would take Covarrubias's men by surprise and wipe out the bandits before they knew what was going on.

Yes, it was a pretty plan, Vaca thought wryly as he watched Tomás disappear around a bend in the ravine. But only time would tell whether or not it would work. Plans seldom survived the first contact with the enemy, as he recalled from his reading of the Prussian military leader Helmuth von Moltke.

Vaca moved over to the foot of the trail that led up to the ledge, leaned the Winchester against the rock wall, and hunkered on his heels with his back against the wall, as well. The sun was high enough now to penetrate into the knife-edge cleft through the hills, and the air was beginning to bake. Vaca knew he would have to guard against the heat making him drowsy. He couldn't afford to doze off.

Giving himself a firm command to stay alert, he settled down to wait for his men.

* * *

The rough terrain meant that it took more than an hour for Smoke, Dean McKinley, and the cavalry detail to approach the spot where the Desert Wolf claimed that Juan Covarrubias's gang was holed up with the stolen horses. They couldn't afford to hurry; the sound of rapid hoofbeats could travel quite a distance in this thin, dry air.

McKinley pointed out several landmarks along the way, including the two hills that resembled a camel's humped back.

"Vaca tried to tell me the army brought camels out here after the war to try them out instead of horses and mules," the young cowboy said. "That just sounds loco to me."

"It's true, though," Smoke said. "I've heard about that."

"Indeed it is, lad," Sergeant Dunn put in. "A friend of mine was posted to Camp Verde, down in Texas, when the Camel Corps was there."

McKinley shook his head. "Pure craziness."

Smoke said, "As it turned out, the experiment didn't really work too well, but I reckon you've got to give them credit for trying."

McKinley laughed. "They ought to put camels in one of those dime novels!"

"As desperate as those scribblers are for ideas, I'm sure they'll get around to it," Smoke said.

A little while later, McKinley led the group toward a low beetling bluff that gradually shelved up into higher terrain. He pointed to it and said, "That ought to be where the trail through the ravine starts."

"We should scout ahead—" Smoke began.

"Wait just a minute," Litchfield said sharply. "If any scouting is going to be done, it won't be by a civilian. Have you forgotten that this is a military mission?"

Smoke valued practicality over modesty, so he said, "I haven't forgotten, Captain, but I have quite a bit of experience at things like this."

That was just a fact. Smoke's argument made sense, but Litchfield didn't look convinced. He said, "All right, Jensen, but take Sergeant Dunn with you. I want McKinley to stay here." He gave McKinley a hostile, narrow-eyed glance. "I'm still not completely sure I trust him. He might try to warn those bandits we're after them."

McKinley opened his mouth to make some response—probably a justifiably heated one—but Smoke stopped him with a gesture.

"You're wrong about Dean, Captain, but I'll go along with you for now. Are you ready, Sergeant?"

"Of course," Dunn replied.

Without waiting for Litchfield to say anything else inflammatory, Smoke heeled his horse into an easy lope toward the bluff. Sergeant Dunn fell in alongside him.

When they were out of earshot of the others, Dunn said, "For what it's worth, Mr. Jensen, I believe Captain Litchfield is wrong about young McKinley. The lad strikes me as quite genuine and trustworthy."

"That's how I've found him to be in the time I've known him," Smoke said. "We've fought side by side, and he hasn't let me down. I reckon I trust him more than I do your captain."

"I can't speak to that. You're entitled to your opinion, of course. But I will say that Captain Litchfield has acquitted himself honorably in several clashes with the Apaches. He's a capable commander in battle."

"That's good to know, considering we're liable to be in a fight before the day's over. What do you think about Vaca's claim that he's not a bandit?"

"I have no way of knowing about that, sir, one way or the other. I suppose we'll see, once the threat of that Covarrubias fellow has been dealt with."

"More than likely," Smoke agreed. "Like I said about Dean, you can tell a lot about an hombre once you've fought alongside him—if that's the way this turns out."

They were close enough to the bluff now for Smoke to be able to see what looked like a black line in the face of it. A crack in the stone, nothing more than that, or so it appeared.

But with each passing yard, the crack became more defined, and eventually they were able to see that it was an opening, a gap angled sharply into the upthrust rock. It was wide enough for two men to ride side by side.

Smoke checked his guns, made sure they slid easily in holster leather. Sergeant Dunn unfastened the flap on his holster. Moving at a slow, wary pace, they entered the ravine. The sun was almost directly overhead and lit up the trail, which probably remained in shadow the other twenty-three hours of the day.

The day was quiet and the only sounds were the soft thuds of the horses' hooves against the sandy ground. The ravine twisted and bent back on itself until it seemed to Smoke as if he and Dunn had to cover fifty yards of ground for every ten yards of progress they made. Every minute lasted three or four times what it really was. All those things combined to stretch a man's nerves until it felt as if they were about to snap.

Then, Smoke caught just the faintest flicker of movement up ahead. It was nothing but a shadow on the ground, there and then gone, right where the trail went around another of those bends.

He knew instantly that someone was waiting for them just on the other side of that bend.

Silently, without stopping his horse, he lifted a hand and pointed at the bend, then motioned for Dunn to fall back behind him. The sergeant grasped immediately what was going on, but instead of doing as Smoke indicated, he pushed his mount ahead and took the lead. If a trap of some sort was waiting for them around the bend, Dunn intended to be the one to spring it.

They were too close to the turn for Smoke to do anything except fall in line behind Dunn's horse. Both men had kept moving without a break, so whoever was lurking up ahead shouldn't have been tipped off that they'd become aware of him.

Smoke held the reins in his left hand and drew his right-hand Colt. Dunn was about ten feet in front of him. The sergeant rode around the bend, and a heartbeat later, Smoke heard a grunt, followed by a thud as something hit the ground.

He jabbed his bootheels into his horse's flanks. The animal leaped forward and cleared the corner.

Two men were struggling on the ground. Dunn's horse had bolted on ahead a few yards. Smoke spotted a small outcropping a few feet off the ground on the right side of the ravine and knew without having to think about it that a man had been waiting there to tackle whoever rode around the bend.

However, he had acted too hastily. He should have waited for the second man to make the turn. As it was, Smoke could get the drop on the ambusher.

But it didn't really matter, Smoke realized, because ten yards up the trail, three more men sat on horseback, pointing rifles at him.

They didn't open fire, and neither did Smoke. It was a standoff as, between the two forces, Sergeant Dunn battled hand to hand against the man who had knocked him off his horse. The cavalryman was older, but he was wiry and experienced. He managed to hook his leg around one of his opponent's legs and flip the man over onto his back. Dunn pounced and hammered a fist against the man's jaw, stunning him for the moment.

Heaving himself to his feet, Dunn backed off. His hand went to his hip, but he discovered that his service revolver had fallen out of its holster when he was knocked off his horse. He eased closer to the wall, giving Smoke a clearer line of fire if gunplay erupted.

Caught in the middle like that, though, Dunn would be riddled with bullets. There was no way he could avoid that fate.

The three men pointing rifles at Smoke and Dunn were vaqueros; that was obvious from their outfits. So was the stunned man on the ground who had knocked Dunn off his horse. Seeing that, Smoke ventured, "You hombres ride for Don José Antonio Vaca, don't you?"

The middle member of the trio lowered his rifle slightly and pushed his horse ahead a little. He said, "You are the Señor McKinley's *patrón*? Señor Jensen?"

"I'm Smoke Jensen," Smoke replied with a nod.

"And this man with you is from the army?"

Dunn said, "I would think that's obvious from the uniform."

The man lowered his rifle the rest of the way and motioned for his companions to do likewise. He rode closer and said, "My name is Tomás. I am *segundo* to Don José."

"Dean McKinley spoke of you," Smoke said. "You're the one who found Juan Covarrubias's hideout in these hills."

That allayed any lingering suspicions Tomás might have had. He looked relieved as he came closer.

"Señor McKinley went to look for you while Don José and the rest of us came here," he said. "You have a search party with you?"

"That's right. McKinley and the cavalry detail waited while the sergeant and I did a little scouting."

Tomás nodded. "I knew you must have talked to the young *señor* or you never would have found this place." He waved a hand up the ravine. "Don José waits ahead, watching the trail to the bandits' hiding place. We were about to join him and attack those dogs who ride with Covarrubias."

"Then it's a good thing we got here when we did," Smoke said. "We can all throw in together. That'll make the odds a lot better."

He was still wary, but his instincts told him to trust Tomás. Joining forces with the Desert Wolf and his men had become his goal, and now it looked as if they were on the verge of accomplishing that.

Their combined group would still have to defeat Covarrubias's men, but they would stand a lot better chance of that if they worked together.

The man Dunn had walloped was regaining his senses. The sergeant stepped over to him and extended a hand.

"Let me help you, my friend," Dunn said. "You fought well."

For a second, the vaquero looked angry, as if he wanted to continue the battle, but then he shrugged that off and clasped Dunn's hand so that the sergeant could help him to his feet.

"*Gracias*," the man muttered.

"*De nada*," Dunn said easily.

"Where are the rest of your men?" Smoke asked Tomás.

"Waiting around the next bend," he replied, motioning with his head in that direction. "We heard riders coming and knew we needed to see who it was."

Smoke said to Dunn, "Sergeant, can you go and tell the captain what's going on? Then the rest of you can join us."

"You're going with these men, sir?"

"That's right. I want to meet this fella Vaca and have a talk with him before we make our next move."

Dunn nodded. "That sounds like a good idea. I'll be back quickly with the others. You won't launch the attack without us, will you?"

Smoke smiled and said, "Don't worry, Sergeant. I expect there'll be plenty of action for all of us to get in on."

CHAPTER 21

As Smoke followed the trail through the ravine, riding with the group of vaqueros who had been waiting around the next bend, Tomás said to him, "I have heard a great deal about you, Señor Jensen. I am glad you are on our side, rather than fighting against us."

"And I'm glad to throw in with you fellas," Smoke said, "as long as your *patrón* is telling the truth about not being a bandit."

"Don José is an honest, honorable man, señor. On this, I would stake my life." Tomás chuckled. "Now, it is true that some of us who ride for him have not always been of the most sterling character, as you gringos might say, but now we stay on the right side of the trail."

"Plenty of hombres out here have done things in their past that might make folks raise an eyebrow. Most of the time, I judge a man by what he does here and now, not what he might have done a while back."

Tomás nodded and said, "A good way to be."

A quarter of an hour later, the riders rounded a bend, and a handsome young man holding a rifle stepped out from the side of the trail. Smoke recognized him immediately from their brief meeting in Socorro.

José Antonio Vaca smiled and said, "Señor Jensen! It is good to see you again. I hoped you might join us, but I didn't really expect that Tomás would return with you."

"Things worked out so I'm able to join forces with you," Smoke said. "I'm glad of that."

"As am I. Where is the fiery young Señor McKinley?"

"He's with the cavalry patrol that should be coming up the trail behind us. They ought to be here in a little while."

Vaca nodded. "Good. We'll wait for them if we can. But for now, we need to keep an eye on Covarrubias's stronghold. You and I will do that, Señor Jensen. Tomás, you stay here with the men and wait for Señor McKinley and the cavalry. As soon as they arrive, join us on foot. We don't want the sound of so many horses alerting Covarrubias that we're coming."

Tomás nodded. "*Sí*, Don José."

Smoke said, "I reckon I should warn you, Tomás, that Captain Litchfield may not cooperate all that well. He won't cotton to the idea that you were left in charge. To his way of thinking, he's in command wherever he is, and that goes for civilians as well as troopers."

"I will try to handle him as carefully as possible, señor, but I will not go against Don José's orders."

"Fair enough. I just thought you ought to know he may give you trouble."

Smoke pulled his Winchester from its saddle sheath and joined José Antonio Vaca as the young man headed up the trail on foot. The ravine was as serpentine as ever and slanted upward as it wound into the hills.

The walls began to recede as they went higher, and eventually the trail was wide enough that four men could have ridden abreast on it. Vaca motioned for Smoke to follow his lead and moved closer to the left-hand wall. He catfooted forward, and Smoke took that to mean they were getting close to their destination.

Vaca knelt when they were about twenty feet from the mouth of the ravine. The walls ended and the ground fell away beyond that. Smoke dropped to a knee beside the young man.

"Tomás scouted this place earlier," Vaca said, so quietly that the words wouldn't reach any farther than Smoke's ears. "He said there are no guards. The ones back down the ravine that he and I disposed of earlier were the only ones."

"Covarrubias must be pretty confident that he's safe here."

Vaca nodded. "You have seen the trail for yourself, Señor Jensen. Two men could hold it for a long time, certainly long enough for reinforcements to arrive." He paused. "And Juan Covarrubias, like most evil men, believes in his power so much that it has made him arrogant."

"Is Covarrubias here himself?" Smoke asked.

"That, I do not know. Sometimes he is, sometimes he is below the border. We probably won't know until we have dealt with the place's defenders."

"You'll know him if you see him?"

"Yes, without a doubt. He once worked as a vaquero for my grandfather." A bitter tinge crept into Vaca's voice. "We were amigos, as much as we could be, given the difference in our station. That bothered him more than it did me. I regret that it was one more thing breeding resentment in him, and that resentment put him on the lawless path he follows now."

"Seems quiet and peaceful down there," Smoke observed.

"It will not stay that way. Covarrubias's men will have to move those stolen horses out today or tomorrow. They could begin doing that at any time."

"The rest of our bunch ought to be here soon."

"I'm going to take a better look," Vaca breathed. He came to his feet.

Smoke rose behind him and drifted forward just as quietly as Vaca did.

The ravine ended at the top of a slope that slanted down into a roughly circular basin surrounded by rocky hills. The ground was steep but not so much that horses would be unable to navigate it down to the level basin. That pocket in the hills was a quarter of a mile wide, dotted here and there with scrubby mesquite trees and clumps of grass. The sparse vegetation provided enough graze to keep alive the horses being held here.

Smoke could see the stolen stock scattered across the basin. They hadn't been gathered back up into a herd, which was a good sign. The bandits weren't on the verge of moving them out through the pass at the northwest corner of the natural enclosure.

On the far side of the basin were several crude adobe huts. Off to one side was a corral with maybe two dozen horses in it. Those would be the saddle mounts used by Covarrubias's men. Smoke spotted a few men moving around the huts, but it was likely most of the bandits were inside, getting out of the sun for their midday siesta.

The slope in front of Smoke and Vaca was littered with boulders and riven with gullies. Smoke said, "We'll have some cover getting down there, but we still run the risk of being spotted."

"It is a risk that must be run. We will leave some of the soldiers here, as well as a few of my men who are good marksmen. They can train their rifles on the huts, and if anyone raises an alarm down there during our approach, the men up here can open fire and provide cover for us as we attack openly. But the closer we can get without that happening, the better, of course."

They continued watching as they waited for the others to catch up. Several minutes had gone by when Vaca suddenly stiffened and caught his breath.

Smoke noticed the reaction and asked, "What's wrong?"

"That man who just came out of the hut at the far left . . .

That's Juan Covarrubias. I would know him anywhere, even at this distance."

Smoke's eyes were keen enough that he had no trouble seeing the man stalking around the bandit camp, although he couldn't make out many details. The figure was tall and broad-shouldered, and Smoke thought the man sported a black beard, but that was really all he could tell.

"You're sure?" he asked Vaca.

"I have no doubt. See the way he limps?"

The man did have a slight hitch in his gait, Smoke noted.

"He broke his leg when he was thrown from a horse, back when he rode for my grandfather," Vaca went on. "The bone didn't heal correctly, and he was left with that slight limp. Yes, that is Juan Covarrubias. I was hoping he would be here. The time for a showdown between us is long since due."

Smoke just wanted to get his horses back and stop the bandits from hurting innocent people. He hadn't signed on to help settle any sort of personal grudge between Vaca and Covarrubias. But if the end result was the same, he supposed it didn't really matter.

"Don José!"

The soft call came from behind them. Smoke and Vaca turned to look as Tomás trotted toward them. Behind the *segundo* came the rest of Vaca's men, followed by Dean McKinley, Captain Litchfield, Sergeant Dunn, and the troopers from the 9th Cavalry. All of them were on foot and moving fairly quietly. The shuffle of their steps wouldn't be heard in the basin down below.

With his lips drawn back in a savage grin, Vaca met Tomás and the two men clasped wrists. Smoke nodded to Litchfield and said, "Glad to see you, Captain." This was one of the few occasions when that sentiment was actually true.

"Is that the so-called bandit stronghold?" Litchfield asked curtly, without returning Smoke's greeting.

"It is, and I can confirm those are the horses stolen from my herd being held down there, too."

Litchfield looked at Vaca. "You're the Desert Wolf?"

"Some call me that," Vaca admitted. "It was not a name I sought."

Litchfield jerked his revolver from its holster and leveled it at the young grandee, taking them all by surprise. "You're under arrest," he said.

Instantly, Vaca's men jerked up their rifles and pointed them at the captain. At the same time, the cavalry troopers raised their weapons and brought them to bear on Vaca's men. Sergeant Dunn sprang between the two groups and held his arms out to the sides as he ordered in a low, urgent voice, "Hold your fire! Hold your fire, blast it! No shooting!"

Smoke, McKinley, and Vaca were the only ones not pointing a gun at somebody. Smoke said, "Captain, what in blazes are you doing?"

"This man is wanted," Litchfield said, his voice and body both stiff with anger. "He's accused of being an outlaw and causing a great deal of misery and suffering in this region."

"Lies, all lies," Vaca grated.

"If that's the case, it'll all come out when you're dealt with by the proper legal authorities. Now, put down your guns and order your men to do likewise."

"Captain," Smoke said, "if you don't back off, there's fixing to be a lot of blood spilled here, and it won't do anybody a bit of good. Not only that, the real bandits will get away, because you're threatening to do their work for them!"

Litchfield glared across the few feet that separated him from Vaca. "You can't believe a word this man says, Jensen," he snapped. "All these Mexicans are liars. It's common knowledge up and down the Jornada del Muerto that the Desert Wolf is a bandit."

"If that's true, then why was he going to help us recover those stolen horses?"

A faint smile appeared on Litchfield's lips. "Haven't you ever heard the old expression 'thieves fall out'? That's what's going on here. If you'd just stop and think about it, you'd know that. Why, this man kidnapped Miss Griffin and Mrs. Bacon!"

"Another lie," Vaca said. "The *señorita* and I are in love—"

"Captain, I don't like this fella any more than you do," McKinley interrupted, "but he's telling the truth. I didn't want to believe him at first, but now I do. He may be the Desert Wolf, but he's not an outlaw, and he didn't kidnap Virginia and her aunt. She'd tell you that herself if she was here."

"Thank heavens she's not here," Litchfield said. "You claim that the women are back at that so-called ranch of yours, mister?"

"They are," Vaca said, "and they are safe. The men I left behind will protect them."

"Where is this ranch?"

McKinley said, "I can take you there, Captain, and then you'll see for yourself that the ladies are all right. But we can do that after we've taken care of those no-good horse thieves down there."

McKinley waved a hand toward the basin and the bandit camp it contained.

The tension inside the ravine stretched out for a moment longer as the two sides menaced each other. Then Litchfield said, "I suppose we should deal with first things first. I'll hold you to your promise, McKinley."

"I'll take you there, don't worry," the young cowboy said.

"That's good enough for me." Litchfield lowered his gun.

Vaca nodded to Tomás and the other men. They still cast hostile glances toward the soldiers, but they pointed their rifles at the ground.

The troopers still had their weapons raised, however. Litchfield turned his head to look at them and nodded as if telling them to lower their guns.

Some sixth sense warned Smoke that wasn't what was happening here. He exclaimed, "Vaca, look out!" and pulled his Colts.

He was too late to stop the troopers. They fired, flame spouting from the muzzles of their rifles. The thunderous volley crashed deafeningly in the ravine's close confines. Heavy slugs slammed into Vaca's men and threw them back against the wall behind him.

Not all the troopers opened fire. A few of them stood there, frozen in total shock, as their erstwhile comrades turned on them, too. Rifle butts slammed into the heads of those stunned troopers, knocking them to the ground. The attackers used the rifle butts again to finish them off.

While that was going on, Litchfield darted behind McKinley and flung his left arm around the young cowboy's neck. Smoke hadn't gotten off a shot yet, and he had to hold his fire as Litchfield used McKinley as a human shield. Litchfield backed against the wall as he rammed his revolver's barrel into McKinley's ribs.

Vaca couldn't shoot without hitting McKinley, and neither could Sergeant Dunn, who looked just as shocked as the other men who were still on their feet.

"Captain!" Dunn cried. "What are you doing? Those men—"

"Those men were in my way," Litchfield said. "It's time we put a stop to all the pretense. Jensen, drop your guns. Vaca, Sergeant, the two of you, as well."

"Drop my gun so that you can shoot me down?" Vaca demanded.

"If you don't, I'll kill this young fool. I'd rather not, since he's potentially of some value to me. All of you are. Except, come to think of it, you, Sergeant."

Before anyone could stop him, Litchfield jerked the gun away from McKinley's side, blasted a shot into Dunn's body, and jabbed the revolver back into McKinley's ribs.

Dunn, taken completely by surprise, reeled back as he pressed both hands to his chest. Blood welled through his spread fingers. He tried to say something, but then his knees buckled and he fell. He stayed half-sitting for a moment and then toppled over onto his side and lay still.

The floor of the ravine was already littered with bloody corpses. One more didn't really make that much difference.

Smoke had to give Litchfield credit. The man was fast and sure in his movements. If he'd had the slightest opening, Smoke would have taken a shot at him. But Litchfield had shielded himself effectively with his prisoner.

The treacherous officer's arm was tight enough around McKinley's neck that the young cowboy had trouble getting any words out. But he managed to gasp, "Shoot this varmint . . . Smoke! Shoot right through me . . . and kill him!"

"You know better than that, McKinley," Litchfield said. "Smoke Jensen has a reputation as an honorable man. Even I know that. He's not going to kill you just to get at me." He laughed. "And neither will you, Vaca. The Desert Wolf! What a ridiculous name, and what a ridiculous comic-opera character to go with it. The noble outlaw! Ha!"

Litchfield turned serious again as he went on. "No more games. Drop your guns, both of you."

Vaca said, "I was right. Covarrubias *is* working with an American. A traitor! You!"

Litchfield's lip curled. "And why shouldn't I work with him? There's no money to be made in the army. And they sent me out here to this blistering slice of purgatory! I should have been a colonel by now, instead of an old fool like Griffin. But my time is coming. When Covarrubias takes over down there below the border—with my help—Mexico can reclaim this territory. I'll be the governor of it, too. My word will be law! I'll be like an emperor, and Virginia will reign by my side as my empress!"

Slowly, Smoke said, "Mister, you're absolutely loco. None of that will ever happen."

"Juan may proclaim himself to be a revolutionary, a liberator," Vaca said, "but he is just a bandit. You'll see. You're mad, just as Señor Jensen says."

Litchfield didn't respond to that except to bark, "Men, prepare to fire!"

The troopers aimed at Smoke and Vaca.

Smoke drew in a deep breath. Surrendering went against the grain for him. He had faced tremendous odds in the past and always come out on top.

But he had seldom been in a trap this tight, with the lives of other men at stake, too. Another tense heartbeat went by, and then he said, "All right, Litchfield." He bent and placed his Colts on the ground. With obvious reluctance, Vaca did likewise. "I reckon you win—for now."

"No, I win for good," Litchfield boasted. "And call me Governor. I might as well start getting used to it!"

CHAPTER 22

As it turned out, not all of the troopers who weren't working with Litchfield were dead. A couple of them had only been knocked out. When they came to, they were added to the group of prisoners.

Vaca was the only member of his party left alive, though. The others, including Tomás, had been riddled by the unexpected attack.

Several of the turncoat troopers went back to retrieve the horses while the others kept their rifles trained on Smoke, Vaca, McKinley, and the two soldiers who had survived the betrayal. Then the prisoners were marched at gunpoint down the slope into the basin.

Litchfield followed behind them. McKinley glanced over his shoulder and muttered, "Look at him, strutting along like a little tin god. Making fun of Vaca when he's so full of himself, he's like one of those dime-novel villains!"

"Take it easy, Dean," Smoke said quietly. "Getting worked up isn't going to help anything. He wants to keep you alive, because he thinks he can make you take him back to Don José's ranch, but if you push him too far, he'll just kill you and figure he can find it himself."

Vaca said, "I would never take him there, no matter how much he tortured me."

"Well, neither will I," McKinley declared.

Smoke knew that both young men meant those bold words wholeheartedly. But he also knew that human beings had limits, and no man truly knew what he would reveal under torture until he was called on to endure it.

Maybe it wouldn't ever come to that. The wheels of his brain were already turning over rapidly as he tried to work out some way of escaping this trap and turning the tables on his enemies.

As they were on their way down the slope, Smoke spotted a sudden glint of reflection from something at the bandit camp. When the blinding light went away, he looked closer and saw a long tube set up on a tripod of spindly legs. They had a telescope down there they used to keep an eye on the ravine.

Men were already running around, alerted to the fact that there was trouble by the crashing volley of gunfire from the ravine. Saddles were thrown on horses, and a dozen riders came tearing across the basin to meet the men coming down the slope on foot. By the time the prisoners and their captors reached level ground, the bandits had arrived, sombrero-wearing hombres milling around on horseback and brandishing guns.

One of them lunged his mount forward, banging his heels against its flanks. He was taller and burlier than his companions, and a thick, black beard bristled from his jaws. Even though the limp wasn't evident while the man was horseback, Smoke was sure this was the same bandit Vaca had pointed out earlier.

This was Juan Covarrubias, former vaquero and current *bandido*, and would-be revolutionary.

Brutally, he yanked his mount to a halt in front of the newcomers. Deep-set eyes under bushy brows scanned the prisoners, and when his gaze landed on Vaca, those eyes widened in recognition. He sat up straighter in the saddle as profane oaths spewed from his mouth. He yanked a long-barreled Remington revolver from its holster and pointed the gun at Vaca.

"You!" he exclaimed. "You pig of a Vaca!" He added some more colorful descriptions of the young grandee's ancestry, then blustered, "I ought to shoot you down where you stand right now! I ought to blow your brains out, you filthy *rico* dog!"

Vaca snarled right back at him and said, "Go ahead! Whether you kill me or not, you'll still be the same dirty border scum you've always been, Juan."

The Remington trembled in Covarrubias's hand. His finger was white on the trigger. But he held off on firing and, after a tense moment, pointed the gun at the sky while he let down the hammer he had eared back. A harsh laugh came from the tangle of beard around his mouth as he slid the gun back in its holster.

"You don't get off that easy, Vaca." He made the name sound as obscene as any of the curses he had thrown out. "No, when you die—and you *will* die—it will be slowly and painfully. You will scream like a baby and beg for mercy, and there will be none!" Covarrubias looked past the prisoners. "Litchfield! *El Capitán!*"

Litchfield strode forward. His gun was holstered now, since he had the troopers to keep Smoke and the others covered. He hooked his thumbs in his waistband and looked very satisfied with himself as he swaggered up to the bandit boss.

"Hello, Juan," he said. "I know you weren't expecting to see me, but there have been some unexpected developments." He jerked his head toward Smoke. "This is Smoke Jensen. He has something of a reputation."

Covarrubias nodded. "*Sí*, I have heard of this Señor Jensen. From all the stories that are told about him, I thought he would be much taller and perhaps would breathe fire."

Smoke didn't say anything.

"He's dangerous enough," Litchfield said. "Once he was involved, I couldn't take a chance on him finding you and ruining everything. I arranged matters so that he would wind up as our prisoner, not a threat to us."

"But this meant you had to reveal the arrangement between the two of us," Covarrubias commented with a frown. "We cannot proceed as we have been."

"That's not the case at all," Litchfield answered instantly. He nodded toward the troopers. "These men are all loyal associates of mine. They realized their lives would be much better working with me than being mere soldiers."

Covarrubias pointed at the two privates who stood with Smoke, McKinley, and Vaca. "Not all of them fell in line, eh?"

"I never even approached those two and a few others," Litchfield replied, with a shake of his head. "I knew they were too stubborn to see what was good for them."

Covarrubias nodded slowly. "So after we kill these prisoners, no one will be left alive to accuse you of anything. Is that it?"

"Exactly."

The bandit boss leaned forward in his saddle and frowned. "Then why do you not go ahead and kill them?"

"Because we can get some use out of them. Let's go on to camp where we can be comfortable, and we'll discuss it."

"Of course." Covarrubias pointed at the prisoners and told his men, "Tie their hands. We will take no chances with the notorious Smoke Jensen and his friend, or with that *maldito* Vaca."

It didn't take long for the prisoners to be secured. They marched across the basin with the troopers behind them. Covarrubias ordered one of his men to dismount so that Litchfield could use his horse. The two of them rode side by side with the other bandits bringing up the rear.

Smoke knew that he and his companions were vastly outnumbered, but he wasn't in the habit of giving up. He didn't see any way out of this mess—yet—but he told himself it was just a matter of time.

As they crossed the basin, he was glad to note that the stolen horses appeared to be well taken care of. That wasn't a surprise; the animals represented a good payoff for the men who had stolen them.

When they reached the camp, the bandits who had been left behind looked curiously at the prisoners. Smoke didn't see any sympathy or mercy on the hard-bitten faces, just speculation about what these captives might be worth.

They were taken to the cabin Covarrubias had come out of earlier and ordered to sit on the ground. Awkwardly, because their hands were tied behind their backs, the men sat. Some of the bandits remained to guard them while the troopers working for Litchfield went off to get acquainted with the rest of Covarrubias's gang.

"Tell them to share their tequila and mescal with you!" Covarrubias called after them with a big grin.

An awning on poles was set up in front of Covarrubias's cabin. Chairs were brought out and placed under it. Covarrubias and Litchfield sat in the shade, while the prisoners, sitting cross-legged on the ground, baked in the sun.

One of the men brought a jug and glasses for the two ringleaders. Covarrubias poured tequila from the jug and handed one of the glasses to Litchfield.

"To our bold enterprise, eh?" the bandit boss said, as he raised his glass. "Soon we will be rich men, eh?"

"Richer even than we dreamed," Litchfield replied, after he had downed a swallow of the fiery liquor. "Vaca's father and grandfather have a great deal of money, isn't that right?"

"*Sí.*" Covarrubias spouted a few more obscene comments about the Vaca family and added, "All rich men should burn for eternity in the flames of the infernal pit! Except for us, of course. We deserve to have piles and piles of gold."

"And power," Litchfield said, "but that goes with the money. The old men will pay plenty to have the boy returned safely to them, won't they?"

Covarrubias's dark brows drew down into a fierce glare. "You mean to ransom him back to them? To let him live?"

"I never said that," Litchfield replied with a smile. "They'll pay to get him back—but what happens after they fork over the money is an entirely different matter."

Covarrubias sat back in his chair and grinned. "Ah, I understand now. And I like the way you think, *mi amigo.* What about the others?"

"Jensen owns one of the biggest ranches in Colorado. His wife can afford a hefty ransom, too."

That brought a laugh from Smoke, despite the misery of sitting in the broiling sun.

"Yeah, you go right ahead and send a ransom demand to my wife, Litchfield," he said. "She'll come down here with about fifty top gunhands and blow you and all of your partners straight to hell!"

Litchfield sneered at him. "Are you trying to convince me to go ahead and kill you out of hand, Jensen?"

"No, I'm just telling you the truth. You don't know what you're about to blow the lid off of."

"Let me worry about that," Litchfield snapped.

Covarrubias pointed at McKinley. "What about the young one? What good is he?"

"He's going to lead us back to Vaca's hideout. We kill the rest of Vaca's men, grab Virginia and her aunt, and bring them back here." Litchfield lounged back in his chair, sipped his drink, and went on, "Or rather, you and your men will do that. I need to remain here as your prisoner."

"But you are not—ah, I see! The *señorita* and the *señora* will not know that you and I are amigos, eh?"

"That's right. Then you'll let me go, so I can return to Fort

Craig and deliver the ransom demand. I'm thinking a mule train of guns and ammunition would be suitable. Colonel Griffin isn't rich like Vaca's father and grandfather, but he *does* have valuable resources at his command."

"Will he cooperate?" Covarrubias asked.

"I'll be honest with you: I don't know. But if we have to, we can arrange things so that I 'rescue' the ladies, and we won't have lost anything. We can carry on as we have been, only we'll be better financed, because of what we'll collect from the Vacas and Mrs. Jensen."

"You're dreaming, mister," Smoke said.

"You are a madman," Vaca added.

Litchfield just smiled. "Mad dreams are what allow men to do great things," he said.

Covarrubias gestured at the troopers and said, "What about those two?"

"They're of no value to us whatsoever," Litchfield replied with a shake of his head. "But your men might get some sport out of killing them."

"We are not Apaches, amigo!" Covarrubias sounded offended by the suggestion. Then he spread his hands and added, "But I suppose some target practice never hurt anything, eh? I will consider this and decide later. For now, we leave them here to, how do you say?—stew in their own juices!"

Covarrubias fished a thin, black cigar out of a jacket pocket and lit it with a lucifer he snapped to life on his thumbnail. He sat there with Litchfield, smoking and sipping tequila and looking quite pleased with himself, for several minutes.

Then he raised a finger and said, "One thing we do different than what you say, amigo. When Colonel Griffin has delivered what we demand, we send his sister back to him—but the young woman stays with me."

Litchfield was finishing the tequila in his glass as Covarrubias said that. He jerked upright, choking and sputtering. The empty glass slipped from his fingers and thudded to the ground. It took him a second before he could speak again.

"What? Absolutely not! I told you, we'll make Virginia and her aunt believe that I'm a prisoner, too, and that way, no suspicion will fall on me. Once we're back at the fort, Virginia is bound to turn to me for comfort after such a harrowing experience, and it'll be no time at all before we're married. Then, after you've taken over in Mexico and made me the governor of the territory, I'm sure she'll enjoy her life in Santa Fe too much to ever question anything." Litchfield smiled. "She's really a shallow little thing, you know, and not very bright."

Smoke saw both McKinley and Vaca lean forward and glare at the renegade captain. They didn't like what Litchfield was saying about Virginia, but such insults were the least of their worries right now. He caught the eyes of both men and gave a tiny shake of his head, just enough to caution them not to react. It might be better to let this exchange play out.

Covarrubias nodded, puffed on his cigar, and took it out of his mouth to say, "You paint a very pretty picture, *Capitán*, but I am in charge here, and I say things will be different. I have never laid eyes on Señorita Griffin, but I know she must be a beauty or else a man such as you would not want her. Now *I* want her, and I will have her."

"Stop this, Juan," Litchfield snapped. "What you suggest is never going to happen, and if you're not careful, you're going to wind up damaging our friendship. And I'll remind you, our arrangement has been quite profitable for you so far."

"Oh, *sí*, very profitable, I agree. And it is thanks to you that I will have much, much more money in the future. So *muchas gracias, Capitán, muchas gracias*."

Litchfield sniffed, looked smugly satisfied with himself, and sat back in his chair.

Covarrubias pulled the long-barreled Remington from its

holster, eared back the hammer as he thrust the weapon across his body, and shot Litchfield in the side of the head.

McKinley, Vaca, and the two troopers all exclaimed in shock and horror. Smoke had sensed that Covarrubias was about to do something dramatic, so he wasn't completely surprised by the brutal execution.

The shot had taken Litchfield by surprise, though. He barely had time to register that before the .44-caliber slug, fired at close range, exploded out the other side of his head in a grisly spray of pink, gray, and white, leaving a fist-sized hole behind it. He toppled out of the chair and was dead when he thudded limply to the ground.

The sudden blast drew the attention of the other troopers. They looked around, saw Litchfield lying on the ground and Covarrubias sitting there with powder smoke wisping from the muzzle of his revolver, and a couple of the men took a step in that direction.

Instantly, the bandits all drew their guns and covered the soldiers, who could only stand there staring at the body of the dead officer.

Covarrubias stood up, pouched his iron, and swaggered over to face the troopers. His limp was barely noticeable.

"You have a choice to make now, *mis amigos*," he told them. "You can be upset over the death of this foolish gringo and try to avenge him, in which case you will all die in the next few minutes. Or you can swear your allegiance to me and trade those uniforms for the garb of brave revolutionaries! Heroes of the people!"

"We're buffalo soldiers, mister," one of the troopers said. "Don't that mean nothin' to you?"

"Not a thing, as long as you are loyal to our cause! If you wish to join us, no matter what color your skin may be, we welcome you to our ranks, *compadres*!"

Smoke could see for himself the magnetism that Covarrubias was capable of. Vaca had said that the bandit boss was an effective leader of men, if nothing else, and that appeared to be true.

The troopers looked at each other for a long moment. Several of them nodded, and the man who appeared to have appointed himself their spokesman said, "If you'll have us, mister, we'll be happy to throw in with you. Cap'n Litchfield never showed us no real respect. He figured we could be bought off with a few shiny coins and would do his biddin' for him. He'd've turned his back on us in a second once he got what he wanted."

"Very true, very true," Covarrubias said, nodding. "I have no doubt of that at all. But now you are our amigos, as good as any man in our brave company. And you can demonstrate your loyalty by killing the two over there who are not with you."

"No, Clyde!" one of the captive troopers cried. "Don't do it! Don't listen to this crazy man!"

The trooper called Clyde shook his head slowly. "Sorry, Hank. We got a chance to do better for ourselves than we ever could've in the army. We got to grab it while we can."

The two prisoners begged and then yelled curses as their former comrades came over to them, grabbed them by the arms, and dragged them off a short distance. They were stood up on their feet, but their legs buckled in fear as their would-be executioners backed off. They fell to their knees and continued pleading.

Those pleas fell on deaf ears. While Covarrubias and the other bandits looked on, grinning eagerly, Clyde pointed to five of the turncoat troopers and called out, "Firin' squad detail, fellas, just like we practiced from time to time at the fort. Ready . . ."

Rifles came up and were lined at the two prisoners.

"Aim . . . *fire!*"

A ragged volley rang out. Flame spurted from the rifles. Bullets smashed into the captives and drove them over backward. They lay there, twisted grotesquely because their hands were still tied behind their backs. They jerked and kicked for several seconds before the stillness of death settled over them.

A cheer went up from the bandits.

The troopers who had carried out the execution looked a little shaken as they lowered their weapons. They knew they had taken a step from which they could never turn back. They were outlaws now, just like the rest of this bunch.

Covarrubias jerked a hand toward Smoke, McKinley, and Vaca. "Throw them in one of the huts and stand guard on them," he ordered his men. In his arrogance, he added, "You can cut their hands free."

One of the bandits asked, "But what if they cause trouble or try to escape, Juan?"

"Make them regret it," Covarrubias said. His teeth flashed in his beard as he grinned. "Make them sorry they were ever born—but do not kill them!"

He jerked his head toward Litchfield's body.

"And drag that carrion away for the buzzards and the coyotes to feast on!"

Chapter 23

The huts had walls of adobe brick, and the roofs were adobe, as well, supported by a layer of interlacing mesquite poles. They probably leaked when it rained, but here on the edge of the Jornada del Muerto, that was an infrequent problem.

Even though the prisoners' knives had been taken away from them, Smoke figured they could break out through the roof of the hut into which they were herded, given enough time.

But they didn't have time. The windowless huts had no doors, so Smoke, McKinley, and Vaca could hear Juan Covarrubias shouting orders to his men, telling them to get ready to ride to Vaca's *rancho*. Clearly, the bandit boss was eager to get his hands on Virginia and Dorothy.

Two men were posted as guards right outside the door. They carried Winchesters, packed two revolvers apiece, and each man had a machete tucked behind the sash tied tightly around his waist. Covarrubias had ordered them not to kill the prisoners, but they could do a lot of damage without it being fatal.

The hut was furnished with several crude bunks and some empty crates to use as seats. Smoke, McKinley, and Vaca sat down. Vaca leaned closer to the other two men and whispered, "We have to get out of here! We have to stop Covarrubias."

"That's not going to be easy, considering we're outnumbered more than ten to one now that those troopers have thrown in with him," McKinley said.

"I don't care about the odds. We have to do something to save Virginia and Señora Bacon."

"I'll never tell that varmint how to find the *rancho*, I know that," McKinley declared. "I don't reckon you will, either."

"Of course not." Vaca grimaced. "Unfortunately, I fear that may not be necessary. Covarrubias and his gang have been operating here along the fringes of the Jornada del Muerto for quite a while. It's possible he already knows how to get there. Litchfield believed he would have to torture the location out of us, but Juan . . ." Vaca's shoulders rose and fell eloquently. "That's why we have no time to waste," he said.

Smoke said, "As hard as it is to just sit and wait, we're better off not trying anything until Covarrubias takes some of his men and leaves. That's what he's getting ready to do, and our chances of escaping will improve after he's gone."

Vaca looked stricken. "But that means giving him a chance to get his hands on Virginia and her aunt."

"Now, hold on," McKinley said. "You know these parts just as well as Covarrubias does, don't you?"

Vaca let out a disgusted snort. "Better! I have explored all of these hills and know every foot of them."

Smoke thought he knew what McKinley was getting at. He said, "If we don't take too long about getting loose once Covarrubias is gone, you probably know some shortcuts that would get us back to your ranch ahead of him."

Understanding dawned on Vaca's face. He leaned forward and said, "Yes! I could do that. At least, we would have a chance to beat him there and warn the others."

All three of them had kept their voices pitched low enough that the guards outside the door couldn't hear what they were saying. Smoke had a glimmer of an idea how they might escape, but before he could tell McKinley and Vaca about it, a burly shape blocked the light in the doorway. Covarrubias swaggered up and propped a shoulder against the side of the door.

"I know better than to waste my time asking you about this, José, but you, gringo"—he looked at McKinley—"tell me how to find this dog's *rancho*, and I promise to let you live. I might even allow you to join our great cause if you cooperate well enough."

"You can just go straight to blazes, mister," McKinley snapped. "I'm not going to tell you a blasted thing. Do your worst!"

Covarrubias laughed. "Bold words, but I promise you, you do not want me to do my worst!" He waved a hand. "But it does not matter. I can find what I'm looking for. I know the general area. It would be faster if you helped, gringo, but it is not really necessary."

The bandit boss straightened from his casual stance and dropped his right hand to his gun.

"So, if you insist on not cooperating, I really have no more need of you—"

Vaca stood up swiftly and stepped in front of McKinley. "You will have to shoot me first," he said, "and I know you don't want to do that." His lip curled. "I am too valuable to you."

Covarrubias didn't draw his revolver, but he allowed his hand to rest on the butt. "It is true. I believe your father and grandfather will pay handsomely to save your life," he said. "But I can put a bullet through your knee and still collect a good ransom."

Smoke stood up. "You'll have to kill me, too, Covarrubias."

"You already said your wife won't pay for you, amigo—"

"But you can't even try for a ransom if I'm dead. Sally would insist on proof that I'm alive."

A scowl drew Covarrubias's bushy eyebrows down. "Why

are you two so fond of some gringo saddle tramp? This boy is nothing to you!"

"He's my friend," Smoke said.

"And mine," Vaca added, drawing a slightly startled glance from McKinley.

"Fine." Covarrubias shook his head in disgust. "He lives—for now. But once I have what I want . . ."

He didn't finish that vague threat. Instead, he turned and stalked away, saying sharply over his shoulder to the guards, "Watch them!"

Inside the hut, McKinley said quietly, "I'm obliged to you fellas for sticking up for me like that. I'm not sure what I've done to earn it." He looked at Vaca. "And I sure didn't expect you to claim that we're amigos."

The young grandee smiled. "There is a saying I learned when I studied Latin: *Amicus meus, inimicus inimici mei*. It means 'My friend, the enemy of my enemy.' That describes us, does it not?"

"I reckon so." Grudgingly, McKinley added, "Anyway, if Virginia feels about you the way she does, you must not be too bad an hombre."

"*Gracias*. But once we are out of here and Virginia and her aunt are safe . . ."

"Yeah, things could be a mite different," McKinley said.

Smoke said, "I'm glad you two have decided to call a truce, but as soon as Covarrubias is gone, you'll have to break it."

McKinley and Vaca both looked at him in puzzlement. "What are you talking about, Smoke?" McKinley asked.

"The two of you are going to do your best to kill each other," Smoke said.

Not long after that, Covarrubias and at least twenty of his men galloped off toward the narrow trail through the ravine. From the open door of the hut, Smoke watched them go.

One of the guards eyed him warily and snarled, "Back away, gringo." He caressed the wooden handle of his machete as if he would like nothing better than to pull the big blade and hack Smoke to pieces with it.

Smoke retreated into the shadowy hut. McKinley and Vaca stood tensely, waiting for him to tell them to go ahead with the plan they had worked out. The minutes dragged by as they listened to the fading hoofbeats of Covarrubias's group. Even when the bandits were gone, they continued to wait, just to be sure. If Covarrubias was still too close, it could ruin everything.

Finally, Smoke nodded to the two men. McKinley faced Vaca and said loudly, "None of this would've happened if it wasn't for you, you dirty no-good rat! If you hadn't dragged Virginia out to that run-down ranch of yours, she'd be safe now."

"Shut up, filthy gringo pig!" Vaca responded. "You're just jealous because she prefers a real man like me instead of a mewling little boy like you."

"You're a liar!" McKinley added some appropriately obscene descriptions. Vaca shot back with some strong, profane words of his own.

As Smoke watched them, he saw their faces darken with rage. They were working themselves up into legitimate anger, spilling out actual resentments they felt toward each other and not mincing words about it. As long as they were able to control their emotions, that wasn't a bad thing. The harsh words sounded genuine because to an extent, they were.

Despite that, the two young men had the presence of mind not to forget the plan. They positioned themselves the way Smoke had suggested during their whispered strategizing, and after a particularly virulent exchange, McKinley took the next step.

He bellowed in fury, lowered his head, and charged at Vaca,

grabbing him around the waist and propelling him backward through the doorway.

Vaca shouted, too, and hammered punches at McKinley as the young cowboy's momentum carried them several yards into the open before both men lost their balance and crashed to the ground. They began rolling around, still grappling and punching.

Everything depended on how the guards reacted. If they stood back and just watched the fracas, that would ruin the whole thing. Smoke was counting on the fact Covarrubias had ordered that Vaca be kept alive and relatively intact.

After a moment, McKinley wound up on top, straddling Vaca's torso. He locked his hands around Vaca's throat as if he were going to choke the life out of him.

That did the trick. The two guards rushed toward them, yelling curses and orders to break it up. Smoke made his move then, charging out of the hut and swinging clubbed fists in a powerful blow that landed on the back of the closest guard's neck.

That powerful blow knocked the man straight down onto his face. He dropped the Winchester as he fell. Smoke snatched up the rifle, and at the same time he brought his bootheel down, once again striking the back of the man's neck, this time with enough force to snap the guard's spine. It broke with a sharp crack.

At the same time, McKinley let go of Vaca's throat and threw himself at the legs of the other guard. He caught the man around the knees and heaved. The bandit let out a startled shout as he went over backward. The rifle slipped out of his hands and sailed through the air.

Vaca was already springing to his feet. He plucked the Winchester out of its flight and whirled toward the other huts. Several of Covarrubias's men, their attention drawn by the shouts, charged toward the escaping prisoners. When they saw that Smoke, McKinley, and Vaca were all loose, they stopped short and clawed their guns out of leather.

Smoke and Vaca opened fire while McKinley was pounding senseless the guard he had tackled.

The deadly crackle of rifle fire filled the basin. A couple of the bandits went over backward, driven off their feet by the bullets slamming into them, while others spun and toppled. But the rest managed to fight back, and Smoke was forced to drop to one knee as slugs whipped past him. He felt as much as heard the ugly wind-rip of the bullets uncomfortably close to his ears.

"Take cover!" he called to McKinley and Vaca. "Get behind the hut!"

McKinley had jerked away both revolvers from the man he had knocked out. He fired the guns toward the bandits as he ran toward the hut. A few yards away, Vaca retreated, as well, heading for the hut's other corner.

"Come on, Smoke!" McKinley shouted, as he reached the primitive structure. "We'll cover you!"

The two young men did so as Smoke surged to his feet and made a dash for safety. He ducked around the corner next to McKinley, who followed him.

Smoke pressed his shoulder against the adobe wall, thrust the Winchester's barrel around the corner, and edged out far enough to take aim as he continued pouring lead at the bandits. He had to pull back as return fire chewed chunks out of the adobe.

"Looked like they were spreading out," Smoke said. "Vaca! Can you cover the other side?"

"I have it!" Vaca responded. His rifle cracked to add punctuation to the reply.

McKinley had emptied the Colts. The bandits had taken his gun when he was captured, but they had left the cartridges in the loops on his shell belt. He plucked them out and began thumbing them into the cylinders of the guns he had taken from the guard.

"Could you tell how many of the varmints were left?" he asked as he reloaded.

"At least half a dozen," Smoke said. "Maybe more."

"So, two to one odds. Maybe three." McKinley grinned. "Those aren't bad odds."

Smoke laughed. "I've seen worse."

McKinley grew more solemn as he asked, "Do you reckon Covarrubias heard all this gunfire? Do you think he'll turn back?"

"We gave him enough time to get a good distance away before we made our move. He should have been all the way through that ravine and out into the open at the edge of the desert. The shots might have carried that far but might not have. I don't think he'll turn back, though. He's too anxious to get his hands on the ladies."

"I hope you're right," McKinley said, "even though I hate to think about him going after Virginia and Mrs. Bacon. That big bunch might be too much for us to handle if they came back, though. At least this way we've got a chance to stop him—assuming we can get out of here."

A sudden burst of rifle fire came from the other side of the hut. "They're circling around!" Vaca shouted over the racket.

McKinley whirled and leaped to the hut's rear corner on the side where he and Smoke were. Seeing bandits darting from rock to rock, he opened fire as well. Bullets slammed into the hut's rear wall and forced him back.

"Here they come from the front!" Smoke called. He snugged the Winchester's butt against his shoulder and began cranking off shots. One of the bandits charging toward the hut doubled over as a bullet punched into his guts. He stumbled forward a couple of steps and then pitched to the ground.

The next instant, Smoke felt a paralyzing impact in his hands as a slug struck the Winchester's breech with a loud *whang!* and smashed the rifle out of his grip. He took an involuntary step backward and grimaced. He was pretty sure he wasn't injured, but he was unarmed now, and the bandits would be on him in seconds.

In the heat of battle like this, they wouldn't remember Covarrubias's orders to keep him alive. They had already come close to ventilating him enough times to prove that. But no matter what happened, he would go down fighting.

No sooner had that thought flashed through his mind than he remembered something else: George Washington had once said that the most effective defense was an unexpected attack.

For Smoke Jensen, to think was to act. He lunged out from behind the hut and left his feet in a long dive that carried him alongside the man Dean McKinley had beaten into unconsciousness. The handle of the man's machete stuck out from behind the sash around his waist. Smoke grabbed it and rolled. The long, sharp, heavy blade ripped free as bullets kicked up dust mere inches from Smoke.

The bandits were almost on top of him by now—but that was their bad luck.

Smoke used the momentum of his roll to bring him back up on one knee. He thrust out the machete and the blade plunged with ease into the belly of the nearest man, who screeched in surprise and agony as he found himself run through. The machete's point stuck out from his back.

Unfortunately, Smoke didn't have time to drag the weapon free of the man's body. He had to abandon it and dive out of the way as the dying bandit toppled toward him.

Another attacker skidded to a stop and flung his rifle to his shoulder to draw a bead on Smoke. Smoke was about to try to throw himself aside when a shot blasted and the man's head jerked, blood spraying in the air from where he was hit. He folded up, dead by the time he hit the ground.

Smoke looked around, expecting to see that McKinley or Vaca had downed that bandit. Instead, he spotted a lean figure standing at the corner of the hut. Sergeant James Elphinstone Dunn lowered the rifle he held. Smoke still curled from the muzzle.

Dunn gave Smoke a nod and a grim smile. Then his knees buckled and he slumped over against the hut, sliding down the wall until he was sitting on the ground.

Smoke wanted to check on the sergeant, but shots were still exploding behind the hut. He bent and snagged a couple of revolvers from bandit holsters. He didn't have time to inspect the cylinders as he ran to join McKinley. All he could do was hope that the guns still had some live rounds in them.

As he came up beside McKinley, the young cowboy glanced over at him, then snapped another shot from one of his revolvers. Smoke saw a bandit poke his head up from behind a rock and let instinct guide his aim as he fired. The bandit's sombrero flew off his head as the slug bored through his skull. He flopped backward, out of sight.

The Winchester being wielded by Vaca cracked again and then fell silent. An eerie, echoing hush settled over the basin.

McKinley broke that hush by asking, "Are they all dead?"

"I don't know about that," Smoke said, "but none of 'em seem to have any fight left in them. You two take a look at the bodies, but be careful about it. Keep an eye on any of them who are still alive. I need to see to Sergeant Dunn."

"Sergeant Dunn!" McKinley exclaimed. "I thought Litchfield killed him."

"I did, too, but the sergeant showed up a minute ago and probably saved my life."

Smoke ran around the hut to where Dunn was still sitting

with his back braced against the wall. The sergeant was conscious and lifted his head as Smoke knelt beside him.

"Sorry I faded out there . . . for a moment," Dunn said. "I got a bit tired."

"No need to apologize," Smoke told him. He looked at the large, dark stain on Dunn's shirt and went on, "How is it you have any blood left in you, Sergeant?"

That brought a weary chuckle from Dunn. "I'm not sure. I must have had . . . an excess . . . to begin with."

Smoke ripped the sergeant's uniform blouse open and saw the bullet hole in Dunn's chest. He eased Dunn away from the wall enough to check for an exit wound in the back and found one. Quickly calculating the angles, he said, "It looks to me like the bullet hit a rib and glanced off before going on through. It must have missed your heart and the lung on that side."

"Or else I'd be . . . dead by now, eh? Do you think you can . . . bind it up?"

"That's what I'm going to do."

Smoke glanced up as a shadow fell over them. Vaca stood there.

"Only one of the bandits was still alive, and McKinley is watching him," Vaca reported. "Is the sergeant going to live?"

"He will if I have anything to say about it," Smoke replied. "Take a look around. See if you can find some tequila."

Vaca looked like he didn't care for Smoke giving him orders, but he didn't argue. He trotted off and was back in a couple of minutes with a jug that sloshed as he hurried up.

Smoke tore off a piece of his shirt, soaked it with the fiery liquor, and used it to clean both wounds. Then he splashed tequila liberally in the bullet holes. Dunn groaned and turned pale but didn't pass out.

While Smoke was binding up Dunn's torso with strips of fabric cut from a dead bandit's shirt, the sergeant distracted himself from what was going on by explaining that he had come to the ravine after everyone was gone and followed them into the basin once he had regained some of his strength.

"I've been hiding, waiting for a chance to help you fellows," he said. "I saw to my great regret that some of the men betrayed their duty and joined Captain Litchfield in working with the bandits. I'm very disappointed in them. Do you think perhaps I could have a swallow or two of that tequila, Mr. Jensen?"

"I don't think it'll hurt you," Smoke said as he pulled the makeshift bandages tight.

Dunn took the jug from Vaca, tipped it to his mouth, and downed a healthy swallow. The bracing effect it had on him was visible.

"Ah, that's much better," he said. He looked around. "What now, gentlemen?"

"Covarrubias has gone to abduct Virginia Griffin and her aunt," Vaca said. "We must stop him somehow."

Dunn looked alarmed. "Miss Virginia?" he said. "And poor Mrs. Bacon?" He started trying to get to his feet. "Help me up. We have to get after them."

"You're in no shape to ride—" Smoke began.

"Nonsense. If one of you will help me onto a horse, I'll be fine. An uncle of mine was a Bengal Lancer, you know. Triumphing over long odds and great hardship runs in the family!"

Smoke and Vaca took hold of Dunn's arms and lifted him. When he was standing, he managed to stay upright on his own.

"If you really think you can ride, the best thing you can do is head for the fort and let Colonel Griffin know what's going on," Smoke said. "Vaca, McKinley, and I are going to try to get back to Vaca's ranch and warn the folks there before Covarrubias shows up, but even if we manage to do that, we're going to need help."

"If you can do this, Sergeant, we may have a chance," Vaca added.

Dunn nodded. "Of course. That's just the job for me, lads." He frowned at Vaca. "But I don't know where your ranch is."

Smoke reached in his pocket and brought out the map McKinley had delivered to him. He held it out to Vaca and said, "Maybe you can show the sergeant on this."

"Of course!" Vaca took the map and held it so that Dunn could see it as he traced lines on it with his fingertip, indicating where in the badlands the old *rancho* was located. "If I had a pencil, I would draw it—"

"That's all right, sir," Dunn said. "I can remember. But even if you reach the ranch first, can you hold out until help arrives?"

"We'll hold out," Smoke promised.

Or die trying, he left unsaid, but that promise hung in the air, too.

CHAPTER 24

The horses Smoke and his companions had been riding when they came to the basin had been put in the corral along with the mounts of the bandits who had been left behind to guard the prisoners. Smoke caught and saddled one of those animals for Dunn and helped the sergeant climb into the saddle.

Dunn's face was pale and drawn, but it was also set in determined lines. He had tucked the map into his pocket, and he had a couple of fully loaded revolvers in the waistband of his uniform trousers.

"I don't expect you'll run into trouble," Smoke told him. "Covarrubias and the rest of his men should be in the vicinity of Vaca's ranch, and you can skirt around it."

"If I encounter any problems, I'll shoot my way through them," Dunn promised. His voice was firmer now. The tequila had given him strength. That reaction wouldn't last, of course, but they all hoped it would sustain him until he reached the fort.

Dunn turned the horse and heeled it into a lope toward the ravine. As the sergeant was riding away, McKinley came up to Smoke and Vaca and said, "I did like you told me, Smoke, and tied up that other bandit so he can work his way loose eventually."

"It would have been better to take care of him permanently," Vaca said.

"By cutting his throat or putting a bullet in his brain?" Smoke shook his head. "I've never killed a defenseless man, and I don't intend to start now. Anyway, I've got a hunch doing that would bother you more than you let on, José."

Vaca frowned and shrugged but didn't argue. Instead, he said, "We should go."

"Our horses are saddled and ready," McKinley said.

The three of them swung up onto the horses, but instead of heading toward the ravine, Vaca started in the direction of the pass at the basin's northwestern boundary.

"Hey, you're going the wrong way," McKinley called after him.

"Trust me, this way is faster," Vaca replied over his shoulder. "Covarrubias doesn't know these hills like I do."

"We did say we wanted him to take us on a shortcut," Smoke pointed out to McKinley. "We've got to trust him."

"I reckon so," McKinley said, "but that doesn't mean I have to like it."

In less than a quarter of an hour, they left the basin behind. Smoke hoped to get back here sometime and round up those stolen horses, but right now he and the others had a more pressing problem.

The hills through which they rode were quite rugged, and as Smoke studied the landscape, he didn't think it looked very promising as a shortcut. They couldn't make the same time through here that Covarrubias and his men would be able to achieve by going up the edge of the desert.

But Vaca continued angling northwest, and it wasn't long before they came to a low escarpment that dropped down to a stretch of level, hard-packed ground several hundred yards wide. From this height, Smoke could see that it extended northward as far as the range of his vision.

Vaca reined in, waved a hand at the flats, and said, "That

trail runs up the western edge of the hills and curves around until it comes out not far from my *rancho*. Once we get there, we'll have a little rugged terrain to get through, but it shouldn't take long. We'll have a chance of getting there before Covarrubias, at least."

"How in blazes do we get down there from here?" McKinley asked as he stared at the drop-off.

"There's a path." Vaca smiled. "If your nerves can stand it, that is."

McKinley bristled. "My nerves are just fine," he declared. "You just show us where that trail starts, and I'll go down it first."

"Might be better to let José go first," Smoke suggested. "He knows the ground better than we do."

"Fine," McKinley muttered. "I'm not any more afraid of heights than he is, though."

Smoke was pretty cool-nerved, too, but even he was a mite tense as the horses picked their way along a narrow ledge that angled down the escarpment's face. The path descended at a steep enough angle that the men had to lean far back in their saddles to maintain their balance. By the time they reached the bottom, their shirts were drenched with sweat, and it wasn't all because of the heat of the day, either.

Having been holding their breath a lot of the way down, they paused to drag in a few lungfuls of air. Then Vaca said with a note of urgency in his voice, "Come on. We have to go."

He rode hard to the north. Smoke and McKinley followed.

Keeping the rugged hills on their right, they followed the flats for several miles. As Vaca had said, the route curved gradually to the east. Eventually, the hills closed in around them enough that they had to slow their pace again.

Every second that dragged past was a reminder that Covarrubias could be closing in on his quarry at this very moment. Possibly as a distraction from that tense anticipation hanging over their heads, McKinley asked Vaca, "What do you call your ranch, anyway?"

"What do you mean?"

"You've got a brand, don't you?"

"No. So far, I haven't really seen the need for one."

"You're going to raise cattle, aren't you?" McKinley asked. "If you're not going to have any stock, why do you even need a ranch? Unless the rumors really are right and you're just a bandit, and that place is your hideout."

"I'm not a bandit! I do plan to raise cattle, and horses, as well. There are already cattle on the ranch, but only a small herd so far, not enough to market, so I haven't given any thought to a brand . . . My grandfather has one down in Mexico, of course. Perhaps he might allow me to use it."

McKinley made a face and shook his head. "All those Mexican brands look like a bunch of snakes squirming around in a hot skillet. If you're going to have a ranch on this side of the border, you need a regular American brand."

Vaca looked like he wanted to argue, but all he said was, "I'll consider that."

"Something like the Bar DW, maybe, for Desert Wolf. Or Box LD, if you want to use the Spanish lingo for what you call yourself. How'd you come up with that name, anyway?" McKinley laughed. "Who ups and decides he's going to call himself the Desert Wolf?"

"The farmers along the river gave me that name, and it stuck. It wasn't my idea."

"I guess that's a little better." McKinley grinned. "You like it, though, don't you?"

Vaca just scowled and didn't say anything—but he didn't deny the accuracy of McKinley's comment, either.

They rode on through the hills, having to detour now and then to get around steep, impassable ridges. Smoke asked, "How much farther is it?"

"The ranch is about a mile from here," Vaca replied.

"We're getting close enough that we might be able to hear gunfire if Covarrubias gets there ahead of us and attacks the place."

Vaca said, "That's right, and I've heard nothing so far."

By now, the sun had begun to drop lower in the western sky. It had been a long day with no food and very little water. The hardships and dangers these three men had gone through had drained them of much of their energy, but not of their determination to press on and prevent Virginia and Dorothy from falling into the hands of Juan Covarrubias and his band of brutal thieves and killers. Smoke, McKinley, and Vaca all drew on inner reserves of strength and kept moving.

Then they rode through a narrow cut that sloped upward, and when they came to the end of it, Smoke saw the red tile roof of the hacienda in the distance. At least, he assumed that's what it was, and Vaca confirmed that a moment later as all three men reined to a halt.

"That's it," he said. "The Wolf's Head, as it will be known from now on. If we had more time, I would dismount and sketch the brand in the dirt for you, Señor McKinley." He added dryly, "Just to be certain you approve."

"You don't have to do that," McKinley replied. "You're just joshing me." Then, with some reluctance, he went on. "I reckon we've gone through enough together now that you ought to just call me Dean. And I'll call you José. But not *Don* José, blast it. You're not my *patrón* or anything."

"Fine. I don't care, one way or the other."

Smoke smiled faintly and managed not to grin. Despite their bickering, their common interest in Virginia Griffin, and natural rivalry over the beautiful young woman, those two hombres were getting to be friends. Fighting side by side and back to back would do that.

They nudged their horses into motion again to start down

the slope in front of them. But the next instant, something slammed into Smoke's back and drove him forward in the saddle. A strong arm looped around his neck as he was dragged off the horse and sent crashing to the ground.

Smoke knew instinctively that some ambusher had been lurking on top of the ridge, ready to jump on anybody who rode through the cut. He didn't have to stop and think about that.

Which was good, because he was too busy fighting for his life.

The attacker must have counted on the hard landing to stun Smoke into submission, or at the very least for his weight to keep his quarry pinned to the ground.

Neither of those things happened. Smoke bucked up hard, his powerful arm, shoulder, and back muscles bunching under the faded shirt he wore. At the same time, he writhed to his left, so the knife that swept down in a would-be killing strike aimed at the back of his neck buried itself in the dirt instead.

Smoke brought his right elbow back and sunk it in the attacker's midsection. Then he reached up behind him and grabbed a double handful of the man's greasy hair. He hauled hard and brought the man toppling forward with a screech of fury, pain, and frustration.

With the weight on top of him mostly gone, Smoke broke free and rolled to his right. He stopped on his belly, pushed himself up a little with his left hand on the ground, and drew his right-hand Colt. A few feet away, the Apache warrior who had tackled him was trying to scramble upright. He still had his knife.

Smoke shot him in the head. The bullet knocked the Apache onto his back. The knife slipped from the warrior's suddenly nerveless fingers. His awkwardly bent legs twitched a couple of times as death caught up to the nerves and muscles.

As Smoke surged to his feet, he saw that McKinley and Vaca had been attacked, too. They were rolling around on the ground, wrestling with the Apaches who had tackled them and knocked them off their horses.

Smoke drew his left-hand gun, too, and was looking for an opening to shoot when the soft scuff of leather on rock from behind him alerted him to more danger.

He whirled and crouched as a rifle cracked. The bullet sizzled through the air near his head. He tipped up both Colts and fired at the figure looming above him on the ridge.

The Apache was trying to work the loading lever of the Winchester he held when one of Smoke's slugs bored into his sternum and the other caught him under the chin, coring an angled path up through his brain. Dead instantly, he pitched forward off his rocky perch.

Unfortunately, he hadn't been alone. More Apaches crowded into sight. More than likely, these were the remnants of the war party that had attacked the wagons and the cavalry escort on the way to Fort Craig. They must have been skulking around the area, waiting for another chance to strike at the hated intruders.

The three warriors who held the high ground opened fire, forcing Smoke to dive to his left as lead stormed through the space where he had been an eyeblink earlier. He triggered both Colts while he was in midair and caught a glimpse of one of the Apaches twisting around from a slug's impact.

Making a shot like that was almost entirely luck, but Smoke would take it.

He landed on his shoulder and rolled again. Dirt flew next to him as bullets plowed into the ground. He raised the right-hand Colt and blasted another Apache off the ridge.

That left just one of them. He yipped in a frenzy of hate and leaped off the ridge, aiming his body at Smoke.

It was such a desperate, unexpected move that Smoke wasn't able to get completely out of the way. The Apache's lower body slammed against his right shoulder, and once again Smoke was driven off his feet.

At the same time, the warrior tried to smash the butt of his rifle against Smoke's head. The stroke missed and struck Smoke instead on the left shoulder. That arm and hand went numb. Smoke found himself on his back on the hot ground with a kill-crazed Apache on top of him, his right arm and gun hand pinned underneath the man's weight, and his left arm unable to move.

That didn't leave him much to fight back with, but giving up wasn't an option. He jerked his head and shoulders off the ground and drove his forehead into the Apache's face, pulping the warrior's nose as blood shot out of it.

That stunned the man long enough for Smoke to pull his right arm free. He crashed the Colt against the Apache's head with all the strength he could muster. Bone crunched under the blow from the heavy revolver. Smoke hit him twice more before he sagged limply in death, his skull crushed.

Smoke shoved the corpse aside and struggled up onto his knees. The dead man's blood covered his face and had gotten into his eyes. He sleeved it away with his left arm and looked to see how McKinley and Vaca were doing.

McKinley had been taken by surprise every bit as much as Smoke. Instead of landing on his belly when he was knocked off his horse, he had come down on his knees, which caused pain to shoot up through his thighs and hips. He ignored that as best he could and tried to twist out of the grip of the man who held him.

The attacker's left arm went around his neck from behind and wrenched his head upward. That drew McKinley's neck taut. He knew what was coming next—a knife blade that would swipe across his throat, cutting deep and allowing his life's blood to spurt out in a crimson fountain.

The instant of sheer panic that caused in McKinley made him spasm upward. He jerked his head forward and loosened it enough for his chin to slip down on the arm that held him. As the attacker's sleeve rubbed against his lips, he opened his mouth and bit down as hard as he could.

The sleeve kept his teeth from ripping flesh as badly as they would have otherwise, but he sank them deep enough to bring a howl of pain from the man who had jumped him. McKinley kept his jaws locked and writhed in the grip of the man's other arm. He broke free and spun away, falling on his side.

When he looked toward the man who had attacked him, he saw an Apache warrior with a bloody left sleeve on the blue shirt he wore. The man's lips drew back from his teeth in a vicious, animal-like snarl. He brandished the knife he held and threw himself at McKinley.

The young cowboy lashed out with his left leg and drove his bootheel into the Apache's chest, knocking him away. McKinley's right hand flashed down to his hip in search of his gun but found only the empty holster. The gun had fallen out when he was knocked off his horse.

The Apache had wound up on hands and knees. McKinley sprang at him and landed on the man's back. It was his turn to wrap an arm around his enemy's neck. He clamped his left forearm in place across the Apache's throat while his right hand groped for the wrist of the hand that held the knife.

He closed his fingers around that wrist and hung on for dear life. The Apache squirmed and bucked, but McKinley didn't let go. He knew that if his grip slipped, more than likely it would be the end of him.

Straddling the lower part of the warrior's back, McKinley

grunted with effort as he hauled the upper half of the Apache's body off the ground. That bent the man's spine the wrong way, but McKinley knew he wasn't strong enough to break the Apache's back. He had to end this fight some other way.

Slowly, he began forcing the Apache's hand toward the man's body. He twisted the wrist, which caused the blade to angle upward. The warrior's struggles became more frantic as he realized what McKinley was trying to accomplish.

All he had to do was let go of the knife, and that would prevent McKinley from carrying out the plan. But the Apache stubbornly clung to the weapon. He must have believed that he could still get loose and turn the blade against McKinley.

The way McKinley had the Apache's arm twisted, though, he couldn't bring his full strength to bear against the young cowboy. Not only that, but McKinley's arm across his throat was cutting off his breath, as well. His efforts began to weaken as the lack of air took its toll.

Sensing that if he waited any longer, the Apache would drop the knife in sheer desperation, McKinley heaved on the man's arm and threw his own weight forward at the same time. That forced the Apache's torso down just as McKinley shoved the man's knife hand underneath him.

McKinley felt the warrior spasm as the blade went into his chest. He hauled the Apache up again and pushed on the man's wrist to drive the knife in deeper. The Apache sagged in McKinley's grip. The knife must have found his heart.

McKinley let go of the dead man and scrambled to his feet. He spotted his Colt lying on the ground not far away and hurried to grab it.

Like Smoke and McKinley, Vaca had been knocked off his mount by an Apache warrior who leaped onto his back from the top of the cut just as the three riders emerged from it. His face scraped the ground as he landed, and he got a mouthful of dirt and gravel. Sputtering and spitting, he writhed over onto his back before the man who had tackled him was able to pin him down.

The Apache lunged toward Vaca, his hands diving for the young grandee's throat. Vaca flung his right leg up, hooked it in front of the warrior's face, and levered the man off him. As a youngster, Vaca had wrestled with some of the vaqueros during his visits to his grandfather's ranch, and that experience proved very useful now.

Vaca leaped after his opponent but had to twist aside at the last second because the Apache came up with a knife and swept the blade toward him. Vaca avoided the slashing steel, but just barely.

He toppled sideways to the ground and landed awkwardly, which gave the warrior an opening for a kick that Vaca couldn't avoid. The man's foot, shod in a high-topped moccasin, slammed into Vaca's ribs and sent pain shooting through him as well as driving the breath from his lungs. He gasped for air and tried to get up, but his muscles didn't seem to want to work.

The Apache crowded in and aimed another kick at him. This one caught Vaca on the hip. Vaca exclaimed in pain. The warrior drew back his leg and tried to kick him in the head, but this time, Vaca finally got his hands up and grabbed the foot before the vicious blow landed. A desperate heave sent the Apache tumbling over backward.

Vaca would have liked nothing better at that moment than to lie there, catch his breath, and try to recover from the punishment he had already taken.

But he didn't have time for that, and besides, he didn't want Smoke and McKinley to see him almost kicked into submission. That would be humiliating! Pride and anger worked together to lift him to his feet.

But the warrior he'd been battling sprang up, as well, and

with considerably more strength and agility than Vaca could muster at the moment. The man leaped at him, knife raised high to strike downward.

Vaca had to grab the Apache's wrist with both hands to stop the blade's descent. The Apache hammered his left fist into the same ribs he had kicked a few moments earlier. Vaca grimaced, turned to throw a hip into the man, and pulled hard on his arm. That flipped the warrior to the ground.

Vaca tried to stomp the Apache's throat while still hanging on to his wrist. The man twisted his head and shoulders out of the way. He hooked a foot behind Vaca's left knee and jerked that leg out from under him. Vaca fell clumsily on top of him but managed to keep the knife away from his flesh.

The two men rolled over and then back, each trying to gain the upper hand. The Apache lifted a knee at Vaca's groin. Vaca writhed away from it so that the warrior's knee sank in his belly instead. That wasn't as bad as it could have been, but at the same time, it was enough to force the air out of his lungs again. The world spun crazily around him as a red haze seemed to drop over his eyes.

Through that haze, he spotted a rock about the size of two fists clenched together. It lay within reach—maybe—but it was at the outer edge of that reach. Vaca would have to let go of the Apache's wrist with one hand to make a try for the rock.

That seemed to be his only option. He had realized already that his revolver was no longer in its holster. Earlier, he had taken the thong off the hammer because he knew they were getting close to the hacienda, but as it turned out, that had been the wrong thing to do. The gun had slipped away from him during the fight.

He had to make the try. Throwing all the strength he had into his left arm, he held off the knife with it as he let go with his right hand and lunged for the rock. He felt his grip slipping as his fingers closed around the rough stone chunk.

Whipping that arm around, he crashed the rock against the Apache's head just as the warrior's knife hand tore loose and the blade flashed toward Vaca's face.

Vaca felt steel slither along his left cheek, but the knife didn't penetrate or slice into his face. Bone crunched under the rock's impact. Vaca jerked it back and hit the man again, and then again. The Apache's arms fell loosely to his sides and the knife slipped out of his hand.

After the third blow, the warrior's head was misshapen enough that it was obvious his skull was crushed and he was dead. Panting, Vaca let the blood-smeared stone fall from his hand and pushed himself up. He raised his head, looked around dazedly, and saw Smoke and McKinley watching him with guns in their hands, ready to step in if they had to.

The rest of the Apaches were scattered around the area, all dead.

McKinley stepped over to Vaca and extended a hand to him. "Are you hurt?" he asked.

Vaca shook his head as he clasped McKinley's hand. "Not really. He landed a few kicks. I'll be stiff and sore tomorrow."

"I know the feeling," McKinley said, as he helped Vaca to his feet. "Those fellas put up a heck of a fight." He looked at Smoke. "I reckon they must have been what was left from that bunch the other day?"

"That's how I figure it," Smoke replied. "There must not have been any more besides the ones who jumped us, after all."

"And they lingered in the area to see what other mischief they could get up to."

Smoke nodded. "That's the only explanation that makes sense."

"They're dead now," Vaca snapped, "and they may have caused plenty of mischief by delaying us. Covarrubias could already be at the ranch!"

Smoke listened intently, but a hot, quiet stillness lay over the late afternoon.

"Still no shooting," he said.

"We can hope we made it in time," McKinley said.

"We can do more than hope," Vaca said. "Let's take their guns, get our horses, and go!"

Chapter 25

The horses had been spooked somewhat from the racket of the fight and the smells of blood and powder smoke, but they hadn't drifted far off. It took the three men only a few minutes to catch them, and then once again they were on their way to the ranch newly dubbed the Wolf's Head.

They approached the hacienda from the rear, dismounting and proceeding on foot when Vaca said they were within a quarter mile of the corrals and barn. The trail ran among some large boulders and outcroppings of rock, and they had just stepped around one such massive stone slab when a rifle barrel thrust into view and the muzzle pressed against McKinley's head.

The tall, lean vaquero named Hector growled, "I knew fate would bring you back to me, gringo, so I can avenge the great injustice you did to me!"

On the other side of the trail, Hector's burly bearded amigo Lupe stepped out from behind a boulder and pointed a revolver at Smoke.

"We have them, Don José," he said triumphantly. "You are free now!"

"I was free to start with," Vaca told his men. "Don't you see that I'm armed just as they are? Señor Jensen and Señor McKinley are on our side now."

Hector's thin lips twisted in a snarl. "They are friends? Not your captors?"

"They are allies," Vaca said. "We have the same enemy—Juan Covarrubias!"

"Covarrubias!" Lupe said. "That dog! What evil is he up to now, *patrón*?"

"The last we know of him, he was on his way here to abduct Señorita Griffin and Señora Bacon. You have seen no sign of him?"

With obvious reluctance and a last hostile glare directed at McKinley, Hector lowered his rifle and turned to Vaca.

"He has not been here," Hector said. "All is peaceful."

Vaca frowned at him. "I thought I told the two of you to stay with the ladies and protect them with your lives."

"I assure you, they are well guarded, Don José. One of the men said he thought he spotted some riders approaching through these hills, so Lupe and I left several men watching over the *señorita* and her *tía*, and came out here to be certain the *rancho* was not under attack from behind."

Smoke said, "Something must have happened to delay Covarrubias. We ought to get the ladies and head for the fort with them. Could be we'll run into a detail heading this way if Sergeant Dunn was able to get there and warn the colonel."

Vaca thought about it for a moment and then nodded. "That's a good idea," he said. "Lupe, Hector, you'll ride with us, and we'll take some of the other men—"

He stopped short and lifted his head to listen intently as the sound of gunshots broke the late-afternoon hush. The others all tensed, as well.

"No!" Vaca cried. "We are too late!"

"Maybe not," Smoke said. "Come on!"

The five men ran toward the hacienda. Vaca led the way, his fear over what might happen to Virginia lending him speed. But Smoke and McKinley were close behind him, then Hector, and finally Lupe, puffing hard, bringing up the rear.

They dashed between the corrals and past the barn. Nothing was moving back here, but gunfire still crackled fiercely from the front of the hacienda. Covarrubias and his bandits had arrived, Smoke knew, with reinforcements in the form of those renegade cavalry troopers.

Suddenly, when Smoke and the others were still fifty yards from the rear wall, a handful of riders swept around the corner. The big sombreros worn by the horsemen told Smoke they were part of Covarrubias's gang, circling the hacienda to launch a rear assault on the place.

They probably would have succeeded, too, if not for the unexpected opposition they found here.

Smoke stopped and raised his rifle to his shoulder. The Winchester already had a round in the chamber, so he settled the sights on one of the riders and squeezed the trigger. The rifle cracked and the bandit Smoke had targeted flung his arms out to the sides and somersaulted backward out of the saddle.

McKinley, Vaca, and the two vaqueros began shooting, as well, slamming lead at the attackers. The bandits might have been surprised to find such fierce defenders back here, but they immediately returned the fire, yelling wildly as they jerked revolvers from holsters and triggered the guns.

They shot hurriedly, though, and the bullets either flew wide of Smoke and his companions, sailed harmlessly overhead, or kicked up dust in front of them.

The defenders were much more accurate. Vaca drilled one of the bandits, and McKinley downed another. One of Hector's bullets struck a galloping horse, and the unfortunate animal crumpled to the ground at full speed, throwing its rider over its head. The man crashed to the ground. Momentum turned him over a couple of times, and when he tried to get up, he ran right into a fatal slug from Smoke's rifle.

Screaming in hate, the fifth and final rider charged straight at the five men. Another volley rang out, and the bandit lifted in the saddle, shredded by multiple bullets. After bouncing once when he hit the ground, he lay there like a limp, bloody bundle of rags.

As the echoes of the shots rolled away over the hills behind them, the sounds of battle continued in front of the hacienda. Vaca cast a desperate glance at the other men and then broke into a run again. They followed closely behind him.

As they neared the house, a shot blasted from one of the rifle slits in the wall around the hacienda. The bullet kicked up dirt and gravel beside Vaca's feet. He skidded to a stop and shouted, "Hold your fire! Hold your fire!"

Inside the wall, someone yelled, "It's Don José!"

"Open the gate!" Vaca ordered as he hurried forward again.

The small, sturdy gate swung open by the time the group reached it. A couple of vaqueros holding rifles waited inside, wide-eyed with excitement.

"A thousand pardons, Don José!" one of them cried. "We thought at first you were part of that band of devils attacking us!"

"That's Juan Covarrubias and his men," Vaca explained as he entered the compound with Smoke, McKinley, Hector, and Lupe right behind him. "Is Señorita Griffin all right?"

One of the men shut the gate and reached for the heavy bar that would hold it closed. The other vaquero said, "She and her aunt are in the courtyard with four men to guard them. That dog of a Covarrubias will never reach them!"

"How many men are defending the front wall?"

The vaqueros glanced at each other and looked worried.

"There were three left alive when we saw the riders circling around and knew they were going to attack back here, too," one of the men answered. "We came to fight them off if we could."

Vaca groaned. "Three men to hold off thirty!"

The vaqueros looked even more dismayed. "We are outnumbered by that much?" one of them asked.

"We will never surrender!" Vaca declared. "The two of you, stay here in case Covarrubias tries to send more men around this way. Hector, Lupe, come with me! We will meet them at the wall!"

"We're coming, too," McKinley said.

"This is our fight as well as yours," Smoke added quietly.

Vaca nodded. "My thanks to you both," he said. "But now, there is no time to waste!"

He ran to an arched walkway in the middle of the house's rear wing. Normally, it would be closed off by a wrought iron gate, but that gate stood open at the moment. Vaca hurried through the passage with his four companions close behind him. They came out in the house's central courtyard.

Virginia and Dorothy were there, along with Estella and the four vaqueros guarding them. Virginia saw Vaca and cried, "José!" She ran to him and threw herself into his welcoming embrace.

Smoke saw McKinley's mouth tighten at that sight, but then a look of resignation came over the young cowboy's face. He glanced at Smoke, grinned, and shrugged his shoulders.

"A smart fella's got to know when he's beat," he said. "Besides, José's not that bad an hombre once you get to know him. I suppose Virginia could do a lot worse."

"He's a mite on the hotheaded side," Smoke allowed, "and I'm not sure he'll ever make a go of this ranch—but he seems to have his good qualities, too."

Vaca continued holding Virginia with one arm while he used the other hand to signal to Hector and Lupe, telling them to join the men defending the front wall.

Dorothy Bacon gave them a weary smile as she came up to Smoke.

"It's good to see you again, Mr. Jensen," she said. "I wasn't sure if help would arrive or not. Things don't seem to be going too well around here."

"We're going to see if we can change that," Smoke said. "Are you and Miss Griffin all right?"

"Vingie and I are fine. José's men are very devoted to him. He told them to protect us, and I feel like they would lay down their lives to do so."

"I'm sure they would." Smoke paused, and then a grim note came into his voice as he went on. "The problem is what happens when all of them are dead and you don't have anybody left to defend you."

"If it ever comes to that, I'm prepared," Dorothy said quietly. She put a hand on a pocket in her dress where a lump was visible. "There are six rounds in this pistol. One for Vingie, four for those dastardly bandits—and one for me." She smiled again. "But now that you're here, that may not be necessary."

Smoke returned the nod she gave him. He would do everything in his power to make sure the faith in him she expressed wasn't misplaced.

Vaca gave Virginia a quick kiss, then ran toward the passage that led to the front of the house. Smoke and McKinley were right behind him. When they emerged into the small open area between the house and the wall, Smoke saw three men kneeling on a parapet at the top of the wall, firing rifles. Hector and Lupe stood at rifle slits and added their efforts to the defense.

As Vaca led them toward the wooden steps up to the parapet, one of the defenders there reeled back, gurgling as blood spurted from a bullet-torn throat. He toppled off and landed inside the wall as life ebbed from him.

Unfortunately, he wasn't the only one who had fallen to Covarrubias's assault. Two men lay sprawled on the parapet, dead or mortally wounded, and two more were bloody heaps where they had fallen off the defensive works after being wounded.

Vaca bounded up the steps and raced to the parapet in a crouching run. He dropped to one knee, thrust his Winchester over the top of the wall, and began firing.

Smoke and McKinley took places on the parapet, too, spreading out so they could cover a bigger field of fire. Using the rifle slits in the wall would have been safer, but they could see their enemies better from up here.

The approach directly in front of the hacienda was fairly flat and open, but slopes rose on both sides. There was plenty of cover on those slopes in the form of rocks, gullies, and clumps of scrub brush that might not stop a bullet but could hide gunmen concealed behind them.

A gray haze of powder smoke hung over the scene, broken by spurts of orange muzzle flame, as the attackers laid siege to the sturdily built old hacienda.

Vaca allowed his raging emotions to get the best of him and fired his Winchester as fast as he could work the rifle's loading lever. Smoke and McKinley took a more methodical approach. Smoke used those muzzle flashes as targets, and after he had squeezed off a couple of rounds, the sight of a man rolling bonelessly out from behind a rock rewarded his efforts. The man came to rest on his back and didn't move again.

A few yards away, another bandit staggered into the open and pressed both hands to his chest. He pitched forward onto his face and lay still.

"I got one, too!" McKinley called to Smoke, as he levered his rifle. A cocky, fighting grin stretched across the young cowboy's face.

A second later, he yelped and ducked, then lifted a hand to his right ear. The fingers came away smeared with red.

"One of the varmints nicked me, doggone it!"

"Keep your head down," Smoke cautioned, "or you'll lose more than a little bit of ear."

Even as he spoke, he was peering over his rifle's sights, lining up another target. When the rifle cracked and bucked against his shoulder, a sombrero leaped high above some brush, spinning from the bullet that had torn through it. Smoke didn't know if the slug had gone through a bandit's head at the same time as it knocked the sombrero off, but no more shots originated from that thorny growth.

Vaca's rifle clicked on empty. Grimacing, he turned and slid down to a seated position, with his back pressed against the wall. His head was just under the top of it, safe for the moment. He reached in his pocket, dug out several more rounds, and thumbed them into the repeater.

"How are you holding out for cartridges?" he called to Smoke.

"Not many left," Smoke answered.

"Me, neither," McKinley put in.

"There should be more ammunition in the house," Vaca said. "I can send a man for it—"

"No time for that," Smoke said. The bandits' guns had fallen silent suddenly, and in that unexpected hush, he heard Juan Covarrubias bellowing orders in Spanish. "I reckon Covarrubias is out of patience, and—here they come now!"

A dozen bandits burst out from where they had taken cover and charged toward the wall, firing as fast as they could. That storm of lead forced the defenders on the parapet to stay down. Hector and Lupe were able to continue firing from the rifle slits, but there was only so much they could do. A couple of attackers stumbled and fell, but two more instantly leaped up to take their place.

Hector reeled back from his position, dropped his rifle, and clapped his left hand to his bleeding right arm. He had been hit badly enough to knock him out of the fight.

Lupe glanced over his shoulder at his friend, yelled, "Hector!" and clearly wanted to go to the lean vaquero's aid, but the big man's devotion to his *patrón* kept him where he was, blasting shots through the narrow opening in front of him.

Then the hammer of his Winchester clicked on empty, and there was no time to reload. Lupe dropped the rifle and turned to run to Hector's side.

"Get him in the house!" Vaca ordered from the parapet.

Lupe barely slowed down as he bent to scoop Hector up in his brawny arms. Then he loped toward the hacienda with his amigo draped over his shoulder.

When the shooting paused for a second, Smoke rose up and emptied his Winchester into the attackers, firing swiftly as he swung the barrel from left to right. Two of the bandits went down, the bullets bowling them over like ninepins.

Farther down the parapet, McKinley followed Smoke's example and fired his rifle until it ran dry. To Smoke's right, Vaca did the same thing. Again, some of Covarrubias's men fell—but the attack continued unabated as more of the bandits joined in.

Smoke hadn't caught sight of Covarrubias himself. The bandit boss was probably hanging back, content to let his followers do the dirty work and risk their lives.

"Fall back!" Vaca called to Smoke and McKinley. "Fall back into the hacienda!"

That was all they could do, Smoke knew. In the past, Preacher had told him about how the defenders of the Alamo had fought on the parapets of the wall around the old mission, battling the dictator Santa Anna's army hand to hand, using their empty rifles as clubs. That effort, valiant though it had been, had ended in death and defeat for the Texans.

Trying to stop Covarrubias's men here at the wall would have the same result.

But before Smoke retreated, he dropped the empty Winchester and drew both Colts from leather. Daring the bullets scything through the air above the wall, he stood up and sprayed slugs through the front rank of bandits, knocking down several more of them as gun smoke and flame gushed from the muzzles of the thundering revolvers.

Then he pouched the irons, turned, and leaped off the parapet, joining McKinley and Vaca in the desperate retreat.

As Smoke landed lithely on the ground, he heard something smash against the gate. Had they brought up some sort of battering ram, or was that simply the shoulders of a dozen kill-crazy *bandidos* crashing into the barrier?

He didn't know, and it didn't matter. The three men raced through the arched opening in the hacienda's adobe wall. Vaca paused long enough to pull the wrought iron gate closed and snap the padlock on it, but Smoke knew that wouldn't hold the bandits for long. Bullets would soon smash that lock and open the way for them to continue their onslaught.

The defenders would make their last stand in the courtyard.

CHAPTER 26

When Smoke reached the courtyard, he saw that Virginia was already in Vaca's arms. He cradled her close, rested a hand on her auburn hair, and murmured words to her that no one else needed to hear.

Smoke glanced at Dorothy Bacon. The older woman was pale and looked frightened, but she summoned up a smile when she saw Smoke looking at her and reached down to rest a hand on the pocket where her pistol waited if it were needed.

And things were looking mighty like it would be.

But Smoke didn't have an ounce of give-up in him. He'd been behind the door when the Good Lord passed out that tendency—and then the Creator had stubbed His toe when he was adding stubbornness to the recipe that was Smoke Jensen.

With his natural instinct for command, he said to Dorothy, "Ma'am, you and your niece had better wait in that little niche over there." He pointed to the place he meant at the rear of the courtyard. It was a recessed doorway leading to one of the chambers in the back part of the hacienda. "Lupe, you and Hector go with them and protect them."

"But Hector is wounded," Lupe protested.

"I can fire a *pistola* with my left hand," Hector snarled. "Just let me have a gun, and give me a shot at that pig, Covarrubias!"

One of the vaqueros who had been guarding the women handed a revolver to Hector, who took it with his left hand as a savage grin twisted his wolfish features. Blood still dripped from the fingers of his dangling right hand as he and Lupe went with Virginia and Dorothy to the niche that would be their last refuge.

Smoke and McKinley reloaded their Colts with the rounds from the loops on their shell belts. Both had enough bullets to fill the cylinders, but that was all. There was no time to look for more ammunition in the house, because at that moment, the gate in the front wall burst open from the steady pounding it had received.

Vaca ran into the passage through the front part of the hacienda and fired through the openings in the interior gate at the attackers who poured into the compound. Two of the vaqueros joined him in taking the fight to the bandits.

But in less than a minute, one of those men staggered and then doubled over as he was shot in the belly. He collapsed, and Vaca waved the other man back. They ran through the passage into the courtyard and split up, using the walls for cover and then firing back around the corners.

Smoke and McKinley knelt beside the low, crumbling circular wall around the dry fountain in the center of the courtyard. From there they had straight shots through the passage at the bandits who approached the interior gate. Several of Covarrubias's men started forward, only to be driven back by the lethal gunfire. One of them fell, kicked spasmodically for a few seconds, and then didn't move again.

"We're whittling them down!" McKinley called to Smoke.

That was true, but they weren't doing it fast enough, Smoke knew. They were going to run out of bullets soon.

Then they had to duck for cover behind the fountain wall as the attackers cleared a path for several riflemen to concentrate their fire on the defenders. Bullets chewed steadily at the low wall. They couldn't penetrate, but Smoke and McKinley were pinned down here, unable to return the fire.

As he had been diving for shelter, Smoke had caught a glimpse of a man crawling forward on his belly, obviously bound for the gate as the riflemen fired above him. A moment later, Smoke heard the dull, booming reports of a handgun, accompanied by the clanging sound of bullets striking metal. Then a triumphant shout went up from the bandits, and Smoke knew the man had succeeded in shooting the lock off the gate.

A second later, that was confirmed by the crash of the iron gate being slammed open. Boot soles slapped rapidly on the paving stones inside the passage as men charged the courtyard.

The attackers spilled into the open area in the center of the hacienda. What had been a cool, peaceful haven from the heat of the surrounding badlands became a killing ground instead. The sharp tang of powder smoke stung eyes and noses as clouds of the stuff rolled through the courtyard. Flashes of orange flame split the gathering gloom of twilight.

José Antonio Vaca seemed to be everywhere at once, darting back and forth among his enemies and striking with the fierce swiftness of a desert wolf. When his gun was empty, he hurled it into the face of a bandit and followed it with the stroke of a knife across the villain's throat. He whirled and, moving almost too fast for the eye to follow in the smoke and shadows, stabbed two more of Covarrubias's men.

The vaqueros who were still on their feet fought hand to hand, as well, emptying their guns and then battling with knives and fists until the sheer numbers of their foes carried them to the ground, where they died with the bodies of their enemies heaped around them.

Some of the bandits broke away from the others and went

for the niche where the women were. Hector and Lupe fired their guns as long as their ammunition held out, then, like their amigos, fought on with what they had.

Even though Hector clutched his knife in his left hand, the blade danced back and forth, opening a vein here, plunging into an unwashed body there, as he gave ground only inches at a time.

Lupe preferred to fight with his bare hands, roaring out his defiance as his great fists smashed skulls and broke ribs. He grabbed hold of one bandit, heaved the futilely struggling man above his head, and flung him with devastating force into three of his fellows. All of them sprawled on the ground, blocking the attack on the niche for the moment.

Then Dorothy Bacon stepped up, thrusting her arm between Hector and Lupe. The little pistol in her hand barked once, twice, three times, and at each report, a bandit's head jerked as a bullet bored into it. Dorothy hadn't used a bullet on Virginia after all, deciding in the heat of battle that she would rather spend them on her enemies.

Smoke and McKinley held their ground beside the fountain. Vaca retreated to join them, and shoulder to shoulder, they fought off the bandits as long as they could. Smoke sensed that the enemy force was shrinking. Covarrubias threw his men forward callously, not caring how many of them died to achieve his ends. Smoke tried to oblige, shedding so much blood with his knife that his shirt sleeve was crimson to the elbow.

Then Juan Covarrubias himself came limping through the swirling clouds of powder smoke. Maybe he wasn't afraid after all but had just been waiting for his moment. He stepped up onto the low, wide fountain wall with a gun in each hand and towered over the melee around him. One of the guns blasted and Vaca cried out as he toppled backward. McKinley leaped to catch the young grandee and knelt there supporting the wounded Vaca.

Covarrubias loomed above them, ready to smash them to bloody rags with the guns in his hands.

Nearby, Smoke sunk his knife into the chest of a bandit and tried to pull it free, but the blade grated and caught on a rib. As the dead man fell, his collapse wrenched the knife out of Smoke's hand. He saw Covarrubias about to kill McKinley and Vaca but had nothing with which to strike at the bandit boss.

Nothing except his bare hands, and he was about to leap in front of the other two and try to get his hands on Covarrubias when he heard someone shout his name.

"Mr. Jensen!"

Smoke's head whipped around. He saw something sailing through the air toward him—*a cavalry saber!*

His hand flashed up and closed around the saber's grip. In a smooth continuation of the same move, he turned and thrust up and out. The saber went into Covarrubias's body under his right arm and drove deep, cleaving ribs, skewering the right lung, and finally splitting the evil heart, stopping it forever.

Covarrubias lived just long enough for his eyes to open wide in horror and amazement, and then he toppled backward into the dry fountain, crashing down like a falling tree. His fingers clenched on the triggers of both guns, causing them to roar, but by then the barrels were aimed at the darkening sky and the bullets soared away harmlessly.

An instant later, Smoke realized he heard the sharp notes of a bugle being blown. A man stepped up and gripped his arm. Smoke looked over at the man and said, "You tossed me that saber just in time, Sergeant."

Sergeant James Elphinstone Dunn grinned, moving stiffly because of the bandages wrapped heavily around his chest under a fresh uniform blouse.

"Aye, that I did. And it appears that we arrived at a fortuitous moment, as well."

That was the truth. The courtyard was filled now with fighting men in uniform, only these were the loyal troopers from Fort Craig, not the men who had turned renegade because of Captain Litchfield's promises of wealth. The 9th Cavalry, under the command of Colonel Andrew Griffin himself, made short work of the remaining bandits.

Griffin bellowed, "Virginia! Where are you?"

She burst out of the niche and ran to him. They hugged each other fiercely for a moment, and then Virginia exclaimed, "José! Where's José?"

"Over here," McKinley called to her.

He was still kneeling and holding Vaca, who sat propped against him, pale and drawn but conscious. Smoke saw the large bloodstain on the young man's shirt but couldn't be sure just how badly Vaca was wounded. Some injuries bled a lot but weren't life-threatening, while others barely seeped any crimson but proved fatal.

Virginia cried out and dropped to her knees beside Vaca, who summoned up a smile and assured her that he would be all right. Colonel Griffin embraced his sister Dorothy and made sure that she wasn't hurt.

Smoke went to check on Hector and Lupe. They were wounded but alive. None of Vaca's other men had made it.

But all of the bandits were dead, too, including Covarrubias himself. His intended revolution had come to an ignominious end, Smoke thought as he paused by the fountain to look down at the body of the dead bandit boss.

McKinley stepped up beside him and said, "You killed that skunk just in time, Smoke. Another second and Vaca and I would've been done for."

"How's he doing?"

McKinley grunted and said, "He'll be all right if Vingie has anything to say about it—and I reckon she does. That girl's kind of like a force of nature when it comes to getting what she wants."

"I know what you mean," Smoke said, thinking of Sally. "I married one like that myself."

And it would be mighty good to get home to her.

"Are you sure about this, Dean?" Smoke asked a couple of days later, as he got ready to mount up. They were back at Fort Craig, and Smoke had already said his goodbyes to Colonel Griffin, Sergeants Dunn and O'Malley, Dorothy Bacon, Virginia Griffin—and José Antonio Vaca, who was recuperating well in the post hospital.

Dean McKinley thumbed back his hat and said, "Yeah, I think I'm doing the right thing. Like I said, ol' José's a pretty good hombre once you get to know him, and with him being laid up for a spell, he'll need some help keeping the Wolf's Head going."

"That ranch is never going to make it, you know. Not right there on the edge of the Jornada del Muerto."

"Maybe not, but he's stubborn enough that it just might. Shoot, he won me over, didn't he? Not to mention Vingie."

Smoke looked at the young cowboy and asked, "Is that going to be a problem? You being around the two of them, I mean."

McKinley shook his head. "No, I don't think so. I'm ready to accept whatever Vingie wants and be happy for her. Of course, if she was to change her mind one of these days . . . No, never mind. I don't plan on stirring up any trouble."

Smoke hoped McKinley was telling the truth about that.

"Well, you know you're welcome back at the Sugarloaf anytime you want to ride up that way again," he said. "And I'm mighty obliged to you for helping round up those horses so I could turn 'em over to the army and finally get paid for them."

"I was happy to do it, and I'm glad you're going to be selling more mounts to the army, Smoke. It'll be good to see you every time you get down this way with a fresh batch."

"I might send Pearlie with the next herd," Smoke said with a grin. "These parts are a little too hot and dry for me. I've gotten used to the high country. But I'll be back one of these days, you can count on that."

The two of them shook hands, and Smoke swung up into the saddle. He raised a hand in farewell and turned his horse toward the gate.

"Hey, Smoke!" McKinley called after him.

Smoke paused and looked back.

"You think one of those scribblers, as you call 'em, will ever write a dime novel about this Desert Wolf ruckus?"

Smoke laughed. "I reckon you can bet a hat on it," he said, and then he rode away, heading north toward home.

TURN THE PAGE FOR AN EXCITING PREVIEW!

THE THREE WISE MEN OF THE WEST—JOHNSTONE STYLE.

The legendary trio of Preacher, Audie, and Nighthawk team up for a Christmas Eve showdown with the not-so-jolly night raider Forkbeard—in this action-packed holiday tale from the bestselling Johnstones. . . .

'Tis the season for family and friends to get together—even for rugged mountain men like Preacher and his buddies. This year, they're planning to visit an old friend, Tall Dog, a half-Crow, half-Viking warrior who lives in the north woods of Canada. Tall Dog's wife is expecting a baby, and everyone's looking forward to the blessed event. What they aren't looking forward to is a treacherous trek through the snow-covered woods—or the unsavory characters who roam there. Preacher figures they can't possibly be more dangerous than what he's seen in the wilds of the American frontier. But he's wrong.

These woods are haunted—by a devilish Dane known as Forkbeard.

He might have a beard like the legendary Saint Nicholas, but Forkbeard is the polar opposite of the jolly gift-giver. He's a deranged madman who raids villages with his merciless tribe of marauders to avenge his ancestors—or so he says. As far as Preacher can tell, the man is just a low-life thief who terrorizes innocent families. But there appears to be more to the story. According to legend, there's a treasure trove of Viking artifacts at stake, and Forkbeard will do anything to claim them.

This Christmas Eve, Preacher and his friends won't be opening presents. They'll be closing ranks on a crazed bearded killer—in the ultimate holiday showdown.

CHAPTER 1

When Preacher heard the faint noise in the brush behind him, he moved his hand just enough to close his fingers around the wooden handle of the big hunting knife tucked behind his belt in a fringed sheath.

The campfire in front of him crackled merrily, and Audie was talking, as Audie often was. Whoever was sneaking up behind Preacher probably thought that would be enough to cover up any slight sounds he might make.

The mountain man's hearing was incredibly keen, however, and sensitive enough to pick out the things that shouldn't be there.

Like the crack, almost too quiet to hear, of a twig breaking under somebody's foot.

Preacher eased the blade an inch or so out of its sheath. Whoever was skulking around, they were going to find a surprise waiting for them: durned near a foot of cold steel.

"And then," Audie said, leaning forward and gesturing as he spoke across the flames to the giant Crow warrior known as Nighthawk, "and this is the amusing part . . . and then he said, 'If I had known you were going to take offense, I would have compared him to Epictetus instead of Marcus Aurelius!' "

Audie slapped his thigh in sheer glee as he rocked back and forth on the log where he sat.

Nighthawk nodded slowly and solemnly and said, "Umm."

"Yes, indeed, the entire room erupted in peals of hilarity, I tell you. It took a long time for Wentworth to recover from those bons mots I assure you."

Another twig snapped behind Preacher, closer this time. He hadn't been looking into the flames to start with. That was a mighty good way for a man to ruin his night vision and get himself killed. But as soon as he had heard somebody sneaking up on him, he had peered intently at the darkest shadow he could find to make his eyes adjust even more. He would be able to see just fine once the varmint got around to making his move.

Which, in a way, Preacher hoped would be soon. Otherwise, Audie was liable to start on another one of those stories that made just about as much sense as a bunch of toad frogs playing fiddles and singing and dancing.

Audie finally stopped laughing at his own story. He dabbed away tears of amusement with his left hand.

"I really shouldn't be making sport of Wentworth like this," he said. "The poor fellow tried to fit in with the rest of the faculty, he really did— Get down, Preacher!"

Preacher threw himself to his left. As he came off the log, he slid the knife from its sheath.

A few feet away, Audie bolted upright to his full height of a little less than four feet and drew a flintlock pistol from behind his belt in the same movement. He thrust the pistol toward the thick brush behind where Preacher had been sitting and pulled the trigger.

The pistol boomed as smoke and flame gushed from its muzzle. The Indian who had burst out of the brush with a tomahawk held high, ready to sweep down and cleave Preacher's skull, stopped short and rocked back as the heavy lead ball plowed into his chest.

The attacker wasn't alone. Another Indian, screeching in anger, crashed out of the brush and brandished a tomahawk as well.

Preacher had used the momentum of his dive to roll over and surge back to his feet. He was ready to take on the second would-be killer. As the tomahawk swept down at him, Preacher blocked the stroke with his left forearm and drove the knife under the Indian's chin into his throat.

The blade grated on the man's spine, but that didn't slow it down. The point ripped out the back of the Indian's neck.

Nighthawk was up, too, towering over everyone with his great height. He plunged into the brush, and a great disturbance followed with the branches jerking and waving back and forth.

When he backed into the open, he had hold of two buckskin-clad warriors. He gripped each man by the neck from behind, an indication that he had caught them as they turned and tried to flee.

As Nighthawk stepped into the circle of firelight, Preacher saw that the moccasin-shod feet of the men the giant Crow had hold of dangled several inches off the ground. Nighthawk growled and shook one of them like a dog with a rat, jerking the man's body one way and then the other so forcefully that his neck broke with an audible crack.

Nighthawk might have dealt with the fourth attacker the same way, but Preacher stopped him by saying, "Hold on there, old son. Don't kill the varmint just yet."

Nighthawk grunted and swung around so that Preacher could see the face of the man the huge warrior held. He studied the Indian's clothing and hair and said, "Ree."

That was a common nickname among mountain men for the Arikara, one of the tribes that lived in these parts.

"I agree," Audie said. "But that's puzzling because I was under the impression the Arikara are friendly."

"They might've been, but Indians are notional folks. Ain't that right, Nighthawk?"

Nighthawk rolled his eyes, nodded emphatically, and said, "Umm."

"Yes, I suppose if anyone has a right to agree with that, it's you," Audie said to his old friend.

Preacher pointed to the ground and told Nighthawk, "Put him down."

The towering warrior growled again, gave his captive a hard shake for good measure, and dropped him to the dirt next to the fire.

He tossed the dead man a few yards away with the callous disregard of a child throwing aside a toy he was bored with.

Preacher knelt next to the still-living Arikara warrior, held the knife to his throat, and asked, "How come you and your pards jumped us, mister? Have the Ree gone on the warpath?"

The warrior just glared up at him as if daring Preacher to go ahead and cut his throat. He didn't answer the mountain man's questions.

Audie was examining the bodies of the men he and Preacher had killed. He looked up and said, "These men are Mandan, not Arikara."

"They're kinfolks, ain't they? Or at least the Arikara, Mandan, and Hidatsa all get along together."

"Indeed, but it's not that common for warriors of the different tribes to be traveling together in a small group such as this. It would be different if a great many of them from different bands had gathered to fight a common enemy—for example, the Sioux."

"What are you gettin' at?"

"I suspect that they're outcasts. Renegades, if you will, forced to leave their respective villages for some reason. They formed an alliance to enhance their chances for survival."

"Renegades," Preacher mused. "I reckon that could be the explanation, all right. They figured they'd kill us and take our supplies and horses."

The prisoner spat angry words in his native tongue. Preacher was fluent in the Arikara language and understood the hate-filled diatribe.

"Yeah, I understand, you're an unfriendly varmint. I reckon the smartest thing for me to do would be to go ahead and cut your throat. Lucky for you I'm in a friendly mood, what with it comin' up on Christmas and all."

Chapter 2

The approaching Yuletide season was, in fact, the reason Preacher and his friends found themselves here in the upper reaches of unorganized territory not far from the border of the British provinces of North America.

This was sparsely settled country, five hundred miles west of the Great Lakes, populated mostly by Indians, fur trappers, and a few hardy entrepreneurs who had established trading posts along the many rivers and streams.

The normal base of operations for Preacher, Audie, and Nighthawk was farther west in the Rocky Mountains, where for many years they had been trapping beaver and other fur-bearing animals.

But they had been in this part of the country before, most recently a couple of years earlier, when they had journeyed north across the border to the village of Skarkavik, which had settled on the shores of a huge lake by Norwegian immigrants who chose to live like their Viking ancestors.

That trip had been in response to a summons for help from another friend of Preacher's, the grandfather of Bjorn Gunnarson, a strapping half-Norwegian, half-Crow warrior who usually went by the name Tall Dog.

After helping save Skarkavik from an evil timber baron bent on taking over the area, Tall Dog had decided to remain at the village with his grandfather while Preacher, Audie, and Nighthawk returned to their usual mountain haunts.

A few weeks earlier, the three friends had been at Dutch Charley's Trading Post, a long way southwest of here, when Audie had said, "We ought to go see Bjorn and celebrate Christmas with him."

They were sitting at a table near the fireplace where flames crackled and danced, warming the big, low-ceilinged room. This half of the building was a tavern, while the other side served as the trading post and general mercantile.

Preacher leaned back in his chair, stretched out his long legs, and crossed them at the ankle. He picked up the mug of beer Dutch Charley Hennenberger had drawn for him a few minutes earlier and took a sip from it, then used the back of his other hand to wipe foam from the gray-shot mustache that drooped over his wide mouth.

"I didn't know that Vikings celebrated Christmas," he said.

Audie had placed a box on his chair so he could sit on it and reach the table, where a glass of mulled wine was in front of him. He had spent many years as a professor at a noted university back east before following a longtime dream and heading west to become a mountain man. Even though he had fit in quite well with the rough frontier life, his educated background gave him more refined tastes, which he indulged now and then.

"Their winter celebration is known as Yule," he said, "but it shares numerous traditions with our Christmas. Or rather, our Christmas traditions borrow heavily from Yule, which began as a pagan festival centered around their harsh northern pantheon. No doubt that borrowing of traditions came about because of the Viking presence in what became England, where many of them decided to settle and become farmers instead of continuing their raiding, plundering ways. And once there, as you know, most of them converted to Christianity, so the two holidays dovetailed neatly together."

Preacher cocked an eyebrow and said, "You give me more credit for knowin' about such things than I've got comin'. Tall Dog used to tell me some o' them old Viking tales. Sagas, he called 'em, and they were sure full of blood and thunder. Made for some mighty fine listenin' around a campfire. But I don't recollect him ever talkin' about Christmas."

"Well, you can trust me about this. There'll be a Christmas celebration in Skarkavik, complete with feasting and a Yule log."

"I always trust you, Audie," Preacher said with a grin. "You know more about more things than anybody else I've ever come across."

"Umm," Nighthawk said in agreement. The big Crow didn't drink alcohol, but he had a small pile of hard candies in front of him, and from time to time, he would pop one in his mouth and suck on it with a blissful expression that seemed to say he was being transported to heaven.

"At any rate," Audie said, "if we set out now, I believe we could arrive at Skarkavik by the winter solstice, in time to celebrate both Christmas and Yule with our friends. I'm sure it's quite a festive occasion for them."

"Let me get this straight," Preacher said. "You want to go *north* for the winter. Ain't that sort of backwards from the way folks usually do it?"

"The weather has been mild so far this year. There's every reason to believe that we wouldn't encounter any conditions that would be too unfavorable for travel."

"Maybe not, but if a blizzard was to blow in while we were up there, we might not be able to get back," Preacher pointed out.

"In which case, you know that Bjorn and his people would be happy to have us spend the winter with them."

Preacher nodded. "That's true."

"And it's not as if we do much more during the winter than just wait it out, no matter where we are."

Audie was right about that, too. Normally, they wintered at some Indian village, mending their traps and other gear and doing a little hunting for meat, but for the most part just taking life easy. Many of the tribes were quite hospitable and even provided a young woman or two for cooking, companionship, and warming an hombre's buffalo robes.

Preacher had a hunch that spending the winter in Skarkavik would offer those same amenities. Now that he thought about it, he liked Audie's idea better and better.

"All right," he said. "We'll go see what Tall Dog's been up to." He grinned. "Wouldn't surprise me none if him and Betsy have themselves a family by now."

Beautiful, auburn-haired Betsy Kingsley had been part of their previous visit to the Norwegian settlement. A romance between her and Tall Dog had developed during the journey northward, and when he decided to remain in Skarkavik, it came as no surprise to any of his companions that Betsy stayed there, too. Preacher, Audie, and Nighthawk had lingered long enough to enjoy the wedding feast before heading back to the Rockies.

Audie picked up his cup of mulled wine, took a healthy swallow, and sighed appreciatively.

"We should start soon," he said. "Just in case we do encounter any inclement weather along the way."

That was what they had done. After stocking up with supplies from the trading post that they loaded on their pack horses, they had headed northeast, skirting around small mountain ranges and then angling across the vast plains.

In another day or two, they would reach the Sheyenne River and follow it to the Red River, a shallow, silty stream that flowed northward all the way to the vast lake where Axel Gunnarson, Tall Dog's grandfather, had founded Skarkavik.

This evening, they had camped on a small rise with a stand of brush and trees set back a short distance from the slope. Not expecting to run into any hostiles, they had built a fire and enjoyed their supper.

The surviving warrior and his three companions had interrupted the pleasant interlude after that meal.

"Any more of you skulkin' around out yonder in the dark?" Preacher asked now as he continued to hold the knife against the Arikara's throat.

Earlier, he had unbuckled and set aside the gun belt that held twin, holstered Paterson Colt revolvers, a gift to the mountain man from a company of Rangers down in Texas he had met a while back.

If he had been packing those irons when the attack began, he wouldn't have needed the knife. He'd have just pulled those hoglegs and gone to work, thumbing off shots until all of the renegades had holes blown through them. With the repeating revolvers, he could dispense a whole heap of lead in a hurry.

The prisoner just stared at him defiantly and didn't answer.

"Nighthawk, maybe you'd best go take a look around," Preacher said. "If Dog was here, he could scout out any more troublemakers, but who knows where that shaggy ol' varmint's gotten off to."

Dog, the big, wolflike cur who was one of Preacher's most steadfast trail companions along with the big gray stallion known as Horse, had wandered off earlier in the evening, bent on hunting prairie chickens or rabbits or whatever else he could scare up for supper.

Nighthawk grunted agreement with Preacher's suggestion and headed off into the darkness, moving with speed and stealth that were uncanny in such a big man.

"Well," Preacher said in English to Audie, "I don't reckon there's any reason to keep this hombre alive any longer—"

"Wait," the prisoner said through clenched teeth. With that razor-sharp blade tight against his throat, he had to be careful how much he moved his mouth.

"Oh, so you do understand our lingo," Preacher said. "I had a hunch maybe you did. If you want to keep breathin', you'd best speak up and give me a good reason why I don't just cut your throat and be done with it."

"You know . . . Black Angus?"

Preacher frowned and glanced over at Audie, who said, "There's a breed of cattle in Scotland called the Angus. I believe some varieties are known as black Angus. But they're not raised in America, as far as I know."

Carefully, the prisoner continued, "I mean . . . Black Angus Vicker . . . My friends and I . . . are his men . . . along with others . . . whites and Indians alike . . . We follow . . . the dark trails . . . together."

"So you're outlaws," Preacher said, "and you belong to a gang led by this fella Vicker. Is that about the size of it?"

"Yes. We were . . . scouting . . ."

"Lookin' for fresh victims, you mean."

The Arikara warrior just glared at him and didn't respond to that accusation.

Audie leaned closer and asked, "Were you and your friends expelled from your own tribal bands as I theorized?"

"Our people . . . are fools. They want to be friends . . . with the white men. Their lives . . . will be ruined . . . and they cannot see it." The prisoner grimaced. "Take your knife away . . . so I can spit on . . . your white man's civilization!"

"You're talkin' to the wrong fella, old son," Preacher told him. "I ain't over-fond of civilization my own self. But that never made me turn renegade and owlhoot. Now tell me, where's the rest of this gang of yours?"

The warrior didn't answer. Preacher increased the pressure on the knife, and a tiny trickle of blood, black in the firelight, ran down the prisoner's bronzed throat.

It was a question of what would happen first: the warrior's nerve breaking, or the blade sinking deep enough to sever veins and arteries.

As it turned out, neither of those things happened because at that moment, gunshots crashed somewhere not far off, shattering the late evening hush that hung over the land.